DADDY'S LITTLE FOREIGNER

MISSOURI DADDIES
BOOK THREE

EVERLY RAINE

Copyright © 2023 by Everly Raine

All rights reserved.

No part of this book may be reproduced in any form or by any electronic or mechanical means, including information storage and retrieval systems, without written permission from the author, except for the use of brief quotations in a book review.

Cover Artist: Scott Carpenter

Editor: Lori Smith & Everly Raine

CONTENTS

	Author Note	1
1.	Chapter One	3
2.	Chapter Two	9
3.	Chapter Three	13
4.	Chapter Four	20
5.	Chapter Five	26
6.	Chapter Six	34
7.	Chapter Seven	42
8.	Chapter Eight	50
9.	Chapter Nine	63
10.	Chapter Ten	76
11.	Chapter Eleven	86
12.	Chapter Twelve	94
13.	Chapter Thirteen	109
14.	Chapter Fourteen	118
15.	Chapter Fifteen	127
16.	Chapter Sixteen	137
17.	Chapter Seventeen	146
18.	Chapter Eighteen	159
19.	Chapter Nineteen	166
20.	Chapter Twenty	178
21.	Chapter Twenty-One	189
22.	Chapter Twenty-Two	196
23.	Chapter Twenty-Three	204
24.	Chapter Twenty-Four	211
25.	Chapter Twenty-Five	217
26.	Chapter Twenty-Six	221
27.	Chapter Twenty-Seven	234
28.	Chapter Twenty-Eight	240

29. Chapter Twenty-Nine 247
30. Chapter Thirty 252
31. Chapter Thirty-One 259
32. Chapter Thirty-Two 266
33. Chapter Thirty-Three 274
34. Chapter Thirty-Four 282
35. Chapter Thirty-Five 287
36. Chapter Thirty-Six 292
37. Chapter Thirty-Seven 299
38. Chapter Thirty-Eight 306
39. Chapter Thirty-Nine 313
40. Chapter Forty 318
41. Chapter Forty-One 325
42. Chapter Forty-Two 332
    Epilogue 342

Keep up with Everly! 351
Acknowledgments 353
About Everly Raine 355
Also By Everly Raine 357

To all my readers. Thank you

BLURB

Sofia's dream of moving to the United States and finding love finally comes true. Life is hard having no family or friends in a new country, but she is determined to make the best of it. Working at BTS is a dream and she loves every minute of it. Most of her coworkers are great and so is her boss, Jaxson.

He is hot, dreamy, possessive, and a Daddy. But he is off limits or so she thought. Too bad a mysterious person is threatening harm if she doesn't stay away from him.

Jaxson, retired police officer, and club owner couldn't help but feel a pull towards Sofia. She is sweet, caring, and everything he is looking for in a person.

She may be the Little he's been looking for, but can he convince her to give him a chance? Will he be able to help keep her safe or will the threat push them apart?

Author note: This is an age play book. If you are comfortable reading about age play, ABDL, spicy scenes, discipline (including spanking, corner time, and more), then this is the book for you

AUTHOR NOTE

Trigger Warnings: Little, Mugging, Kidnapping, Hateful comments, Cursing, Threats

This is an age play book. If you are comfortable reading about age play, ABDL, spicy scenes, discipline (including spankings, corner time, and more), then this is the book for you!

CHAPTER ONE

SOFIA

Moving to the United States was hard. Moving to a small town was even harder. Everyone knew she wasn't American when she went to the store to grab something or when she got gas.

People were nice in Springfield, Missouri, but no one wanted to be her friend. Sofia thought it would have been easier to make friends, but she quickly learned how very wrong she was.

It had been two months since she moved to Springfield from Santiago, Chile. Sofia went to work, home to sleep and eat, and that was all. She tried to get out and meet new people, but everyone tended to keep to themselves.

Well, unless the person was born and raised in Springfield. It seemed like a lot of people that moved to Springfield had a hard time making friends until they had lived here a while or knew someone here before.

These things did not work in her favor.

She had only been here two months, and she didn't know anyone.

Sofia had found a job at the local club, Behind the Scene, as a bartender and she loved it. When she was in Chile, Sofia had worked several jobs to earn enough money to move to the United States. When she was a little girl, her uncle had told her about the U.S. Ever since hearing all of his stories, she dreamed of moving here.

The interview had been weird. She knew it was a club that catered towards kinky people, specifically Littles, Middles, Mommies, and Daddies. It was like the club was made just for her. Back in Chile, Sofia had dipped her toe into the lifestyle with some Daddies and she loved every minute she experienced.

"How long is your shift tonight?" Juliet asked.

Sofia looked at her, placing down the cup she was drying. "I close tonight." She didn't mind closing, but it did get dangerous at night when she walked from the club to her apartment. Having no car was proving to be difficult, but she had to make do with what she had. Right now she was saving up for a car, that was the first thing on her list.

"Good luck, girl. I don't envy you," Juliet said.

"I honestly don't mind working until close," she replied.

"But? There's a but in there."

"But it gets dangerous walking home. There are drunks out and I'm small with not a lot of muscle."

"That's why I asked to have the earlier shift when they asked for my preference. I didn't want to walk home alone when my boyfriend took my car. Thankfully, I got a couple dollars from my boyfriend to get a cab."

Sofia cringed at the mention of Juliet's boyfriend. She had only met him once, but she never wanted to meet him again. He gave off a bad vibe, and she didn't want to be around that.

Juliet lived in the same building as her. It was nice, but at the same time it wasn't. They weren't friends by any means, more like acquaintances. Sofia had tried to befriend her, but Juliet was hot and cold. At the club she was all buddy buddy with Sofia but when they saw each other at the apartment complex, it was like she didn't exist.

Several times Sofia had wondered if it was because of her boyfriend but she couldn't be too sure and she didn't want to ask. She didn't want Juliet's boyfriend to hear about it if he was the reason she acted that way. He knew where she lived and that could be dangerous.

"Jaxson had asked if I could work the later shift and I said yes. I need the money and I don't have anything else to do," Sofia replied. "He did ask me if I had reliable transportation and I said yes."

Juliet snorted. "You don't have a car."

"But I have my feet. They are reliable for transportation. Walking." She hadn't specified what type of transportation she had to Jaxson and he hadn't asked. She just hoped he didn't find out.

Jaxson was intimidating but there was also something about him that turned her on. There was a connection between them, or she felt like there was one. She had no clue if he felt the same pull she did, but she felt like he might. Other than her, he didn't really interact with a lot of people in the club. Why would he do that if he wasn't interested in her or didn't feel something?

Sofia knew nothing romantic could happen between them. He was her boss, and she knew that was something most companies didn't allow. It was forbidden. She needed to remember that because, several times, she had found herself daydreaming about him. She dreamed about what it would be like for him to be her Daddy.

But daydreaming wasn't that bad, right? As long as she didn't act on it, there was no harm. Or that's how she looked at it right now. Someone else might tell her she's not even allowed to have those thoughts.

"If he finds out you lied to him, it's not going to end well," Juliet said. "Does he know that you're a Little?"

Sofia shook her head. "I don't know. He asked me if I knew what kind of club this was, and I told him I did. I explained what I knew about BTS, to show my knowledge, but I don't know if he knows that I am a Little."

"There are some Littles who work here that, if they lie or have an infraction, they'll get spanked. Obviously with their consent and they signed on with the understanding they were allowing one of the owners to punish them. Just wanted to know if you signed off on that because you might want to tell him now if you did."

Sofia looked at Juliet in shock. Really? She hadn't heard anything about that.

"He didn't say anything about that. So I guess I didn't sign it," she said.

"You're lucky. I've seen one of the other workers get spanked and then sent to corner time because they lied about their transportation home at night. The owners are very serious about safety. It's their top priority for the members that come but also for the staff," Juliet said. "I would just be careful. They could give you a write-up or something like a warning if they found out you lied."

She started to worry that Jaxson was going to find out that she walked home late at night. What would he do? Was he going to fire her?

She really hoped he wouldn't fire her, because she was on a work visa right now. If Jaxson fired her, and she wasn't able to find a job quick enough, she worried about being sent back to Chile.

The process for getting a Green Card was hard. She needed references and to fill out a lot of paperwork. She was currently getting all of her things straight before she submitted it. Hopefully, she would get accepted on the first try, but she didn't know for sure.

There were several people she knew who had applied and were rejected. Some of them had been trying to get a Green Card for over five years now and were still unsuccessful.

She hoped that wasn't going to be her.

"All I can say is good luck. If you're not going to tell him, then you need to make sure you're really good at lying and nothing happens," Juliet said before she walked away.

Sofia let out a sigh and started to clean the cups again. She wasn't going to be able to think about anything else for the rest of her shift. She had already been here four hours, and she had another four to go.

Tonight seemed like it was going to be one of the slower

nights, which meant she was left to her thoughts. She loved it, but she also hated it because half the time she thought about how lonely she had been since she got to the United States.

In Chile, she had several friends she hung out with. They didn't know she was a Little, but it didn't bother her. She missed hanging out with people and having conversations.

It wasn't the same having a conversation with Juliet because it was normally work related. There was just something about talking to someone about their life or what was going on or what a person was going to do soon.

Whenever something exciting happened, she didn't have anybody to share it with. She just had to almost internalize the happiness.

Sofia looked over to her right to see Jaxson talking to one of the Littles. Sadness filled her as she saw both of them smiling and laughing. Was that his Little? She didn't know if he had a Little or not, and she didn't want to think about it. Just the thought of him having a Little made her sad.

Grabbing some of the juice boxes, she bent down and started to stock the fridge as she waited for somebody to ask her for something. She didn't like slow nights because there's only so much restocking and cleaning she could do before she just was cleaning clean surfaces or standing there.

She stood up, a startled gasp leaving her lips when she saw somebody standing in front of her.

"Hello, Little one," Jaxson said.

CHAPTER TWO

SOFIA

Butterflies filled Sofia's stomach when Jaxson called her Little one. She was always fond of that nickname and it turned her on. There was just something about a Daddy Dom calling a Little 'Little one.' She thought it was sweet.

There's no way of telling if Jaxson knew she was a Little without outright asking him. He hadn't asked her in the interview if she was a Little, only if she knew what the club catered towards.

In Chile, she had worked in a bar, but it was just a regular bar. When she saw BTS was looking for a bartender, she looked into the position. When she realized it was a club for people who were interested in age play, she immediately applied.

It was like her dream was coming true. She'd always wanted to go into a club that catered towards age play, and she wanted to continue to work as a bartender.

"How are you?" Jaxson asked.

She blushed and looked down at the bar, picking up a glass and started to clean it. It was already clean, but she needed something to do while she talked to him.

"I'm good, and you?" she replied.

"I'm doing well. How are you liking it so far in the United States and working here?"

"It's nice. It's definitely a culture shock from Chile to here but it's nice. Working here is amazing," she said. "It's like a dream come true." She put down the cup that she was cleaning and picked up another one.

"If there's anything I can do, let me know and I'll help," he said. "I'm glad that you like working here. If anything goes wrong, be sure to call me."

That was another thing. He was so nice, and he also wanted to take care of her. Make sure that she was doing okay coming to the United States for the first time. He had told her when he hired her that if she needed anything to let him know.

She wasn't going to do that, because he was her boss, but also because she didn't want to grow attached to him. What if she got fired, then who would she rely on?

"Okay," she whispered.

She had several more cups that needed to be cleaned before she could move on to anything else. This had been the task she was doing before Juliet talked to her. There were a few other things she needed to get done. For instance, a couple of Littles had been eating and drinking down the bar and she needed to go clean up the mess.

Most Littles try to keep things clean but she understood that sometimes it just didn't happen. When she let loose and let her Little out, her apartment got trashed. They try to clean up to their best ability but if they spill a drink, it just gets sticky, and that's when she steps in.

"Have you taken a break yet?" Jaxson asked.

"No," she replied.

"Sofia."

That's all he said, and she stopped what she was doing to look at him. Why would he just say her name and not anything else?

"Yes?" she asked, setting down the cup.

"You need to remember to take your break. This is the second time that you've forgotten and it's unacceptable."

She sighed and looked at him. There were things that needed to be done that the other bartenders didn't do.

"I'll take it later," she said as she picked up a wet cup and started to dry it.

"You need to take your breaks. They're paid breaks so you don't have to worry about not earning money in those thirty minutes," he gently said, trying to get his point across.

"There are things that need to be done."

She didn't know why they were having this discussion because she was getting paid to do her job. She didn't want to start slacking and make the other co-workers start to not like her.

"And those things will be there when you come back from your break," he said. "Come take your break with me. I would like to get to know you."

Sofia looked at Jaxson and couldn't believe what he said. He wanted to get to know her? She reminded herself that it was strictly business and nothing else. It couldn't be anything else.

She kept reminding herself of that even though she was wondering if he was attracted to her. Did he feel the connection she felt with him? It was hard for her to ignore but if he didn't feel it, then he wouldn't know any different.

"I'm okay. I can just finish what I'm doing and then go to the break room," she said.

If she went with him and had her break, she knew that slowly she was going to fall for him. It was already hard whenever she saw him not to let her thoughts wander. Anytime she saw him with a girl, it made her sad.

"Please have your break with me?" he coaxed, giving her one of his dazzling smiles.

She opened her mouth to decline but, before she could, he lifted his eyebrow.

"I have other things I want to talk about as well. Grab something to eat and drink and meet me in my office," he said as he stood up from his chair. "If you aren't in my office in five minutes, I will come down and get you."

Sofia looked up at him and nodded her head. The promise in his words was real, and she knew he would come downstairs and get her.

"Yes, sir," she whispered.

CHAPTER THREE

JAXSON

Jaxson sat in his chair, waiting for Sofia to come into his office. There was just something about her that made him want to protect her, cherish her, and take care of her. He didn't know what it was, but it was hard not to act on those impulses.

The other day he had caught Sofia not taking her break when she had an eight hour shift. That was unacceptable, and he told her that. He needed her to understand that she needed a break, but she didn't seem to realize that.

He was worried she was going to work herself to death. She had taken several shifts when other employees couldn't work. Those extra shifts had put her into overtime hours.

Jaxson had told all of their employees they could cover other people's shifts. He did let them know that he didn't necessarily want them to work overtime. Everyone deserved a break and shouldn't be working themselves too hard. He also understood everyone's life was different and encouraged those who needed the extra money to pick up other shifts.

He wondered if Sofia was in that situation. Did she need money? He didn't want to ask and make her uncomfortable or embarrassed if she did. At the same time, he wanted to make sure she was taken care of, if she needed some help.

There had been several times Jaxson told her she didn't need to work so hard, but it always seemed to fall on deaf ears. She said she understood, but did she really? From the way she acted, it didn't seem like she did.

A knock sounded on his office door. "Come in," he said.

Sofia's small frame walked into his office. He took her in as she walked over to the chair in front of his desk.

She was a little pale, and he didn't know why. What could have happened in between her grabbing a snack and walking to his office? Was somebody bullying her?

Neither Jaxson nor any of the owners tolerated bullying at all. It was something all of them talked about with everybody who walked in through the doors.

It was never okay to bully somebody.

"Are you okay?" he asked, as she sat down.

He watched her closely to see if she would give off any indications that she was lying to him. He didn't know if she was going to tell the truth or not, and it wouldn't surprise him if she didn't. A lot of employees were scared to tell their bosses things, out of fear of getting in trouble, but Jaxson didn't want that. He wanted all of his employees to know that he was there for them and would listen to all of their concerns, look into things, and find the truth.

"Did I do something wrong?" she asked in a shaky voice.

His eyes went wide as he stared at her. She thought she did something wrong.

"You didn't do anything wrong, that I'm aware of," he said. "Why would you think that?"

She looked down at her hands where she held her snack and drink.

"You said you had something to discuss with me," she quietly said.

He didn't think telling her that would have made her scared. If he had known, he would have told her it was nothing bad.

"Are you going to fire me?" she asked.

"No!" he raised his voice. "Nobody's getting fired today or tomorrow. You're not getting fired."

He watched as her body relaxed.

"I just wanted to talk to you about taking breaks and making sure that you're looking after yourself," he said.

Sofia looked at him with a confused face, her head tilting to the right side.

"Do you need me to open that packet for you?" he asked, pointing to the packet of goldfish in her lap.

She looked down at the goldfish and shook her head. All he wanted to do was help her open it. He watched as she struggled with it for thirty seconds before she finally opened it.

"What exactly did you want to talk about that?" she asked.

He loved hearing the slight accent she had every time she spoke. It wasn't prominent like he thought it would be. Who had taught her English? Did they speak English in Chile?

"I just need you to know that you don't have to work every waking second that you can. We don't want to make you sick. I don't want you to be sick," he said. "That also means taking care of yourself and not taking your breaks could harm you in the end."

"How?" she asked, taking a mouthful of goldfish.

"You can exhaust yourself in a shift when you don't take your breaks. You are standing for your entire shift. You need your break to sit and relax. It gives you time to collect yourself if things get busy," he explained. "But it also allows you to have time to eat and drink. It's important to nourish your body and going too long without food can hinder you."

Jaxson knew it was important. When Michael gave everyone a rundown on the body and how it can actually affect them, Jaxson cracked down on the employees making sure they were taking their breaks. He even implemented that it was a paid break so people would. He didn't want the employees to work through their break because they needed the money.

Sofia nodded her head, and he was hoping he was getting through to her. She wasn't the first person he had this conversation with. There had been several people who worked here and didn't take their breaks or stayed an hour after they were supposed to leave.

It was always a hard discussion to have with any employee because he didn't know their situation outside of working. Were they in need of money? Were they living in a safe place? Were they trying to pay off something? So many questions he didn't have the right to ask.

"Okay," she said.

"You're valuable to BTS. You're a hard worker that gives your all. Something we, as the owners, love to see but not at the expense of you getting sick. We want you to have fun working here and not working you like a slave, because you're not one," Jaxson said. "I need you to understand that."

"I do," she whispered.

"So from now on we're going to take our breaks on time?"

Sofia looked unsure, and Jaxson had a feeling it was going to go like this. He didn't think that, with him telling her all of this, she would miraculously change. He had no clue what work was like in Chile. Did they have breaks or did they work through shifts and only get to eat when they got home?

There were so many things he didn't know and he had no doubt, for the next several times she worked, that he would have to remind her to take a break and eat.

That was fine with him because it meant he got to see her and talk to her. He found himself walking around the bar a lot more than he normally did just to get a glance of her or talk to her. Jaxson needed to stop but he couldn't help himself. He felt a connection to her, and he wanted to explore the possibilities of being with her.

Yes, he was her boss. He knew some people thought it wrong and should be forbidden to have a relationship with his employee. At the club they had decided it wouldn't be, as long as they showed up for their shift and didn't get any special treatment.

"It's okay," he said. "I'll just remind you every once in a while. I've done it with some other workers so it doesn't bother me. I just want you to be healthy and taking breaks is important."

He'd only done it with two or three other employees and it didn't last long because they realized he was serious. Part of Jaxson hoped Sofia would take a while for her to get used to the idea of taking a break and remembering on her own. He wanted to see her every time she worked and having this as the 'excuse' was perfect.

Her face screwed up in distaste. He knew she probably didn't like it, but it was going to happen. He needed her to know he was being serious about her taking breaks. It was important for employees to take breaks when they had a long shift, to fuel their body but also to give it rest.

Jaxson watched as she finished up her snack and drink. He wished she would have gone slower, so she could stay and talk. He knew she was probably eating faster than she normally would so she could leave. If she was worried he was going to fire her in the beginning, there was no doubt that she didn't want to be here.

He wanted to ask her a million questions about her life. Where was she living now? What did she like to do in her free time? He had many more questions, but he knew she would want to get back to work and he couldn't hold her here forever.

"Can I go?" she whispered.

"You may," he said.

He watched as she got up from her seat and left his office. Everything inside of him wanted to call her back and tell her to rest, but he knew he couldn't right now. She wasn't his, *yet*. Soon though, she would be his and she couldn't do anything about it.

He had seen a couple times when she thought he wasn't looking and she stole a glance. It wasn't just one time but several since she started to work here. He found himself walking out onto the floor in front of the bar more often, so he could see it again.

Soon he would make his move, but he needed to give her a little time to adjust and get used to the idea. He was slowly showing her he cared and wanted what was best for her. Hopefully she was catching on.

CHAPTER FOUR

SOFIA

*L*ast night had been slow once she left Jaxson's office. There had been several of those nights and it always left her to her thoughts.

Which could be a good thing or a bad thing. Last night it seemed that it was a bad thing, well not really a bad thing. It just left her with her thoughts about Jaxson. So many thoughts about what he would be like as a Daddy, *her* Daddy.

She'd only been brought out of her thoughts two times last night. The first time she didn't even realize she had been daydreaming about him. She tried to keep it to a minimum after that realization but it was hard. Jaxson had just been so dreamy, and it was hard not to think about him.

Sofia tried her hardest but working at the club he partly owned wasn't easy. Everything around her reminded her of him.

This morning she had off, and she had planned on going to the store to buy some essentials; milk, eggs, bread, and maybe some ham if she had enough money.

She had gotten paid last month, but she still had a couple weeks until she got paid again which meant she had to make the little amount of money she had to work. She was used to living like this, unfortunately. In Chile, she didn't have a lot of money. While she was trying to save up to come to the United States for a better opportunity, she had to skip some meals.

It wasn't ideal, but she knew she would find a rhythm and things would get better for her. It was the United States, after all, and this was the land of opportunity. Sofia was already getting paid more than she did in Chile but she hadn't factored in the cost of living.

She didn't live in a poor neighborhood but she also didn't live in the richest one either. She knew her safety was important, so she had found an apartment building that had a room within ten to fifteen minutes walking from the club.

It was okay during the light of day, but as it grew dark, it wasn't. She hadn't been there long, but she already knew that after dark, people walked as fast as they could to get wherever they were going. Many people took cabs to avoid the streets after dark.

She couldn't blame them. Several times she wanted to take a cab, so she didn't have to walk, but she was keeping the money left over after rent for food.

Sofia walked into the grocery store and pulled out the bills from her pocket and counted them. Twenty dollars. She had no clue what she could get with twenty dollars, but she was going to try to get as much as she could from her list.

Something that was different, here in Missouri, was they added tax onto her purchase after she got all rung up. In

Chile, the prices were with tax so she didn't have to think about adding extra to cover them. Just another thing for her to worry about.

Sofia went and grabbed milk first, before finding the eggs and bread. She had no clue if she had enough money to buy ham or not. For now, she was just going to make do with milk, eggs, and bread.

She turned down the aisle where the candy was and stopped.

Shit.

Jaxson was standing there, looking at some candy.

Right before she could turn around and leave, he looked in her direction.

"Sofia?" he called out her name.

She gave him a small smile and waved. How was she going to get out of this? She didn't think he would shop at this store.

"Do you work tonight?" Jaxson asked as he walked closer to her.

Sofia looked at him funny. Wouldn't he know if she worked tonight? He was the one that scheduled her and all the other employees.

"I'm trying to make conversation," he softly said.

Her mouth opened slightly when he said that. Crap. Right. People had conversations with other people.

"I do," she replied. "I come in later and work till close.."

"Do you enjoy working until closing?" he asked.

The question caught her off guard. He had asked the same question when she was in the interview with him, and she told him she didn't mind. Was that partially a lie? Yes, it was, but she had needed and wanted this job. She was going to say anything she could to get it.

"Yes," she replied, keeping up her little lie.

He studied her face before he nodded his head. Was he trying to see if she was lying? Sweat formed on her forehead and she so badly wanted to wipe it away, but she didn't want to bring any attention to it. Then he would know she was lying.

"If it ever changes, you let me know," he said.

"Yes, sir."

She wasn't going to and part of her thought he knew that as well.

"I mean it," he said, looking directly into her eyes.

Crap. He knew.

"I know," she whispered, trying to ease his worry or whatever he was feeling right now.

It was hard to read him and what he was feeling. She was normally good at reading people, but Jaxson was different. He was closed off and didn't give away much. Well, most of the owners were like that.

"Doing a little shopping?" he asked as he looked at what she was carrying in her arms. Worry flashed over his face.

Why was he worried? It could look like she was buying just the staple things because that was all she needed. But Jaxson always knew things, even if people didn't tell him those things. Sofia had witnessed it several times while she was working.

It was freaky.

"Yes," she whispered.

She didn't like the worry on his face. She needed to leave

soon or else he was going to start asking questions, and she knew that she couldn't lie.

Jaxson was like a lie detector.

Again, freaky.

"Sofia," he said, pulling her from her thoughts.

"I've got to go. I have some things to do around my apartment," she rushed out.

A feeling inside of her stomach told her he was going to ask some personal questions, and she didn't know if she would be able to handle those questions. She didn't want to have to lie, especially since she was a terrible liar. It would just show Jaxson she wasn't doing well, and she didn't want that.

"Okay," he said. "I'll see you tonight."

"See you."

Sofia felt so bad for lying to him, but she knew it was for the better. He would just worry about her if he knew the truth. She didn't want him to be worrying about her. He was her boss, not her Daddy or boyfriend.

She quickly walked to the front of the store and put her stuff on the belt and walked up to the cashier.

"Will this be all?" she asked as she scanned her last item.

"Yes," Sofia replied.

"That'll be fifteen dollars and twenty-seven cents."

Sofia handed over her twenty dollar bill and waited for the change and receipt. She knew it was important to buy this food because she needed to eat. At the same time, her heart broke a little because she wanted to save the money for something else.

She could feel his eyes on her as she got back her change

and receipt. After she picked up her bag of groceries, she glanced over in his direction and she was right. He was staring at her with a concerned look.

Giving him a small smile, she walked out of the store and started her walk to her apartment. It wasn't a far walk, and she was used to walking, since she walked everywhere in Chile.

With each passing step, her thoughts got a little sadder. She had talked with her grandma about moving to the United States for an opportunity. Her grandma had urged her to get away from Chile. It was one of the hardest decisions she ever made. Now she was wondering if it was a mistake.

Yes, she had landed an amazing job, but she lived in a run down apartment and didn't have a lot of money left over for food.

She thought by now she would have made a couple friends she could hang out with outside of work but that hadn't happened either. She had been here for two months already and had been looking forward to so many different things. A lot of them weren't coming true.

Sofia unlocked her apartment and walked in and headed straight for the kitchen where she put away the groceries. She had a couple hours until she needed to head into work.

Walking back into her living room, she sat down on the old armchair and leaned back. She didn't know what she was going to do, and it sucked. She felt like she was drowning underwater, not able to take a single breath.

She didn't know how much longer she could do this.

CHAPTER FIVE

SOFIA

Sofia was absolutely exhausted as she started her shift. Today had not been a good day at all. Being reminded, when she went to the grocery store, that she didn't have a lot and then being left alone to her thoughts didn't help either.

She felt depressed, and all she wanted to do was lay in her bed and do nothing. But that couldn't happen.

She didn't have anybody to take care of her, which meant she had to take care of herself. It was exhausting, and she longed for the day she found a Daddy who would want her. She didn't think it would be soon, which made her even more sad but she had to get used to this. If she didn't take care of herself, then nobody would and she would find herself out on the streets.

Sofia grabbed a tray of fruit cups and restocked the mini fridge where they kept them. Every Little in the club loved fruit cups, and she found herself restocking the fridge every couple of hours when it was busy.

The fruit cups came from a farm about thirty minutes away from the club and they delivered once or twice a week. The fruit was amazing and Gene was super nice, definitely a Daddy. She hadn't spoken to him personally. He always talked to the owners when he made deliveries, and she had caught some of the conversations.

At one point, she thought she heard that all the workers on the farm were Daddies, but she had to be mistaken. That was super rare to have so many Daddies in one spot.

She had eaten a fruit cup on one of her breaks and she couldn't deny that it was delicious. It was an assortment of fruit. Some of them had strawberries, cantaloupe, grapes, and pineapple. Others just had an individual fruit in case somebody was allergic or didn't like something.

She personally had grabbed one that had everything in it because she loved all of the fruit. They were so delicious and so juicy. If she had it her way, she would eat these all the time. That was how good they were.

Two girls walked up to the bar and looked at her, giving her a big smile. Sofia loved working here because almost all the Littles were super sweet and polite when they asked for things. Sometimes they were impatient and annoyed but their Daddies normally set them straight pretty quickly and made them apologize.

There were a couple Littles who, in her opinion, were spoiled and their Daddies or Mommies didn't do anything about it. They let them be rude, but Sofia just dealt with it. It came with every job.

"What can I get for you?" she asked them.

She knew their names were Janie and Charlotte. She had

seen them several times at the club, and they were always super kind and respectful.

"Two apple juices, please," Charlotte said.

Sofia walked over to the fridge, and grabbed two apple juices.

"I can't wait for the playdate tomorrow. It's going to be so much fun! Are you coming?" Janie asked.

She looked at both of them as she walked back over.

"Of course I am! I wouldn't miss it for the world! It's going to be amazing," Charlotte responded.

Sofia handed them their juice boxes and put it on their tabs, well Charlotte's Daddy's tab and Janie's tab.

"Thank you!" Charlotte said as they walked back to their group.

She longed for the day when she could go to a playdate with her friends. It looked like so much fun.

"Put her juice box and anything else she gets tonight on my tab," Mac said.

He was another one of the owners. He usually walked around the Little's area whenever Janie was here. Sofia knew they weren't together but she wasn't sure if Janie was aware of Mac's interests in her.

"Okay, sir," she responded and quickly changed it.

"Thank you," he replied before walking away.

She thought it was a cute gesture. Who knows if Janie realized he was paying for her drinks and snacks, but Sofia thought it was a sweet thing. Not many Doms did that for people they weren't in a dynamic with, or at least that wasn't something she normally saw happening during her shifts.

Sofia really wanted to go to the playdate Charlotte and

Janie were talking about, but she knew she wasn't invited. She also didn't know anyone there, they weren't her friends. Sure, she had served them several times and saw them play together, but that was all.

She didn't even think the girls knew her name, but she sure knew theirs. She longed to be friends with other Littles but was afraid to talk to them. Sofia worked here, and they came here to play. She didn't know if Jaxson had a policy on who her friends could be at the club. Would it be a conflict of interest or was it okay?

Sofia had thought about asking him, but she always stopped herself. Even if he had said yes to her being friends with them, she didn't even know how she would go up and talk to them. Would they want to be friends with someone who had just moved to the United States?

She didn't know for sure about them, but she knew some people didn't like people from other countries coming to the United States and living here. She didn't want to befriend the wrong people and get bullied or reported when she had done nothing wrong. Sofia didn't think Charlotte and Janie were like that, but she wanted to be sure.

They hadn't said anything, and she hadn't heard any whispers either. Maybe they were okay.

She was also worried because, even in Chile, she didn't feel like she connected with anyone. She felt like she had to force herself to be something she wasn't. She didn't want to pretend with anyone about who she was or how she acted, and it was stopping her from talking to people and making friends.

Sofia looked over at the group of Littles and saw all of

them laughing, not having a care in the world. She wanted that. She wanted to not be stressed with worry about money and just hang out with friends. But she didn't think it was going to happen soon.

Sofia went back to cleaning off the counter, making sure everything was spic and span. She didn't like messes. She wanted to show Jaxson she was a good employee, and he could rely on her. She didn't want to give him any reason to fire her.

"Are you okay?"

Sofia jumped and turned around. Jaxson was standing right in front of her across the bar. She stared at him, not registering that he had asked her a question.

"Sofia," he said. "Are you okay?"

She slowly nodded her head and turned back around. She needed to get back to work, and she didn't want him to see how exhausted she was. It weighed her down. She knew if he stared at her long enough, he would find out and tell her to go home.

She wasn't going home.

"Sofia," he said. "Turn around and look at me."

She really didn't want to turn, but the way he said her name made her want to obey. It was soft but demanding.

"Sofia," he said her name again, almost like a warning.

Slowly turning around, Sofia didn't look Jaxson in the eyes. She couldn't.

"Eyes," he said. "Now."

She brought her head up and looked into his eyes. Her shoulders slumped when she realized he was going to find out how tired she was.

"I don't like being lied to," he said.

Her eyes went wide. How did he know she had lied? Just because she was tired it didn't mean she wasn't okay. But she wasn't only tired, she was also feeling slightly nauseous. Probably because she hadn't eaten anything to fill her stomach.

"If you don't want to answer a question, don't lie," he said. "Just tell me you don't want to answer."

Sofia stared at Jaxon for several seconds, trying to figure out what to say. She knew Daddy Doms didn't like lying. Most of them encouraged Littles who didn't want to talk about it to say so instead of lying. Well, that's what Sofia read, and she had seen some Doms do that while she was working.

She normally tried not to eavesdrop on people's conversation. It was difficult not to, though, when she was serving them drinks and they were talking right there. They had to know she could hear them talking if they were sitting at the bar.

Sometimes she felt guilty, but other times she couldn't help herself but listen to them because it was so interesting. Sometimes it made her glad she didn't know other people, and sometimes it made her long to know people. To have that conversation with someone.

"Sofia," Jaxson said.

"Sorry," she whispered. "Sir."

It wasn't mandatory for her to call him sir, but she just felt like it was right. He was a Dom, and she was a sub and Little. It was a sign of respect and she did respect him.

"What's on your mind?" he asked, sitting down in a seat.

She looked around, trying to see if anyone needed a drink or a snack. No one else was at the bar. Part of her wondered if, while she was in her head, Jaxson had given everyone a look to not come up. She didn't think that was possible, but somehow, she felt like he would.

From her observations, whenever he was down in the main area, he only interacted with the other Littles who had Daddies. Well, besides Janie, but Sofia was pretty sure Mac was going to be her Daddy. It was weird that he talked to her all the time.

Jaxson didn't talk to other people who didn't have a Daddy or a potential Daddy. What made her different? Why was he always down here when she worked? Why was he always coming up and asking her questions?

"Sofia," Jaxson said, sighing. "Are you okay? Do we need to go into my office so you can talk?"

She shook her head and looked down at her hands. She needed to stop spacing out while he was right next to her.

"I'm okay," she whispered. "Just thinking about life and work."

Work was her life right now. She didn't really have anything else going on. No friends to hang out with and all she did was sleep, eat what little food she had, and work. That was all she had time for right now.

"Okay," he said. "If you ever do want to talk, you can always come to me. I'm always free if you need to talk."

She nodded her head and looked at him again. Sofia hadn't heard him say that to anyone else. Maybe he only said that when there weren't people around so other people didn't worry. It was kind of him if he did that.

"Thank you," she said. Who knows if she was actually going to take him up on that offer or not. She didn't talk to many people about her problems, well, she didn't talk to *anyone* about them. Sofia didn't want others to be worrying about her.

Jaxson stayed sitting there, and she wondered if he needed anything. He normally didn't sit at the bar.

"Can I get you anything?" Sofia softly asked.

"Nope," he said. "I'm just going to sit here for a while. Watch people to make sure everything is running smoothly."

She nodded her head and turned her back. That was odd, he never sat there and just watched people. He was normally interacting with some other Doms or walking around, but not sitting at the bar, *her* section of the bar.

Sofia started to dry some cups she had been doing earlier, but completely forgot when the girls came up and then Jaxson. Nerves ran through her body as she peeked over her shoulder and realized Jaxson was still looking at her.

Why was he looking at her? Was she doing something wrong?

She had never felt his eyes on her this much since she started working here. She didn't know if it was a good thing or not. It worried her that he might be trying to find something so he could fire her.

"You're okay," he said. "Just pretend I'm not here."

That was easier said than done. He made her nervous and turned on with his stare.

CHAPTER SIX

JAXSON

Jaxson sat in the chair as he watched Sofia work. He had said he was going to look around to see if things were running smoothly, but he hadn't taken his eyes off of her. She was so mesmerizing with everything she did.

He could watch her for hours and hours, but he knew he had work to do. He also didn't want to freak her out.

Sofia looked over at him once again, dry glass in her hand.

"You're okay," he said. "Just pretend I'm not here."

Did she not like the attention? Did she want him to go?

He thought about asking her those questions, but figured it was best not to. He had asked her questions before, and she either got lost in her head or she avoided the question. Jaxson wondered if it was a normal thing for her to do or if it just happened around him.

Jaxson looked around the room and saw several Littles

playing alone or with each other. He loved being here and seeing people let go and having fun.

Everything in him was so thankful now that he had said yes when his friends had come to him with the idea of opening this place. Well, they had all been talking about how it would be cool to have a place like this. Then, they made it happen. At first it was just for them and the few Littles they knew at the time. Through the years, it had become so much more.

They hadn't realized it back then, but looking at it now, this was such a needed place. He was thankful they decided to do it. When they first started out, he didn't think a lot of people would be interested, but he was so wrong. Springfield was such a small town. Yet they had so many members and people visiting from all over the country.

Jaxson looked back at Sofia who was taking an order from Diana, a Domme and Mommy. She was a nice lady who was looking for her baby boy and Jaxson hoped she would find him soon. He saw her coming in several nights a week, watching, but also interacting with some of the Littles.

She used to come in with Charlotte, but that was before she met Finn and they fell in love. At first he thought Diana and Charlotte were in a dynamic, then he really saw how Diana would look over at the boys. She wasn't looking for a Little girl, but a Little boy.

Sofia was always so respectful and kind to anyone who came up to her and asked for something. He knew it was part of the job to be respectful and kind, but he had a feeling she was always like that. She was genuine with it. Still, he wondered if she had a different side to her, a more mischievous and naughty side.

He had a feeling she wasn't going to show that side of herself, if she had it, unless she was really comfortable around the person. Maybe soon he could get her comfortable around him.

"Jaxson," Leo said, sitting down next to him. "How are you?"

He didn't pay attention to Leo but to Sofia who was walking towards them.

"Hello, Sir," she softly said. "Can I get you anything?"

"Just a water, please," Leo said.

Jaxson watched her as she got a water bottle out of the fridge and handed it to him.

"Thank you," he said.

"Can I get anything for you?" she asked, not meeting his eyes directly.

He would have to work on that with her. He liked it when she looked him in the eyes, but it seemed like she was avoiding it.

"A water," he replied. "Please."

She placed a cold water bottle in front of him and briefly looked him in the eyes.

"Thank you, Little one," he said.

Her cheeks turned pink, and she walked away. Ah, he loved the way her cheeks reacted whenever he called her Little one or any endearing name.

He wondered what her other cheeks would look like pink, or even a nice rosy red. To know that he was the one to make them that way.

"So, is everything okay with the new bartender?" Leo asked.

Jaxson looked at him confused. What would be wrong with Sofia?

"Yes, why?" he asked.

Did Leo know something that Jaxson didn't know about Sofia? Was she a danger to the club and him?

He put that question away from his mind. Sofia couldn't be a bad person. She didn't have a mean bone in her body. Jaxson had a gut feeling about her, even though he didn't know her very well or for that long.

"Well, you've been looking at her and talking to her a lot more," he replied. "I wasn't sure if the rest of us also needed to watch her and make sure she didn't do anything."

Jaxson shook his head. "No. I don't talk to her a lot."

Leo raised his eyebrow at him. Why was he doing that?

"You're normally never down here unless you absolutely need to be. Then after you hired the new bartender, you've been down here a lot."

"She has a name," Jaxson said through clenched teeth. Leo kept calling her the new bartender and he didn't like it, at all. Yes, she was new, but she had a name.

A beautiful name.

He chuckled. "Want to tell me what her name is?"

Jaxson wanted to keep it to himself, but he knew Leo was going to find out, anyway. He could just look in the system and figure out who the new hire was. Any of the owners could.

"Sofia is her name," Jaxson finally said. "And I haven't been down here a lot."

"Don't lie to yourself. We all hate it and you know it," he replied.

Jaxson let out a sigh and looked over at Sofia. He *had* been coming down more frequently since she started working here. He couldn't help it. There was something about her that was calling out to him, and he wanted to figure it out.

He needed to figure it out.

"Fine," he said, looking at Leo. "I have been. But don't come at me for that when you and Oliver have been glued to your phone for the past month."

Leo chuckled. "Noticed that, have you?"

"You bet I have. You two are hardly on your phone and all of the sudden you can't go without it. But, tell us when you want."

"So, why are you around her more? Are you interested in her?"

"There's something about her, but I'm also worried about her."

Both of them looked at Sofia and Jaxson realized she was looking over at Charlotte and Janie. The longing look in her eyes as she watched them play together.

"Why?" Leo asked. "You've never been this worried about any of our other employees."

"She just moved here a couple months ago. She doesn't know anyone, and I want her to feel welcome. I want her to know that she has people in her corner, and people who want to be friends with her," Jaxson replied.

He was worried she wasn't getting enough interaction with people on a deeper level than just taking their orders when she worked. He wanted her to be happy and lively but it seemed like she was always exhausted and down when she came to work. No matter how hard she tried to hide it, he could always see it.

Before Leo could respond, he started to talk again. "I've noticed her looking over at Charlotte, Janie, and the other Littles several times tonight with a longing look in her eyes. I want to get rid of that look. I want to help her."

"You could always invite her to the playdate they have coming up. Those girls won't mind if you invite her," Leo said. "But the first question is, do you think she's a Little?"

"I don't know," he sighed. "Sometimes I think she is and sometimes I don't think she is. She knew what this club was for and seemed comfortable with it. So either she has a friend who is in the lifestyle or she is."

"So why don't you ask her? You won't know until you do."

That was very true. He just didn't know how to approach it with her. Did he just ask and get it over with or did he try to gently talk through it?

"Well, I'm going to go see if anyone needs help over with the ropes," Leo said. "Good luck!"

"Thanks," he replied.

Jaxson looked over at Sofia and they made eye contact. She had been here for a couple of hours and he knew she was due for her break soon. He wondered if she was going to take it or if he was going to have to remind her, like last time.

He didn't know how they did it over in Chile, but here at BTS, they took employee breaks very seriously. They didn't want anyone overworking themselves and made sure they ate and drank enough.

"Sofia," he called out her name.

She hesitantly walked over to him, and he gave her a small smile.

"Yes?" she whispered. "Do you need anything else?"

"Yes, I do. Did you forget something?"

Her eyes went wide as she stared at him. He wondered what she was thinking about. Was she remembering that she needed to take her break?

"I-," she started and looked off into the distance.

Did she not remember?

"Your break?" he said. "You've been here a couple of hours already and you need to take your break."

He watched as she let out a breath of relief. Was she thinking she forgot to do something else? What could she have possibly forgotten?

"Right," she whispered. "My break. I'll take that."

"I do have a question before you take your break," he said.

Sofia stiffened in her spot, and he didn't like that. He assumed she was thinking the worst thing right now, and he wanted to change that. She needed to start thinking positively and not think the worst is always going to happen.

He really wanted to figure out her thinking process, but that would have to come at a later date. Right now, he needed to focus on asking her if she was a Little.

He didn't know if this was the right place or time to ask, but he needed to ask before she got sucked away into her break, and then back into work. Jaxson knew, once she came back from her break, he needed to leave so people didn't get even more suspicious than they already were.

Maybe he could take her back into the employee lounge and ask her or he could take her to his office. But he shouldn't because people would see them walking towards his office or the employee lounge.

If anything was to happen between them, he wanted to take it slow at first. He didn't want her to be rushed into anything or people come up to her and ask several questions since he technically was her employer.

He could ask to see her after she worked when everything was closed. But he knew she would be tired at that point and ready to go home and sleep. There wasn't a good enough time to ask and the playdate the girls had planned was coming up soon.

Jaxson needed to ask sooner than later in case she was a Little and wanted to come. He didn't want to tell her and Sofia not have any time to think about it.

"Yes, sir?" she asked, briefly looking into his eyes.

He had decided he was just going to flat out ask her. He noticed she didn't very much like questions and he didn't want to beat around the bush.

"Are you a Little?"

CHAPTER SEVEN

SOFIA

Sofia stared at Jaxson in shock. How did he know? She hadn't told him she was a Little. She made sure to hold tightly onto that side of herself while she was working.

Had he seen right through her?

That wasn't possible. She was good at hiding her Little and any emotion she wanted to hide. She had years of practice and Jaxson wasn't going to be the first person to see through her.

Right?

Panic welled up inside of her at the thought of him seeing through her. She didn't know why she was panicking. Maybe it was the fact that no one else had seen through her, and the thought of someone finally being able to, scared her.

Sofia remembered Jaxson asking her about the club in the interview. She said she knew it was a place for Caregivers and Littles. She knows that Jaxson is a Daddy Dom. She also knows she didn't say anything about being a Little.

He had figured that out on his own.

Jaxson wouldn't have asked if he didn't suspect her of being a Little. She wanted to know what gave it away. What had she done to make him see she is a Little?

"Sofia?" he softly asked.

Her eyes tracked to his. Did she lie and say she wasn't or did she tell the truth? She knew he didn't like lying, but she didn't know if he was going to fire her because she was a Little. Would that be a conflict in interest?

She didn't know, and it scared her.

"Are you okay?" he asked.

How was she supposed to answer that? She didn't feel great about him knowing and her possibly losing her job.

"I am," she whispered. "Is that going to be a problem?"

She closed her eyes and took several deep breaths. What if she lost her job right then and there? She didn't know what other places were hiring right now or if they would even take someone who wasn't a US citizen yet.

Jaxson had asked her that in the interview. She had replied honestly, saying she wasn't. She let him know she was here on a work visa and was hoping to gain full citizenship while she was working.

She loved Chile, but she wanted to live in the United States and have more opportunities. She didn't know how long it was going to last, since she was only on a work visa instead of having her Green Card.

Jaxson's eyes went wide. "No! It isn't a problem."

Her shoulders relaxed at his words. She was so glad it wasn't going to be a problem, but why was he wondering if she was a Little?

"I'm sorry if I made you panic. That wasn't my intention, and I promise you being a Little won't affect your job," Jaxson said.

He was reassuring her, and she liked that. It was like he could read that she was panicking, and he didn't want her to.

"W-why did you w-want to know?" she stuttered. She didn't enjoy asking questions, but she needed to know why.

"Some of the Littles are having a playdate in two days and I wanted to invite you," he said. "I know the girls who have put it together. Well, their Daddies really put it together. I wanted to invite you. You could meet the girls and boys who are Littles and make friends."

She blinked several times, not expecting him to say that. He was inviting her to the playdate she had heard the girls talk about earlier in her shift?

She couldn't believe it.

Sofia took a step back. Why was he *really* inviting her to the playdate? Could he do that? From her slight knowledge about him, he didn't have a Little. Was he allowed to do that if he didn't have one?

"I may be completely overstepping here, but I think you would get along with the other Littles and be great friends," he said. "I just wanted to invite you in case you wanted to go. I saw you looking over at the group of Littles."

Why was he so observant? He seemed to be able to read her, even when she was trying to hide things, and now he was observing where she looked. Sofia hadn't really realized she was looking over at the other Little so much. Not until he said something.

She continued to look at him. He sounded so genuine with what he was saying, but she wasn't sure. Could he be lying and just saying these things so she got her hopes up?

No.

He couldn't do that. Sofia didn't think he would do that. Jaxson didn't seem like the type of person who would be mean. Granted, she didn't know him really well, but the little she did, he was super nice.

Sofia looked over at the Littles once again. She didn't know if she should say yes or no. She so badly wanted to say yes. At the same time, they all looked like they were best friends, and she didn't want to be left out. No one liked to be left out or not get things. It didn't make a person feel good.

"I don't know," she whispered, looking back at him.

Everything in her wanted to say yes, so she could make friends. She could also be Little at the same time, but she didn't want to intrude on anything. The Littles hadn't invited her, and she was worried she would be overstepping.

"Why are you hesitant?" he asked. "If you don't mind me asking."

She shrugged her shoulders, but she knew.

"I think you do know. Are you worried you won't be welcome? I can always get Finn to come over and we can talk to him," Jaxson said.

Before she could say anything, he turned around and waved at Finn to come over. Her palms started to get sweaty just thinking about talking to another Dom. She had never been around so many, and it was nerve wracking.

Finn walked towards them. She so badly wanted to run away, but she couldn't when Jaxson looked at her. It was like he knew she was going to bolt, and he needed to make sure she was still there.

"Hey, Jaxson. What do you need?" Finn asked as he sat down in one of the chairs.

Sofia looked at both of them with wide eyes, not knowing what to do. Did she say something or did he let Jaxson handle it? Should she intervene and tell Jaxson she didn't want to go?

That would be a lie, but she didn't want him to ask Finn in front of her, or ask at all.

"Hey! I was talking to Sofia here about the playdate you guys have been organizing," Jaxson started to explain. "I told her she was invited, but I think she's worried. You know I don't have a Little yet. Part of me feels like she's worried that since I don't, I can't invite her."

She wanted to shake her head when Finn looked over at her, but she held still. Jaxson was right in everything he said, she just didn't want him to be right. How did he know what she was thinking? How could he read her so well?

"Sofia, it's nice to finally meet you," Finn said. "I want to let you know you are more than welcome to come to the playdate. Jaxson was telling the truth. You are more than welcome to come, and the Littles would love to have you."

Sofia looked down at her feet, not able to hold eye contact anymore. She didn't want to see their body language right now. It could all be an act, but she didn't think it was.

Her palms didn't stop sweating, and she felt her breathing pick up. Was she supposed to respond? What was she supposed to say?

She had never interacted with so many Doms, especially Daddy Doms, at one time. She was worried she would mess things up. She knew some of the basic things, but there was so much more she didn't feel like she knew well enough.

Jaxson was the one to initiate things with Finn. She didn't know if she was supposed to say anything or let Jaxson take care of it. Sofia knew Jaxson wasn't her Dom, but it felt right, especially in this situation.

He had just taken over, and she didn't mind.

"Little one?" Jaxson said.

She lifted her head a little and looked at him. She absolutely loved it when he called her that. It made her feel special and all gooey inside.

"You really are welcome to come. They would love to have you and be friends with you," he said. "But it's up to you. If you want to go, you're more than welcome. If you aren't ready yet, the girls have a playdate here at least once a month. You'll be welcome at those, too."

"I've got to go. I can see Charlotte getting into the glitter," Finn said.

Jaxson kept his eyes on her the whole time Finn talked and left. She started teetering on her feet, not comfortable with him staring at her for so long.

"What are you thinking?" he softly asked. "You can tell me anything and I won't judge. I'm a good listener."

"I don't want to be the odd one out," she whispered.

She didn't know if he heard her and she didn't want to repeat what she said again.

"You won't be the odd one out. New Littles to the club are always welcome. They become great friends within the first couple of seconds," he said. "They'll include you in everything."

Sofia still didn't know what to do. Charlotte and Janie seemed super nice when she got them drinks, but she wasn't sure. Getting drinks and playing while they were Little were two different things.

"I don't know how to really act around other Littles," she softly said, feeling embarrassed.

"What do you mean?" he asked.

"I've only ever interacted with one other Little," she replied.

Sofia didn't know why she was telling him this. She shouldn't be because he didn't need to know. Still, part of her was comfortable around him, and she felt like she could tell him anything.

He felt safe.

"Back in Chile?" he asked.

She nodded her head. They had never had a lot of Little time together. She knew her best friend was a Little, and they talked about it several times.

"Someone you were comfortable with?" he asked.

"My best friend," she replied.

Sadness filled her at the thought of her best friend being back in Chile. It was a very sad day when she left Chile without her. Sofia was still sad about it, but her best friend supported her moving here. She even said maybe someday she would join.

Sofia knew her best friend was just saying that. No way was she moving to the United States. Both of them knew it, but it was a comfort thing.

"I know you don't know the other Littles, but they'll accept you for who you are. You don't have to change or be worried and act a certain way," he said.

She nodded her head. Jaxson knew them, and she trusted him. Maybe she should go and see if she would have a good time. She could always leave if she needed to.

"I'll be there every second to keep an eye on you," he said. "You'll be safe. If anything happens, you can come to me and I'll take care of you."

That comforted her knowing he would be there, watching over her. It made her feel safe. She knew she would be taken care of, but would this change things between them? Before she could think any further on it, she found herself responding.

"I'll go," she whispered, shocking herself.

CHAPTER EIGHT

SOFIA

It had been two days since Jaxson had invited her to the playdate with the other Littles. Something had changed between them since he told her he would be there every second for her, watching over to make sure she was okay.

Her feelings for him before had just amplified whenever he said those words. She was trying so hard not to let those feelings grow, but he just kept saying the right things to her. He was making it so difficult.

Sofia had no clue why she said yes. Well, she did, but it surprised her. Just knowing he was going to be there, watching her specifically, did things to her. It made her feel even more safe to say yes.

It was weird.

Ever since that moment, when she came into work, she couldn't look him in the eyes. It was hard for her because he normally gave her a smile and started to talk to her, but she didn't want the feelings to escalate. She needed them to go away, because it was inappropriate.

He was her boss.

That was forbidden and looked down upon. She didn't want the other employees to start nasty rumors about her or treat her any differently. Some had been wary around her and she only concluded it was because she was a foreigner.

Jaxson had mentioned to her at the interview, after she got the job, that if anyone was rude to her because she was Latina, to come to him immediately. Sofia wasn't going to talk to him unless it got terrible. Besides, maybe the other employees not wanting to talk to her was because she was new.

It may not even involve her ethnicity.

He hadn't asked her if anyone was giving her a hard time and she was thankful. Jaxson could tell when she was lying, and she knew he would pick up on it again. She didn't want to get anyone into trouble when nothing really bad had happened to her.

Sofia looked around the main room in front of her. The club wasn't closed, but not many people were here. There were some people setting up for the playdate that was about to happen, getting things all ready. They would come over every once in a while and get a drink but it wasn't often.

Her shift was supposed to end in thirty minutes and she planned on slipping into her onesie, grabbing her highland cow –Trixie– and heading out. Sofia knew she wouldn't be able to go out there with all the other Littles if she didn't have Trixie.

That was suicide.

Trixie helped her with so much. She comforted her when she needed it, and helped her be brave in times of need. Sofia brought her everywhere, or well everywhere she could fit into her bag, if she had one.

Each shift at the club, she had Trixie safely in her bag which was in a locker. The first night she had ever worked here, Sofia had made a trip to her bag a couple of times on the way to the bathroom so she could hug her.

It was a comfort thing, she needed it then, and she needed it now.

Nerves ran through Sofia's body as she continued to take the room in. Everything was becoming real and super fast.

Did she have time to slip through the employees' room and out the door?

Sofia didn't know if she had it in her to go to this. Everyone knew everyone, but she didn't know anyone. What if she made a fool out of herself? What if she said the wrong thing, offended someone, and they wanted nothing to do with her?

She turned her head to the right, looking at the entrance all the owners use to get to their office. She didn't know if Jaxson was really going to come down before the event and be there for her.

Well, that was a lie.

Sofia knew he was going to show up. He had never lied to her and had told her before that what he said would happen. Unless he had a huge emergency, but he didn't plan on having any of those.

Maybe part of her didn't want him to show up, so her hopes wouldn't go up, and she wouldn't be attracted to him anymore. But part of her hoped he would, to show her he actually cared and wanted this.

Whatever this was.

"Sofia?" Jaxson said.

Her head turned to the left to see Jaxson walking towards her, but she quickly glanced away. She didn't realize Jaxson had already walked down from his office and into the main room.

When did he come down? Was it before she arrived for her small shift or was she so lost in her thoughts she didn't see him?

"You can't keep ignoring me," he said.

She went back to stocking up the snack section behind the bar for the next bartender. She didn't like to leave things unstocked for the person who worked after her. It didn't seem fair to them when she wasn't busy and could do it now. Who knew if the next person would get slammed with people ordering things.

"Sofia Espinoza," Jaxson used her full name.

She stopped moving and took a deep breath in. Sofia knew at some point she wasn't going to be able to ignore him, but she wanted to see how long she could go for. She knew if she interacted with him any more, that her feelings for him were going to heighten.

She already had trouble right now looking into his eyes without feeling things. The look he always gave her turned her on, and she didn't want to see that. She didn't want to be turned on while she was at work. Then she was all needy and frustrated the rest of the day until she could take care of herself.

Jaxson sighed. "The playdate starts soon. So, if you want, you can go ahead and get ready for it."

She stood up and lifted her head a little to where she was looking at his chest. "I just need to change my clothes and grab Trixie."

Sofia didn't want to leave the bar unattended while she went and changed. She could wait until the next employee came to take over.

"Well, you can leave now to get changed if you want," he said.

"I don't need to," she whispered.

It felt nice to talk to him again, and it worried her. She didn't want to get attached to him. Then him say they couldn't be anything or do anything because he was her boss. But it was so hard. She felt so comfortable around him and like she could say and tell him anything.

"Come around the bar," he said.

She stayed in her spot, trying to process his words. Why did he want her to come around the bar? What could he possibly want?

"Sofia, now," he commanded.

She felt her legs start to move at the command. Part of her hated that her body was listening to him. The other part of her knew that whatever he was going to do was probably for the best.

Even if she didn't like it at the moment.

It seemed like Jaxson knew what was best for her. Did

she like that? She didn't know yet. Sofia hadn't had that in a long time and it was weird. She's had to take care of herself for years and someone stepping up to take care of her, was odd.

"Between my legs," he said, pointing.

While she had walked around the bar, he had sat down in one of the chairs, spreading his legs far apart so she could fit in between them. It was intimate. She had never done this before with anyone.

"Sofia," he said.

She hesitantly stepped forward, in between his legs, but she kept her head down. She didn't want to look him in the eyes.

"Why are you ignoring me?" he asked. "What happened?"

"I wasn't," she whispered, closing her eyes at the lie.

Sofia didn't know why she just lied right then and there. It was an instinct, but she knew it was wrong. Jaxson had told her he didn't like lying and there she was, lying to him.

Why did she have to do that?

"Did you just lie to me?" he asked.

She shook her head and sucked in a breath of air. She was just continuing to lie but she couldn't help it. Once she started, she had to keep it up in case he believed her.

But she knew it wasn't going to work either. Even if he did magically start to believe her, she knew she would feel so guilty after a couple minutes and end up telling him. The guilt was already starting to form in a ball in her stomach, weighing down with each second that passed.

"Naughty girls get punished. I'll give you one more chance. Did you just lie to me, twice?" he asked.

She shook her head once again, denying that she just lied. Sofia also didn't believe he was going to punish her. She had never seen him punish someone, so why would he start with her? She was a new hire, and she had seen other employees do way worse than lying to him.

"You just landed yourself corner time for lying to me," he said.

Her eyes went wide as she looked up to stare at him. He was giving her corner time? Sofia opened her mouth to say something, but she was stunned silent. What was she supposed to say to that?

She didn't think he would actually punish her. He had never done it before, and she always thought it was an empty threat.

Jaxson grabbed her chin with his fingers and she stared into his eyes. He meant business.

"If you lie to me again, your punishment will be worse," he said.

Sofia opened her mouth to tell him she wasn't lying, but he raised his eyebrow like he knew she was about to lie again. She quickly closed her mouth and slightly nodded her head.

Corner time sucked, and she didn't want time added on. She didn't know what he would do to make the punishment worse. Her first thought was time added on but he could do other things. Jaxson could make her write lines, get a spanking, ginger, and more. There were endless possibilities, and she needed to keep her mouth shut so she didn't make it worse.

"Now, are you going to lie to me again?" he asked.

She shrugged her shoulders. Lie to him right now, probably not, but she couldn't promise she wasn't going to lie in the future. That would be silly to promise she wouldn't lie when she couldn't control it. What if she was in a dangerous situation and the only way to keep him safe was to lie?

She didn't want to break a promise. That was one of the worst things she could do. Sofia hated breaking promises. When she did, it was normally her last resort and she always felt guilty after.

"Sofia?" he asked.

She closed her eyes and took a deep breath. How was she supposed to answer that? Did he mean right now or forever?

"Talk to me. What are you thinking?" he asked.

Sofia opened her eyes and looked at him. He wasn't mad but looked slightly concerned.

"Now or forever?" she whispered, scared of what his answer would be.

She didn't want to disappoint him but she knew if he said forever, she would have to say no. There was no way she wasn't going to lie again in her life.

"What do you mean, Little one?" he asked.

"Am I going to lie to you again now or forever?" she asked.

Realization filled his face, and he cupped her face with his hands. She leaned into his touch, loving the warmth that came off of them and seeped into her skin.

"Oh, Little one," he softly said. "I would never expect you

to promise that you weren't going to lie to me forever. That would be a tall order. I just meant now, in this moment, while we have this conversation."

Her shoulders relaxed. She was relieved it wasn't for forever, but just this moment.

"But I don't expect you to lie to me again. You know I don't like lying and it's bad," he said. "I know some circumstances lying is warranted, but that's only some circumstances, not all. Hopefully we are never in those circumstances."

She nodded her head, understanding. She was glad he brought it up because she was going to ask if he didn't. Sofia knew that communication was key to life, and she needed him to know that, in some cases, she was going to lie if it meant keeping him safe.

"Now, are you going to lie to me again?" he asked.

"No, Sir," she softly replied.

"Good girl."

A shiver ran through her when he called her that. It was hot, and she felt herself getting turned on.

His thumb ran across her cheek and she leaned into his touch even more. He had never touched her before, and she loved the feeling.

Now she didn't know if she was going to be able to go back to not touching him. She was going to crave the feeling of his hands on her skin.

"Can you tell me now why you were ignoring me?" he asked. "It wasn't very kind of you. What if something happened, and I needed to talk to you urgently?"

Sofia hadn't thought about that. What if something had

happened and every time he tried to get close to her, she walked away or didn't pay attention? She felt guilty about ignoring him.

She was just thinking about how communication was important to life and here she was not communicating with Jaxson. He had tried multiple times, and she didn't want to. She thought it was for the best, but it wasn't.

"I felt something change between us and it scared me a little," she whispered, not looking into his eyes.

It was weird uttering those words out loud. She was acknowledging something had changed between them and it was becoming real. Too real.

"I felt that too. Why were you scared?" he asked.

She shrugged her shoulders. There were so many things she feared. He could find out she wasn't worth it, dump her, and make her get a new job. He could find out she had never had a Daddy, but had scenes with several when she was in Chile.

Jaxson could not like that.

She didn't know, and it scared her. How was this going to work out between them? He was her employer. It was forbidden, but she couldn't deny the feelings she started to develop towards him.

And now they were becoming impossible to ignore.

She felt the little sparks when he touched her face. She felt safe around him and like she could tell him anything.

"I think you do know," he softly said. "Can you look at me?"

Tears built up in her eyes. She didn't want to cry in front

of him, but him saying that she knew why, made her want to cry.

"It's okay, Little one," he whispered, bringing her in.

She sniffled and grabbed onto his shirt. She didn't expect this whole situation to go like this, and she didn't know if she should be grateful or angry.

"Can you tell me?" he kindly asked.

"You're my boss," she whispered. "I've never had a Daddy, but I've done scenes with them. I'm a lot of work."

He pulled away from her and wiped away the tears on her face. Everything in her wanted this to work out, but what would the employees say? She knew Monty wouldn't mind at all. She was super sweet. Lucy on the other hand could have a problem with her dating or having anything with Jaxson.

No words had been exchanged between Lucy and Sofia, but the looks Lucy gave Sofia was enough to know that she didn't like her. She would always glare at her and whisper behind her back.

"That's okay," he whispered. "No one is going to judge you for dating me. That's how Noah and his Little, Frankie, met. She was a cleaner here and got to know him. They've been together for about a couple years now."

"Does she still work here?" she asked.

Sofia hadn't seen any cleaner here, but she could come when she wasn't here. She also hadn't heard anything about Frankie.

"Sadly, she doesn't. She got diagnosed with a neurological disorder and isn't working right now," he said. "But you may see her around soon. Noah may bring her here to play with some other Littles."

She still didn't know if anyone would judge her for being with Jaxson. She hadn't met Frankie or knew the atmosphere of the club when Frankie and Noah were talking. Had other people whispered behind her back?

"I also want to let you know that I'm not going to judge you for having some scenes with other Daddy Doms," he said. "I'm interested in you. I have been since you walked into my office for the interview. I feel a connection to you and I know you feel it as well. And I would love to see where this goes."

She blinked a couple of times, trying to process his words. He wanted to explore what they have? Should she do it?

"If you want, we can give this a try but if you really don't want to, then I'll leave you alone. It's up to you," he said.

"Okay," she whispered, sounding so unsure.

She really was interested in seeing what they could be like together, but she was still worried. What if something happened, and he fired her?

"Are you sure?" he asked. "You don't have to decide right now. We can talk later about the worries you have."

"That sounds good," she softly said.

"Great. Maybe tomorrow before your shift we can?" he asked.

"Okay."

"Now, how about you go change into your clothes and bring out Trixie. I would love to meet her."

Sofia blushed and looked down. She had forgotten she mentioned Trixie.

"Don't be embarrassed. I'm serious in that I can't wait to meet her," he said. "She's important to you so that means she's important to me."

Her eyes went wide. She never had anyone tell her that before.

"Come on," he said. "Or else you're going to be late to the playdate."

CHAPTER NINE

SOFIA

Sofia stared at herself in the mirror. She was wearing her highland cow onesie and holding Trixie, a highland cow stuffie.

To say she was obsessed with highland cows was an understatement.

They were the best and so cute. One day she was going to go visit some and she couldn't wait for that day.

"Sofia?" Jaxson said as he knocked on the door. "Are you okay?"

She looked at the watch on her wrist and realized she had been in the bathroom for ten minutes now.

"I'm coming," she called back.

Sofia didn't mean to worry Jaxson, and she felt bad. But nerves were running through her. She had only dressed up like this four times in front of other people and it wasn't for long. The scenes never lasted long, and she always ended up changing really quickly and leaving.

What would Jaxson think? Would he find her cute? Was

he still going to want to be there the whole time after he saw her?

"Sofia," he said. "You're worrying me. Do I need to go get the key to unlock the door?"

"No!" she rushed out.

Sofia quickly pushed her work clothes into a bag and unlocked the bathroom door. Before she could attempt to open it, Jaxson was already opening it for her.

He racked his eyes up and down her, almost like he was checking for injuries before he looked at her in the eye.

"You're so cute," he softly said. "Come out and give me a twirl?"

She blinked several times, not believing she just heard him ask her to twirl for him.

"Come on," he said. "Don't be shy."

She blushed and looked down at her feet for a second before she walked out of the bathroom. Sofia could hear some of the Littles outside in the main room, talking and screaming. Were they dressed the same? Were they going to see her when she twirled?

Jaxson held his hand out, and she hesitantly placed her hand in his. What did he want? Why was he holding her hand?

"Twirl?" he kindly asked.

She nodded her head and started to twirl around, giving him a view of everything.

"Adorable," he said.

She giggled and tightly held onto his hand when he tried to let go. She didn't want to let go of him right now.

"That's okay," he said. "Whenever you're ready to let go

of my hand, you can. And if you want to hold on to it for the next hour, go for it."

Sofia relaxed at his words. She was worried he wasn't going to like that she still wanted to hold his hand. She just couldn't let go. Ever since he grabbed her face, it was like something went off in her and she wanted to have contact with him all the time.

"Can I meet Trixie?" he asked.

She held out Trixie. "Da, I mean Jaxson, this is Trixie."

She closed her eyes and took a couple deep breaths in. She almost called Jaxson 'Daddy'. It was hard not to since he was acting like her Daddy.

Everything in her longed to call him Daddy and to actually have him as her Daddy but they needed to talk first.

"You can call me Daddy right now since I'll be looking over you for the next couple hours. Just if you want and no pressure," he said and her heart skipped a beat. "Can you tell me your safeword?"

"Pina," she whispered, her cheeks heating up. "It's pineapple in Spanish."

"Good. If I do something tonight that is a hard limit or things get really overwhelming for you, you call out your safeword and we'll talk about it."

She nodded her head.

Was she going to call him Daddy tonight? She didn't know if she wanted to because, if she did, she may get attached and what if it didn't work out? She didn't want to get her hopes up, but she also really wanted to see how it would feel to call him Daddy for the first time.

"Now, I need to properly meet Trixie," he said before

turning to her stuffed cow. "Hello Trixie, I'm Jaxson. It's so nice to meet you and I'm so glad Sofia has you as a friend."

Her blush deepend as he continued to talk to her. No Daddy had ever talked to her stuffie like she was her friend. It made her feel good though because he didn't just see Trixie as a stuffed toy but as her friend. Trixie was special to her.

Jaxson looked back at her and gave her a smile. "Are you ready to go meet the other Littles and have some fun?"

She shrugged her shoulders. While she was happy and excited to meet the other Littles, she was also really nervous. What if they didn't like her? That was going to make things really awkward at work when she had to serve them.

"It's going to be okay. I'll be here the whole time," he said.

"Okay," she replied. "I guess I'm ready."

"Before we go, I do need to set some rules. No cursing, no lying, no throwing things, be kind to others, and no putting yourself down. Any of these broken will result in getting punished. You already have corner time for lying to me."

She nodded her head. She didn't plan on doing any of those things.

"I is a good girl," she said.

He chuckled. "You're a good girl right now."

"No naughty."

"We'll see. Maybe if you're a good girl the whole time you can get a reward."

She perked up at the talk of a reward. She loved rewards so much.

"Someone likes rewards," he said. "Be a good girl for me and you can get one."

She nodded her head and gave him a smile. "Good girl."

"Now, let's get you to the playdate."

Her heart started to beat faster as they walked towards the main room where all of the other Littles were. She didn't know if she could do this.

"Jaxson!" Littles started to yell.

Sofia immediately went behind him, still clutching onto his hand. There were a lot more Littles here than she thought there would be.

"Who's behinds you?" One Little screamed.

"I've got someone special to me that's hiding behind me," Jaxson said. "Now, before she comes out from her hiding spot, I want to let you know that she's super nervous to meet you all."

A whimper escaped past her mouth. He didn't need to tell everyone she was nervous about meeting them. They didn't need to know

Jaxson squeezed her hands.

"Shows!" another Little yelled. "Meets her!"

She felt Jaxson start to turn around and panic went through her. She wasn't ready to meet all of them yet.

"Sofia," he softly said. "It's okay. They can't see you yet. Can you open your eyes?"

She hadn't even realized she closed her eyes. Everything was becoming overwhelming, and she didn't know if she wanted to continue to do this. Maybe it wasn't supposed to happen today.

"That's a good girl," he whispered. "Such a good girl for Daddy."

Sofia started to relax as she stared into his eyes.

"Ten seconds of courage," he softly spoke to her. "If you really don't want to be here after, just let me know and I'll take you somewhere else. But I need you to try it first. Do you think you can do that for Daddy?"

"Y-yes," her voice was shaky.

Her eyes darted to the side of him and she caught a glimpse of a couple Littles looking over in their direction. Maybe she could do this if Daddy stayed with her the whole time.

"Ready?" he asked. "Take a deep breath for me and let it out. Good girl."

She watched as Daddy turned around. "I want you to meet Sofia. You might have seen her behind the bar, serving you drinks and snackies."

He tugged her hand, and she hesitantly walked out from behind him. The first thing she noticed were all the eyes on her. There must have been at least ten other Littles here, some she knew, and some she didn't.

A shuddering breath fell from her lips. There were so many people just staring at her. The few Daddies who were here were also looking at her.

"Sofia!" Charlotte called out. "It's so nice to see you agains!"

Janie was standing right next to Charlotte and Monroe. She knew those three girls, but the other Littles, she had no clue who they were.

"Can you introduce yourselves one by one?" Jaxson asked.

"You know I'm Charlotte or I go by Charlie."

"Janie."

"Monroe."

"Christine."

"Echo."

"Tucker."

"Kyle."

"Elsha."

"Blaise."

"Valentine."

Sofia blinked several times as everyone introduced themselves. She had seen Kyle around here, but had never talked to him before. Everyone else except Charlotte, Janie, and Monroe were new to her.

"Little one, introduce yourself," Daddy prompted her.

She looked up at him, and he gave her an encouraging smile. She gave a little wave with her hand that held Trixie. "Hellos, I'ms Sofia."

All of the Littles said hello back to her and started to talk all at once. Sofia started to get overwhelmed and gripped onto her Daddy's hand.

"Everyone!" Finn yelled. "One at a time. We don't want to overwhelm people."

Everyone went quiet as Finn talked. She was glad he had said something because she didn't know how she was going to deal with all ten of them talking to her.

"Sofia would love for you to talk to her, but please not all at once. She gets a little anxious at that," Daddy said before he went down to her level and got closer to her. "The only ones with Daddies or Mommies are Monroe and Charlotte. All the other ones are either talking to someone or don't have anyone at all. Just be respectful."

Sofia nodded her head and looked back at all the other Littles. She was glad she wasn't the only one who didn't have a permanent Daddy. While Jaxson said she could call him Daddy while they were here, it didn't mean he was her long term Daddy.

No matter how much she wanted it to be true, she needed to remind herself it was temporary.

The Littles looked at her and nodded before Janie took a step forward.

"Come plays with us?" Janie held out her hand.

Sofia looked up at her Daddy. She didn't exactly know why, but she wanted to make sure if it was okay with him.

"Go on," he softly said. "I'll be right over there with the other Daddies."

She looked down at their hands for a couple of seconds. She didn't know if she wanted to let go of his hand yet. She wanted to continue the physical touch, but she also wanted to go play with them.

"When the playdate is over, we can cuddle all you want," he said.

She nodded her head and let go of his hand. Janie latched onto her hand and dragged her over to the group of Littles. Sofia didn't know how she was going to remember all of their names tonight.

"Dos you wants to colors or tea partys?" Echo asked as they walked closer.

"Colors," she said as she looked around.

Echo was beautiful with her braided pink hair that went past her shoulders. It looked so pretty with all the different colors of pinks in her hair.

"Soooo prettys," Sofia said, pointing to her hair.

"Thanks! Pink is my favorite color!" Echo replied.

Janie dragged Sofia to the coloring table, and they both sat down. All the other Littles sat around the table and they started to peacefully color.

There were so many different things on the table. Paint, glitter, markers, color pencils, crayons, pastels, colorful tape, and more! It was a Littles dream all on the table and they could use whatever they wanted.

Sofia went for the purple marker and started to color on her blank piece of paper. She had no clue what she was going to draw, but she was just going to let her mind take her wherever.

"Sofia," Elsha whispered.

She turned her head to the right and saw Elsha sitting right next to her. She had a pixie cut hairstyle that suited her. She had always loved looking at women who had pixie cuts. They were so brave to cut their hair short.

"Yes?" she whispered back.

She didn't know why they were whispering, but she needed to keep it up in case of something.

"No secwets!" Valentine raised his voice.

"Shhhhh!" Blaise said. "Keeps it downs. No want Doms to hears."

Sofia was so confused. Why didn't they want the Doms to hear?

"Asks!" Kyle said. "Asks her!"

Sofia looked back at Elsha. What was she going to ask her?

"Is Jaxson your Daddy?" Elsha asked.

Her cheeks started to heat up at the question.

"Wells?" Valentine asked. "Is he?"

She shook her head. "No."

Everyone let out a gasp and looked at her. He technically wasn't her Daddy. Maybe just for tonight, but Sofia thought they probably meant full time.

"No?" Elsha asked.

"Wells, why nots?" Kyle asked. "The way he looks at you."

Sofia started to fidget with her fingers. She looked over at her Daddy for tonight and he was already looking at her with a worried face. Giving him a smile, she slightly waved before looking back at the group.

"He's my boss," she whispered.

"Bullshit," Blaise quietly said.

"We just talked about it today and we'll be talking about it later. Nothing has happened."

"Get it!" Charlotte said. "You make him happy and I think you're happy too."

She shrugged her shoulders. Yes, she was happy when she was around him, but there were other things to worry about. Lucy wasn't kind to her, and she felt like Lucy would give her trouble. Maybe even Lucy's friends.

Sofia didn't want that. She didn't want the drama or rumors Lucy would spread about her but Sofia also had feelings towards Jaxson.

"You've gots to tells us what happens," Christine said.

She nodded her head and smiled. Maybe they want to be her friend now and they could have other playdates or meet up and have coffee.

Sofia started to get excited with all of those thoughts. Things were starting to look up for her and she couldn't wait to see where it took her.

"Pinky promise!" Valentine said.

She lifted her pinky and connected it with Valentine. Once they were done, they went back to coloring and making comments every once in a while. Sofia felt more relaxed around them since they had included her into the conversations. She was worried they wouldn't, but she was wrong and shouldn't have worried about anything.

Sofia looked over at the bar to see who was working and she saw Lucy, glaring at her. Before she could do anything, Sofia felt something hit her cheek. She turned around towards the table and saw Charlotte holding blue paint in her hand.

"Did you-" Sofia started but stopped when she saw glitter fly across the room.

Oh my she thought.

Before she could even think about what she was doing, Sofia grabbed the green paint, dipped her hand into it and flung it at Kyle.

A burst of giggles flew out of her mouth as she watched the horror go on his face. It was priceless.

"Sofia!" Kyle screeched.

Paint and glitter started flying across the room, hitting

every Little in sight. Yelling and laughter filled the room as they continued to make a mess out of everything.

This was so much fun. Sofia was having the time of her life right now.

"Enough!" Jaxson yelled.

Everyone stilled in the room and turned their gaze towards the group of Daddies standing before them.

Oh no.

She had nodded her head when he told her the rules, and she had completely ignored them. When Charlotte had first thrown the paint, it hadn't even crossed her mind that Daddy had told her not to throw things and to not be naughty.

"Littles, go to your Caregivers. And if you don't have one, go to a Dom or Domme for your punishment," Finn calmly said.

Sofia stayed in her spot. Was her Daddy for tonight supposed to punish her or was she supposed to find another Dom to do it?

"Come here, Little girl," Jaxson said.

She looked over at him and saw the disapproval on his face. Sofia hung her head as she slowly walked towards him. She didn't feel good about this.

Why had she gotten involved throwing paint and glitter at the other Littles? Because it was fun and as Sofia thought about it, she did feel guilty but she also had so much fun. She couldn't remember a time when she had so much fun.

"You knew better than to throw paint and glitter," was the first thing Daddy said to her.

She continued to look down at her feet, not wanting to

see the disappointment or disapproval from him. She didn't know if her heart could take it.

"You knew it was a rule and yet you decided to still go through with it," he continued to speak. "Do you have anything to say?"

"Charlotte started it," she whispered, not knowing what came over her.

"What was that?"

She looked up at him, a pout on her face. "Charlotte started it and I had to get back at her. Well, it didn't hit her but it hit Kyle but I did manage to hit Charlotte at some point. And I shouldn't get in trouble for it."

He raised an eyebrow at her and crossed his arms.

"You wouldn't be getting in trouble if you didn't throw paint and glitter, but you did and you knew it was against the rules," he said.

She stuck her bottom lip out even more. It was not fair.

"Pouting won't do you any good, Little one," he said. "Now, go clean yourself up and get into some clean clothes. Once you're done, I expect you to come right back to me for your punishment."

She nodded her head and started to walk towards the employee room. As she was walking, she looked around at the other Littles and saw their Daddies, Dom, or Domme's were helping them get cleaned up.

Jealousy ran through her at the sight. She wanted Jaxson, her Daddy for tonight, to clean her up and help her make sure she got everything.

But he wasn't.

CHAPTER TEN

SOFIA

Sofia stood nervously in front of Daddy. She had changed into a new onesie and tried to the best of her ability to get all the paint and glitter off of her. She was pretty sure she had missed several spots on her.

The mirrors in the bathroom or the employees' lounge weren't the best, and it was hard to see her back and hair. She just hoped she didn't have paint or glitter in big glops on her. She didn't want the other Littles to laugh at her because she didn't have any help.

"Sofia," Daddy said. "Can you turn around?"

Her face heated, and she stayed in her spot. She didn't want to turn around because she knew she had missed a spot.

"Sofia," he said her name again.

She let out a small sigh, putting her head down, and turned around.

"Oh, Little one," he whispered. "Daddy's sorry for not

insisting that he should help you clean up. I didn't want to overstep any boundaries, but I should've."

Tears formed in her eyes at those words. She wished he *had* insisted that he help her clean up. She would've allowed him to help her.

"Let's get this out of your hair and neck and then we'll get to your punishment," he said.

She kept her face down the whole time he helped clean her hair and neck, silent tears streaming down her face. It had been a long time since she had someone help clean her and she felt cared for.

"Little one," Daddy softly said. "Can you turn around?"

Sofia turned around, but didn't look up. She didn't want him to know that she was already crying, and he hadn't even started her punishment.

How pathetic was she?

She felt his fingers on her chin, lifting her head up. She tried to struggle against his grip on her chin, but he wasn't allowing it.

"Oh, Little one," he voice was so soft and caring. "It's going to be okay. Do you need a hug before we get started on the punishment?"

She started to shake her head, but when he gave her a look, she nodded her head instead. She needed one, but she didn't know if it was okay before her punishment.

He wrapped his arms around her and held her tightly against him. Tears continued to run down her face as he held her tight. She couldn't remember the last time she had a hug like this. Well, she couldn't remember when she last had a hug, at all.

Her best friend from Chile never enjoyed being physical, which left her not getting any hugs. And when she would go scene with a Daddy Dom, they didn't do much aftercare that involved physical touch. They would make sure she was alright, had food and water, and got home safely, but they wouldn't touch her.

She had been deprived of physical contact and being taken care of. Jaxson doing little things for her like this was making her emotional.

Sofia was never emotional.

She could feel the warmth from him seep into her skin and she sighed in contentment. She felt safe, at home, whenever he was around her and especially when he had his arms around her.

"Now," he said, pulling away. "Are you ready for your punishment? We're going to do both punishments, corner time and a spanking."

Nerves ran through her body as she thought about getting spanked. She had only ever been spanked once, and it was when she was a child and she never got spanked again. Sofia made sure she was a good kid and didn't get into much trouble.

"I'm giving you an option. Would you like your spanking in front of everyone else or private?" he asked.

Sofia looked around the room and realized some of the Littles weren't there anymore, but Charlotte and Monroe were and they were getting over their Daddies laps. She didn't know how she felt about getting spanked in front of the other Littles. What if they saw?

"Sofia?" he gently asked.

"P-private," she replied.

For her first spanking, she didn't want to be in front of other people. What if she screamed and started to bawl her eyes out? She didn't want to be in front of everyone when she did that.

It would be embarrassing.

"Okay," he said. "We'll go into a different room and once we're done, corner time will be with all the other girls."

She nodded her head. She didn't really want to do corner time, but she knew she had lied to him and there was still a little guilt inside her for doing that.

Daddy stood up, grabbed her hand, and started to walk to the back.

"We'll be back," he said to Finn and Michael.

Sofia looked over to find Charlotte and Monroe, pants and underwear down, and laying over their Daddy's lap. A shiver ran through her at the thought of being out here where everyone could see her and Daddy spanking her.

It was a turn on, but it also scared her. She didn't know how she was going to react and didn't want to embarrass herself or Daddy. Would Daddy be mad at her for embarrassing him? Every Daddy was different, and she didn't know what Jaxson would do.

"Ready, Little one?" he asked.

She hadn't even realized they had walked into a different room and were standing next to a chair. She looked around the room, trying to take everything in but there wasn't much. It had a couple chairs, but that was it.

"This room is used for when a Little just needs to be held in a quiet room," Daddy said. "But since it's not being used, we're going to use it and you can make as much noise as you need when I'm spanking you."

Sofia looked up at him. Was she going to make a lot of noise? She hoped she wouldn't scream, but this was going to be different from when she got spanked as a kid.

This was Jaxson, someone she was attracted to and not her parents.

"We can't delay the inevitable," he said as he sat down on the chair. "Can you tell me your safe word again?"

"Pina," she softly said as she took a step forward.

"Good girl. And if this gets too much, you yell out your safeword and I'll stop right away. We'll talk about it and figure out what to do next, okay?"

"Yes, Daddy."

He stared at her with a fond look on his face as she said those words. That was the first time she had called him Daddy out loud, and it felt so right. She wanted to do it again and forever, but knew tonight was the only night for now.

She didn't know if he would still want her after today. She had been naughty and he may not want her for that.

"Ready?" he asked.

She shook her head, but he gave her a small smile and tugged her towards him.

"Let's get this onesie and underwear off," he said.

Her eyes went wide, and she took a step back. She knew Monroe and Charlotte were getting spanked on a bare bottom, but she didn't think she was going to.

"Onesie and underwear on?" she asked.

"I'm sorry, Little one. I spank naughty Little girls on their bare bottom," he said.

She felt her hands start to shake. She didn't know how to feel about this whole situation. Sofia had heard several times of Littles who got turned on by the spanking, or some of them did. She didn't want Jaxson to see her getting turned on.

That would be embarrassing.

"What's wrong?" he asked.

She shook her head. She didn't want to talk about it.

"I can't get spanked with my undies on? It's my first spanking," she softly said, trying to get him to reason with her.

She had worn black panties today, and she was glad. Maybe if he spanked her with her underwear on, he wouldn't be able to see the arousal on her panties. If she got turned on by it.

"No can do, Little one," he said. "Now, let's get the onesie and undies off of you and get this punishment started."

She forgot she was wearing a onesie which meant he had to take the whole thing off of her to get her bottom bare. She definitely didn't want him to see her nipples perking up or the arousal on her pants.

She tried to take a step back again, but he quickly grabbed her hand and gently pulled her towards him. She didn't know how he managed to hold her still and get her onesie off of her. But he had done it and now she was in her bra and nothing else in front of him.

Her arms went out and wrapped around her body, trying to cover everything up. She hadn't thought through wearing a onesie to this play date. Maybe she should've brought her pajamas instead, but they weren't as soft as her onesie.

"No covering up," he said as he pulled her arms away from her body. "You're perfect just the way you are."

She stared at him as he looked over her body. Her skin started to tingle as she saw his heated gaze move over her figure. She started to rub her thighs together, trying to get some friction.

"Ah, naughty baby," he said. "No rubbing your thighs together."

A whine fell from her lips at that. She wanted all the pleasure.

"No pleasure for you right now. You were naughty tonight," he said as he led her over to his right. "And now you're going to get a spanking."

He helped her lay over his lap, her ass in the air. He started to palm and rub her bottom as she laid there.

"After the spanking and corner time, all will be forgiven," he said.

She nodded her head. She wanted the guilt to leave her for lying and disobeying the rules he had set out before. She didn't want to disappoint him any more.

"Ready, Little one?" he asked.

She wasn't ready, and she didn't know if she ever would be.

"No," she whispered.

He chuckled and rubbed her bottom again.

"I think you are," he said. "I'm going to start. Remember, if things get too much, you yell out your safeword and I'll stop."

"Yes, Daddy," she whispered.

"What's your safeword again?"

"Pina."

"Good girl."

Pleasure rushed through her body as he called her a good girl. If he could call her that all day every day, she would be perfectly content. She loved the way it rolled off of his tongue and made her feel all warm and fuzzy inside.

Pain spread across her ass cheek as his hand connected with her bottom.

"Owwww!" she yelled, wiggling around.

She didn't like this one bit.

"Lay still for Daddy as he spanks you," he said.

Sofia didn't know how she was going to stay still for this. It hurt so bad and she wanted no part of it.

Several more swats landed on her bottom and she yelled out in pain as it radiated across her bottom.

"Please, Daddy," she begged.

She didn't want any more spankings. She wanted it to be over.

"Daddy," she cried out.

"Just a couple more," he said.

She didn't know if she could do this for a couple more. Her bottom was on fire and aching so bad with each spanking. She tried to wiggle around to get away from his hand, but they just kept connecting.

"Stay still," he said.

"Dadddyyyyy," she whined.

"The next ones are going to be a little harder."

Before she could protest, several hard smacks landed on her bottom, sending her over the edge. She sobbed and her body went limp against him. Her bottom hurt so bad.

"Shhh," he said. "It's going to be okay."

He helped her stand up and held her against him for a couple seconds.

"You're going to be okay."

She didn't know if she was going to be okay or not. Sofia definitely knew that her bottom wasn't going to be. It was going to hurt for hours and she won't be able to sit on it comfortably.

"Let's go finish off the punishment and then afterward we can snuggle and cuddle as much as you want," he said as he stood up.

She went to grab her onesie to put it on, but before she could, Daddy grabbed it and held onto her hand.

"Little girls do corner time with no pants on," he said. "Their bottoms are sticking out as their nose is in the corner."

"Nooo," she whined.

She didn't want to be on display when she walked into the room. Everyone would see her red bottom.

"Don't worry. All the other Littles will have their pants off as well while they stand in the corner. You won't be the only one," he reassured her as they walked into the room.

Tears were still streaming down her face as Daddy walked her over towards the corner she was going to stand in. She made sure to keep her head down the whole time so she wouldn't see anyone looking at her.

"Legs parted with your bottom out and nose in the corner," Daddy said, helping her get into position. "If you move or talk, the time will start over. Do you understand?"

She nodded her head and sniffled several times.

"As a reminder, if it gets to be too much, say your safeword and I'll come get you. We'll talk about it and go from there."

"Okay, Daddy."

He gently tapped her bottom, making her hiss as she stood in the corner.

"Think about what you did wrong while you're here," he said. "I'll come get you when the time is done."

Sofia heard his footsteps leaving. She knew lying was wrong, but she couldn't help it sometimes. It was a natural thing to do when she was uncomfortable or uncertain about situations. She didn't want to make things worse if she couldn't read the situation right.

As she looked back on the punishment, she knew it hurt a lot and her bottom was still on fire, but it also brought a sense of ease over her. She didn't know what it was, but she liked it. Maybe it was just the guilt leaving her, but this felt different.

It was peaceful.

CHAPTER ELEVEN

JAXSON

Jaxson sat down in the chair next to Michael and Finn. He did not expect Sofia to get into trouble tonight. She seemed like a Little who never wanted to get into trouble.

When he first saw everything happening at the table, he couldn't believe his eyes. She looked like she was having a lot of fun, but she had broken a rule. He had struggled with whether he should punish her for a second.

Just a second.

But he remembered telling her not to throw anything at people and not to be naughty and there she was, throwing paint at the other Littles.

The look of shock when he said he was going to punish her was comical. He had to stop himself from laughing because he didn't want to show it to her in a serious time. She needed to know she wouldn't be able to walk all over him if they got into a dynamic.

"Charlotte has been getting even more mischievous and

naughty," Finn said. "I should've known not to put the paints or glitter out, but I had hoped maybe she wouldn't start something."

"She's really comfortable around you," Michael said. "Monroe has gotten out of her shell more as time goes by."

Before Jaxson could say anything, Mac walked over and sat down. He looked exhausted.

"What's up?" Jaxson asked. "You alright?"

"Janie," he said. "She's keeping me on my toes and keeping me at arm's length."

Jaxson knew Mac had feelings for Janie for a long time now. He was just trying to figure out the right time to make his move.

"Doesn't she have a kid?" Michael asked.

"Yeah, she does," he replied. "But I don't know if that's why she's keeping me at a distance. It's just so exhausting. I want her. I want her to be my Little but she won't let me get fucking close to her."

"Have you told her that?" Jaxson asked.

"Not flat out, but I've given her hints. I've shown her that her having a kid doesn't bother me."

Jaxson looked over at where Sofia was standing in the corner. He loved seeing her red bottom sticking out, showing all the Doms and Dommes in the room that he had taken care of her punishment.

"If you think it's right, maybe you should sit her down and have that conversation with her," Finn said. "Show her you're serious about this. Ask her for a weekend to show her what it would be like."

Jaxson thought about that with Sofia. Maybe he should

sit them down and have a serious talk about having a relationship with her. He knew he already said he was attracted to her, but he wanted to be clearer, so she didn't have anything to overthink.

He knew he needed to be gentle and slow with her, but at the same time, he didn't know if that was right. Jaxson didn't want to overwhelm her with everything, but he also didn't want her to think about it too much and talk herself out of it.

She had stared at him several times with *that* look in her eye. He knew she was attracted to him and felt the spark between them.

"What are you going to do with her?" Leo asked as he sat down right next to him.

"Off punishing one of the Littles?" he asked.

"Yeah, Kyle," he replied. "Don't avoid my question."

Jaxson let out a sigh. There was no beating around the bush with Leo or his brother Oliver. They asked questions until the person gave the answer, thanks to the military.

"I want her to be mine, I see her as mine already," he replied.

"So what are you going to do about it?" Leo asked.

"I'm going to have a talk with her. Tell her how I feel and give her a choice."

He didn't know if it would be tonight. He had a feeling she would be exhausted after all of this, but he wanted it to be soon. He didn't want to wait too long and miss his chance at being with her.

Jaxson looked down at his watch and stood up from his seat. Time to get her.

"Sofia," he softly said as he walked up to her.

She flinched but kept her face in the corner.

"You can come out now," he said.

Sofia turned around and flung herself into his arms. He held her closely as he picked her up and walked back over towards the chair. He could feel her starting to shake as she cried in his arms.

"Shhh, it's okay," he whispered in her ear as he ran his hand up and down her back. "All is forgiven."

She continued to cry in his arms and he whispered sweet things into her ear, trying to comfort her. He wanted Sofia to know he still cared for her and everything was going to be alright. He didn't want her to think for a second that he was mad at her or disappointed that she was naughty.

"I'm sorry!" she cried out as she pulled away from his embrace. "I'll never do that again!"

He chuckled and held her closely. "Don't promise something you may not be able to keep."

She shook her head, tears streaming down her face. He watched as she brought her hand up, rubbing her eyes with her closed fist and wiping away the tears.

"I promise! I'm not going to be naughty again. I don't want to get another spanking," she said.

"Shhh, it's okay," he said as he tried to calm her down. "Sometimes Little girls find themselves being naughty because they might be feeling icky, need to release some stress, and that's okay. Just know that Daddy will punish you."

"Daddy," she whimpered. "No bad girl."

"No, you aren't a bad girl. Sometimes you're just

naughty, but you'll always be my good girl," he whispered to her.

Sofia laid her head down on his shoulder, and snuggled into his body. He could get used to this and he wanted to. He wanted her with him at all times.

He wanted to be her forever Daddy.

Jaxson just needed to talk to her. He wanted her to continue to call him Daddy, come to him with her worries, let him take care of her, and let him love her. He had only known her for a couple of months. They were some of the best months, even if they didn't talk a lot, and it was starting to get better.

He rocked his body back and forth, trying to sooth her as they cuddled.

"She fell asleep fast," Michael softly said as he held Monroe. "Exhausted from playing and getting punished?"

"That and I don't know if she's sleeping well through the night. She works a lot and always gets off late," Jaxson whispered, trying to be quiet for Sofia.

He knew she needed a little rest and it wouldn't hurt her.

"You gonna do something about it?" Leo asked.

Jaxson looked over, and he was holding Kyle. If any other Dom walked into the room, they would probably think they were together, but Jaxson knew better. Not once had Leo or Oliver looked in Kyle's direction when he was in the club. Kyle was looking for a Mommy, or that's what Jaxson had heard from Charlotte. They didn't look at anyone, but they were on their phones a lot. He couldn't wait to see who they were talking to.

"Yes, I am," he replied. "I just need to have a discussion with her before I go all overprotective on her."

Leo chuckled and nodded his head. There were so many things Jaxson wanted to do to help Sofia. He wanted to make sure she ate enough, slept enough, she was taking time to be Little, and not working all the time. He didn't know why she was working so much, especially the late shift. Once he had the talk with her about his feelings, he was going to talk to her about all that stuff as well.

He needed to.

No. He *had* to.

Jaxson couldn't live with himself if he didn't talk to her about those things and she ended up getting sick or hurt somehow.

"You're going to have that talk soon?" Michael asked. "She looks a tad bit underweight, and she has some dark circles starting to appear under her eyes."

Jaxson knew about those and she did look small. He wanted to address those things, but he didn't want to scare her off.

"Yes, soon. I was going to talk to her tonight, but she's exhausted so it may wait until tomorrow when she comes in for her shift," Jaxson replied.

He had hoped they would get to the conversation tonight, but he hadn't thought that he would have to punish her. He knew punishments could take a lot out of Littles and he suspected, since it was Sofia's first one, that it was going to be even more exhausting.

"Take care of her," Kyle whispered as he snuggled into Leo's embrace.

Jaxson stared at him in shock before he cooled his expression. Kyle hadn't known Sofia for more than a couple of hours and they were already sticking together and making sure they were being treated right.

"I will, don't worry," he softly said. "She deserves the world."

Jaxson looked down at Sofia and smiled. She looked so peaceful sleeping in his lap, but he knew she probably needed to head home now and get some rest.

"Good luck waking her up," Leo said as he got up from his seat, Kyle in his arms. "I'm going to go drop him off at his house."

That was one thing Jaxson liked about their club. They made sure unattended Littles got home safely. They never wanted something to happen to them because they didn't go with them.

"Sofia," he gently said as he rubbed her back.

She whined and wiggled around on his lap. He groaned as she brushed up against his dick. Think of unattractive things. It wasn't the time to get a boner with her in his lap.

"Sofia. It's time to wake up," he said.

She whined again and shook her head.

"No, Daddy. Sleepy," she said.

"I know, Little one, but you need to wake up so you can go to bed," he said. "We need to get you home."

He continued to rub her back, trying to get her to wake up. Sofia slowly started to rouse from her sleep. He watched as she pulled her head back from his shoulder and yawned.

"Adorable," he softly said. She was absolutely adorable

when she had just woken up. He hoped someday soon he would be able to see it more often.

"No Daddy," she giggled. "No adorables."

He kissed her nose. "Yes, adorable."

She shook her head. No matter how much she denied being adorable; he was always going to tell her because she was.

And nothing was going to change his mind.

"Let's get you home," he said. "Let me go get my car keys."

She shook her head again. "You don't need to take me."

"Yes, I do. I want to make sure you get home safely."

"I already have a ride and they should be here by now."

He didn't want to let her go with whoever her ride was. He wanted to be the one to take her home and make sure she was in her place safely.

"Okay, give me one second and I'll walk out with you," he said.

Jaxson needed to tell one of the other owners he would be right back. Sofia pushed herself off of him and stood up and he followed suit.

"Let me go tell Michael and I'll walk you out. Sit here and don't leave until I walk with you," he said.

He quickly made his way over towards Michael.

"I'm taking Sofia to her ride outside but I'll be back," he said.

But when Jaxson turned around to walk back towards her, she was nowhere to be found. Oh, she was going to be in trouble.

CHAPTER TWELVE

SOFIA

Sofia felt exhausted when she came to work today and that was hours ago. She still had thirty minutes to an hour left of her shift and she didn't know how she was going to make it through, but she had to. She needed the money.

When she had gotten to work, Monty had told her Jaxson was looking for her. Sofia knew what it was about, or well, part of it at least. She was supposed to wait for him to walk her out last night, but she left before he could do that.

Sofia didn't want him to know she didn't actually have a ride, and that she was walking to her apartment building. He would've insisted that he give her a ride and she wasn't ready for him to see where she was living. It wasn't in the best location, but it also wasn't a terrible location.

But Sofia had a feeling that if Jaxson saw it, he wouldn't approve and would try to get her to go somewhere else. She didn't have money to move anywhere else and she didn't want to take his money.

Any time he had walked into the room, she always made sure she was super busy so he couldn't talk to her. Or she would hide but she knew that wouldn't last for a long time and, sooner or later, he was going to talk to her.

They still had to talk about the spark between them and what they were going to do about it. She didn't know what to do now. She knew if they got into a dynamic, he was going to ask several questions. Questions she didn't want to answer and show how much she was struggling with money.

She didn't want him to take pity on her.

"When are you going to talk to him?" Monty asked.

"I don't know," she softly replied, sounding so unsure. "He's not going to be happy when I talk to him."

"You ignoring him is just going to make it worse."

Sofia knew that, but she had already managed to ignore him for several hours. He must be livid by now and she didn't want to face his wrath.

"Maybe he'll fire you," Lucy sneered at her as she walked by. "Good riddance."

Monty turned towards Lucy and glared at her.

"You really need to tell Jaxson or any of the other club owners about Lucy being mean towards you," Monty said. "It's unacceptable."

"It's fine. She'll get over it soon and she hasn't done anything bad yet," Sofia replied.

"Yet. Just wait until she does do something. Who knows how bad that's going to be."

Sofia knew Monty was right and she probably should tell someone about it, but she didn't want to create any problems. Jaxson was already mad at her and she didn't want to give him another reason.

He had told her to come to him if anyone was being rude and she hadn't.

She was just adding another thing to the list of him being mad at her for. If he found out about that, but if she kept her mouth shut, maybe he wouldn't find out about it.

"If you don't tell him soon, I will," Monty said.

"Please don't," she replied. "I don't want to cause any problems."

"No. People shouldn't be rude to you and it's unacceptable."

Sofia nodded her head. She knew that if she put up any type of fight against it, Monty would push her to tell someone or she would tell one of the Doms about it. Sofia didn't know what to do, and she didn't want to think about it right now.

She was so exhausted, and all she wanted to do right now was go back to her apartment and sleep until tomorrow. Nothing sounded better than snuggling up to Trixie and falling asleep under her covers.

"Incoming," Monty whispered before she walked off.

What did she mean incoming?

"Sofia," Jaxson said.

Her whole body stiffened. That's what Monty meant by incoming. Jaxson was walking over to them and she didn't have time to hide or walk away from him.

She turned around and smiled at him. Maybe if she was nice and smiley at him, he would be less mad at her. But as she took him in, she realized it wasn't going to change anything.

"We need to talk," he said. "No ifs, ands, or buts. We are talking in my office *now*."

Sofia stood there, staring at him. He sounded serious, but not really angry. Maybe this was going to be about them and their dynamic and not her walking out last night.

"Don't you dare try to find a way out of this. You won't," he said. "You're going to walk around the bar and follow me to the office."

She nodded her head. She knew she wasn't going to be able to get anywhere, not when he was keeping a close eye on her. There was no point in avoiding it now.

"Grab Daddy's hand," he said as she walked from behind the bar.

A gasp was heard, and her head turned to the left. Lucy was standing there with her mouth wide open.

Shit.

This was not good. Lucy had heard Jaxson call himself Daddy. What was he thinking? He wasn't technically her Daddy right now. They had talked about it, but they hadn't solidified it yet.

Before Lucy could say anything, Jaxson grabbed her hand and started to walk towards his office.

"We have a lot to talk about," he said.

She kept her head down as they walked. She was toying with looking back at Jaxson. Sofia knew she looked exhausted and she could play that to her favor or it could backfire on her.

She didn't want to leave work. Though, if he saw her

face, he could insist on it. She would get out of this talk but then she would *have* to leave work. She needed the money right now. There was no way she could afford rent and food if she skipped out on an hour's pay.

It didn't seem like a lot, but it was to her. It meant the difference between her being able to eat meals this upcoming week or not.

"Take a seat," Jaxson said as they walked into his office.

She sat down on the couch, the furthest spot from his desk. She didn't want to be close to him in case he blew up after she said something. Somehow Sofia managed to make people mad when she talked. Well, not all the time, but a good majority.

That's why she kept to herself a lot.

"Sofia," he said. "Do you know why we need to talk?"

She shook her head. She had several ideas why they could possibly need to talk, but she didn't want to offer any up and be wrong.

"I think you do," he said. "Are you lying to Daddy?"

"No," she whispered. "I've got several ideas but don't want to pick the wrong one."

"Just name one. You won't get punished for picking the wrong one. Unless you are purposefully picking the wrong one to avoid the conversation."

She took a breath in and looked over in his direction, making eye contact. "We didn't get to talk about our dynamic?"

"Yes, but not what I had in mind," he said. "We'll get to that one in a couple of minutes. There's something more important that we need to discuss first."

"Me leaving last night?"

She was so afraid to say that, but she had a feeling that it was the correct answer. How could it not be? She couldn't remember her doing anything else that would warrant a conversation.

"Yes," he said. "I specifically told you to wait for me until I got back from talking to Michael and what happened when I turned back around? You were gone. I searched for you."

Guilt started to form in her stomach as he talked. She didn't mean for him to search for her.

"You didn't put a phone number down in your application or where you're staying. I was worried about you," he said.

"Sorry," she whispered, feeling terrible now.

She really didn't mean to make him worry and do all of that. It wasn't her intention.

"Why did you leave when I told you not to?" he asked.

"My ride was there and needed to be somewhere. I didn't want to keep them waiting," she whispered. "I really am sorry. I didn't mean to make you worry."

She knew she was still lying to him because she didn't have a ride. But he didn't need to know that because she would get into even more trouble than she was already in. Jaxson would be livid if he found out that she had been walking home every night since she started working there.

She couldn't do anything about it. She didn't have enough money to take a taxi every night to and from work. That would get crazy expensive and she wouldn't be able to pay for rent or eat anything.

"I could've taken you home," he said. "You could've told

the person that you needed to wait for me and they could've gone wherever they needed to go. You knew I offered to take you home and was available."

Tears formed in her eyes the longer he talked. The guilt was getting to be so much and she didn't want that.

"I'm really sorry," she whispered, the tears running down her face.

Maybe last night she should've just called the taxi, so he saw she had a ride home. Then he wouldn't be worried. She hated that he worried so much and even tried to find her.

"Next time, when I tell you to stay somewhere until I come back, I mean it. You have corner time but if you do it again, the consequences will be worse," he said.

"Yes, sir," she whispered.

She wanted to call him Daddy, but she didn't know how he would feel about that. They hadn't talked about their dynamic yet and she didn't know if it was okay to call him that. Yes, he had called himself Daddy when they were out in the main room, but she didn't know if he meant it or if he was just angry and it came out.

"Let's get the punishment over and then we can talk about our dynamic more," he said. "Legs spread, bottom out, and your nose in the corner. This time I'll let you keep your pants on, but don't get used to it."

She made her way over towards the corner and got into position. She hated corner time.

"Think about what you did wrong," he said. "I'll call you when the time is up."

She really hadn't meant to make him worry and look for

her last night. She thought she was doing something okay and that he really wouldn't care.

She was wrong. So wrong.

Why did she not think things through very much? She always seemed to think that it was going to be okay but then several hours later, she finds out it wasn't. There had been countless times that this had happened and she needed to stop that, however she could.

"You can come out now," he said.

She didn't know how long she stood there, thinking about what she had done wrong. If Jaxson offered to walk her outside again, she would just have to get a taxi. Hopefully, he didn't make it a thing.

"Come here," he said as he opened his arms.

She quickly walked over towards him and snuggled into his embrace. She loved his hugs, the way his arms felt around her.

Safe.

Comfortable.

Protected.

All the things she hadn't felt in a while and he was making her feel with just a hug. She was worried that if things went sour between them, that she would lose this and she didn't want that to happen.

Not when she just started to feel this way.

"Now, let's talk about our dynamic," he said. "Do you want to sit on my lap or on the couch?"

She so badly wanted to sit on his lap again, but she knew if she did, she would either fall asleep or not be able to pay attention at all. Her cheeks flushed at that thought.

"Ah, what's that thought?" he asked.

"The couch, please," she softly said, ignoring his question.

"Naughty thoughts?"

She blushed even more and made her way over towards the couch and sat down; him sitting right next to her.

"Now, I know you feel the spark between us. I've asked before and we both can agree on that. The other night you had been hesitant and I want to know why," he said. "Do you think you can tell me?"

She took a deep breath. She didn't really want to tell him why, but she knew communication was important and in this instance, she really needed to do it. He wasn't going to let this slide, and they needed to have this conversation.

"People will start talking about it," she softly said. "What if people think I'm just dating you to get benefits from you being my boss?"

That was the last thing she wanted someone to do. She didn't want any special treatment and make the other people hate her. Though, she knew Monty wouldn't do that, but Lucy definitely would.

"No one will talk or think bad about you. This has happened a lot more than you think, people who work here finding someone they want to be with. If someone is being mean and making nasty comments, you come to me or one of the other owners right away," he said. "What are your other concerns?"

"What if this doesn't work?" she whispered. "Will I be out of a job? I love working here and I don't want to risk losing it."

Sofia felt him grab her hand.

"If this doesn't work out, which I know it will, you will still have your job here. We are mature adults who can do this," he said. "And if we can't, then someone else will take over scheduling so you can continue to work here."

Her mouth fell open at that. He was going to get someone else to schedule the employees if they didn't work out? Oh my goodness. Part of her didn't believe he would actually do it. But the other part of her knew he was being serious and he was going to do what he said.

"I," she started to speak, but stopped herself. What was she supposed to say to that?

"I never want you to think that your job will be in jeopardy if we start a dynamic together. No matter what happens between us, you'll still have your job here," he said.

"Thank you?" she sounded so unsure. Was she supposed to say thank you or was she supposed to change the subject and move on?

Jaxson chuckled and looked at her. "Do you have any other concerns or hesitations?"

She shrugged her shoulders. She couldn't think of anything right now, but that didn't mean she didn't have any concerns or hesitations.

"I don't know," she whispered, looking down at her hands.

"That's okay. If you ever have anything, come to me and we'll talk about it," he replied. "But if you need anything, and I mean anything, please let me know. You have my phone number and I'll always answer."

She nodded her head and let out a yawn. She was

exhausted, but she still had at least thirty minutes left in her shift that she needed to do.

"We can talk about rules, hard limits, soft limits, and all of that tomorrow before you come into work. You need to go home and get some rest," he said.

Sofia shook her head. She couldn't go home right now, she still had part of her shift to finish.

"Why not?" he asked.

"I still have thirty minutes of my shift," she softly said. "I need to finish it."

"You'll still get paid for the thirty minutes," he said. "It's slow out there anyway. Monty and Lucy can handle the last thirty minutes."

Her shoulders slumped. She didn't like thinking about not working and still getting paid for that time.

"Please. I can see how exhausted you are," he said. "Do you need a ride home?"

She shook her head. "I've got a neighbor that drives by who is coming to pick me up. She's normally early so she should be here by now."

Sofia's gut clenched at the thought of lying to him again. She didn't like it, but she didn't want him to know where she lived just yet. She was trying to save up some more money, so she didn't have to stay there.

She had walked to her apartment so many times that she knew it by heart. Nothing was going to happen to her and a little white lie wouldn't hurt either.

"Okay," he said. "She's right out in front of the door?"

"She is," she replied.

"I'll walk with you."

"You really don't need to. She always picks me up right in front of the door. It's very well lit, and the bouncer watches me the whole time."

"Are you sure?" he asked.

She crossed her fingers that were under her legs. "I'm sure! Pete always makes sure I get into the car safely."

It was a total lie. Pete did watch her as she walked away, but she never got into a car. He had asked her if she was ever going to take a taxi or get a car, and she had replied with soon.

"I don't like this, but just this one night I'll let you go. After this, I'm walking with you. That'll be one of your rules," he said.

She let out a breath she was holding and nodded her head. Next time she'll just have to remember to call a taxi before she gets off of work that night. And come up with an excuse why her mysterious neighbor couldn't pick her up.

"I'll see you tomorrow. Remember, text me if you need anything and I mean anything," he said. "Come to work earlier tomorrow so we can talk about rules and limits."

"Okay," she whispered and got up from her seat.

"Give Daddy a hug," he said.

She wrapped her arms around him and melted into his embrace. She loved his hugs.

"I'll see you tomorrow," he said. "Text me when you get home."

"Bye," she replied.

"Sofia."

"I'll text you when I get home."

If she remembered. She had a hard time remembering

things sometimes or they would just slip her mind until several hours later.

"Good girl," he replied.

Sofia walked back towards the main room, quickly grabbed her purse from the employees' room, and then to the front entrance.

"I'll see you tomorrow!" Monty yelled.

"See you later," she replied.

Monty lived in the same apartment building as Sofia did so they saw each other even when they weren't at work. From what Sofia knew, Monty had a younger brother that she was taking care of. She didn't know all the details, but she knew Monty's brother was dependent on her right now.

"Sofia," Pete said as she walked out.

"Hey Pete," she replied. "Have a good night?"

He grunted. "Slow."

Tonight was slower than normal.

"You work tomorrow?" she asked.

She really liked Pete. He was nice, even if he didn't talk much.

"No, I don't. I've got tomorrow off," he replied.

Her whole body went stiff. "Who's working?"

There were a couple bouncers the club had and out of all of them, Pete was her favorite. Well, and Ben.

"Ben is," he replied.

She felt her body relax at his name. She could handle both of them, but Dominic was the one she didn't really get along with. He never talked and always glared at her.

"But I heard Ben was feeling a little bit under the weather today so Dominic may fill in for him," Pete said.

She groaned but nodded her head. Hopefully, Ben was feeling better by tomorrow night so she didn't have to deal with Dominic.

"I'll see you later," she yelled as she started to walk towards her apartment building.

The further she walked, the more her hairs tingled at the back of her neck. What was going on? This had never happened before.

Sofia turned her head to the right and then left, looking around to see if anything was off, but nothing was. No one was out here. Nobody was ever out here.

"Give me the purse!" Someone yelled, yanking the purse from her arms.

She grabbed onto the strap, trying to pull the purse back towards her.

"Bitch!" the person yelled. "Let go of the purse."

But Sofia didn't. She tugged on the strap, hoping it wouldn't break and that the person would let go.

Before she knew it, pain shattered across her face as the guy's fist connected with her face. She screamed as she let go of the purse and fell towards the ground.

Tears brimmed in her eyes, and she watched the man walk towards her. He kicked her stomach, and she groaned as the pain radiated across her body.

"That'll teach you a lesson," he said. "You're not wanted here."

Tears ran down her face as the man ran off with her purse. What did she do to deserve this? Why did he say she wasn't wanted here? Did she know that guy?

So many questions ran through her head as she pulled

herself off from the ground. She needed to get to her apartment and look at the damage. Thankfully, she kept her keys to her apartment and her phone in her pocket instead of her purse. Bad news was, the only extra cash she had was in her purse.

What was she going to do until she got paid? It was several days until payday, and she needed to eat. Maybe she could pick up some extra shifts and eat some snacks at work while she was there.

Groaning, she walked up the stairs to her apartment and unlocked her door. She didn't know if she wanted to look at her face or not, but she figured she should see how bad the damage is.

Not that she'll be able to do anything. She didn't have any cold things in her apartment and she couldn't run the water and wrack up the water bill that she could barely pay for right now.

Sofia walked into the bathroom and let out a gasp at her skin already turning different colors. It had settled into an ache, but she knew tomorrow it was going to be worse.

So much worse and Jaxson was going to ask questions. Shit. This wasn't good.

With that thought, Sofia laid down on her bed, sent the text to Jaxson, and fell asleep.

CHAPTER THIRTEEN

SOFIA

Sofia's face ached even more when she woke up this morning. Her face was purple and deep blue, almost black, from where the guy hit her. She hadn't even attempted to look at the rest of her body, but she knew she had some other bruises.

Her bottom hurt from where she landed on it and she knew she had a couple minor cuts on her hand from hitting the ground. Had she cleaned them when she got back or this morning?

No. She didn't.

She didn't have anything to clean them, and she didn't have any money to buy what she needed. Jaxson's words rang in her head about texting him about anything. Several times she had thought about texting him asking if he had anything, but she didn't want to worry him.

Not that she would be able to hide this bruise when she got there. Sofia had planned on wearing a hat to work to cover up most of it and not talking to Jaxson. She didn't know how well that was going to work.

Jaxson seemed to be keen on when she was trying to hide things and she just knew that he would walk up to her. She had never worn a hat to work before and maybe she should've started every once in a while. Then this wouldn't have been so bad or weird for her.

Part of her wanted to call out of work and tell him she was sick, but she knew he would insist on coming to help her out. She didn't want him to see her like this. The other part of her knew she needed to go to work because she needed the money.

She couldn't skip and lose all that money, no matter how tempting it was to hide away. She would have to skip several days and she couldn't do that. The money was precious to her.

"Sofia!" Monty yelled. "I know you're in your apartment. Can we talk?"

Sofia sighed, grabbed her hat, and put it on before she opened her door. She didn't want to talk to Monty right now, but she knew Monty only bothered her if it was important and it must be important right now.

"Yes?" Sofia asked.

"Why are you wearing a hat?" she asked.

"My hair is greasy and I haven't washed it yet," she replied.

It wasn't a lie, but her hair wasn't so greasy that she needed a hat.

"Could you cover my shift for me? It's right before yours,"

Monty asked. "My brother isn't feeling well, and he's running a fever. I don't have anyone to watch him."

Sofia really didn't want to do Monty's shift as well as her own. It was going to be a long and exhausting day but Sofia couldn't say no. She knew Monty took care of her brother and that he was important to her.

"I would ask you to watch my brother and I could pay you in food, but I don't want you to get sick," Monty rushed out. "If not, I can try to call someone else to cover my shift."

She started to feel bad. "I'll cover for you."

"Thank you so much. I can make you a meal to say thank you or I can do something else," Monty said.

"No worries. You just take care of your brother."

Sofia didn't have any siblings, but if she did, she would want to be able to take care of them without having to worry about anything. Though, Sofia didn't know how Monty was going to pay for rent or food. She didn't know how much money she was earning or anything about her finances.

She had thought about asking, but she knew money was a touchy subject. Or at least it was for her. She didn't want people to ask her how her situation was going because it wasn't going well.

"Thank you so much," she said. "If you need anything, you let me know."

Monty walked off and Sofia closed her door. Now she had even less time to think about how she was going to cover up the bruises.

"Sofia," Dominic said as she walked up to the front door.

She had gotten here a little early because she didn't know how well her body was going to take walking from her apartment to work. She had really considered getting a taxi after everything happened, but by the time she actually thought about it, she wouldn't be able to get one in time to cover Monty's shift.

"What are you doing here? Your shift doesn't start for several more hours," he said.

She kept her head down as she walked up closer to him. She didn't want him to see the left side of her face and ask a lot of questions.

"Monty asked me to cover for her," she softly said.

Dominic was normally quiet and didn't say anything. He always seemed to be in a bad mood and she didn't know why.

"Why are you wearing a cap?" he asked.

Her whole body went rigid at that question. She was hoping no one would notice or ask her that.

"My hair is greasy, and I didn't have enough time to wash it," she said, giving the same lie she gave to Monty.

Sofia didn't know if it would work, but she hoped it would. Maybe she could actually get through this night without any incidents.

"Lift your head then," he said.

"I'm going to be late for my shift," she replied.

She didn't know why he was suddenly asking so many questions. This wasn't like him at all.

"Stop," he said as she started to walk past him.

DADDY'S LITTLE FOREIGNER

Sofia looked up a little, making sure to keep the left side of her face away from him so he couldn't see anything.

"Happy?" she asked, starting to get into a bad mood. "Now, I need to go for my shift."

"No," he said. "You're hiding something and I don't think I'm going to like it."

"You aren't my Dom or Daddy."

She was hoping he would back off, but he didn't seem like he was going to. Sofia took a step towards the open door, but Dominic grabbed her arm.

"Stop!" she yelled. "Don't touch me."

"Then show me your face," he said. "Or I'll tell Jaxson you're hiding something."

"Tell me what?" Jaxson said. "What's going on here?"

She put her head down so he wouldn't be able to see her face. Sofia didn't want Jaxson to get involved with this.

"She's hiding something," Dominic said. "Something about her face. She's wearing a hat."

"Shut up," Sofia hissed.

She was tired, in pain, and now in a bad mood. She didn't want people getting into her business and yet here everyone was.

"Sofia," Jaxson said. "That is no way to talk to Dominic."

Biting her lip, she tried her hardest not to say anything. She was getting agitated and just wanted to be left alone. Maybe she should've called in sick and told Monty that she wouldn't be able to cover her shift.

If only.

"Sofia," Jaxson said. "Can you look at me?"

She kept her head down and tried to get her arm out of Dominic's hold.

"Let go," she growled out.

"Be kind," Jaxson scolded her.

Sofia so badly wanted to glare at him, but she knew once she looked up, he was going to ask a million questions.

"Tell him to let go of my arm!" She raised her voice. "I'm going to be late for my shift."

"Dominic," Jaxson said. "I'll take it from here."

"I want to see what she's hiding," he said. "I watch her come and leave work and something is definitely wrong."

She felt touched for a second that he recognized that, but at the same time, she didn't need it. She wanted to go on with work and get it over with so she could go home and sleep. This day was beginning to become exhausting, and she just wanted it to end.

"Sofia," Jaxson said. "Can you look up at me?"

She brought her head up slightly but knew with the angle he wouldn't be able to see anything on her face. She hoped this would suffice, but deep down she knew that it wouldn't.

"More?" he asked. "Or you can take your hat off."

Sofia didn't want to do that. She thought both of them knew that and wanted it even more.

"Sofia," he said. "Hat off. Now."

"No," she said. "I need to get to work."

"Freeze!" he commanded as she took a step to the side.

She closed her eyes and winced as the skin around her eyes started to hurt. The bruise just seemed to get worse as time went on.

"What's going on with you?" he asked. "You've never acted this way."

"I just want to get to work. I'm covering for Monty and my hair is greasy. There isn't anything wrong. Will you two just leave me alone now?" she raised her hands in the air.

Jaxson grabbed one of her hands before she could pull it back to herself.

"Let go of my hand," she said. "Please. Just let me leave so I can get to work."

"Your hands have little cuts on them," Jaxson said before he turned to Dominic. "You weren't working last night?"

"No," he said. "Pete was."

"What happened, Little one?"

She bit the inside of her cheeks to stop herself from spilling her guts. Jaxson needed to know that she got mugged last night, but she didn't really want to tell him. It was so hard when he got all soft for her and asked her what was wrong.

It made her want to spill her guts to him. To tell him all of her worries and what was going wrong with her life.

"Little one," he softly said. "I can't help unless you talk to me."

She shook her head as tears filled her eyes. She wasn't going to tell him what happened. Sofia just needed to keep her head down the entire night and make sure no one else saw her or asked questions. It wasn't going to be easy, but she was up for the challenge.

"Sofia," he said. "If you won't tell me, then I'm going to take the hat off of you. You're worrying me and I want to make sure that you're okay."

She took a calming breath in. He wouldn't take the hat off of her. Would he? She didn't think he would, but he had surprised her the last several times when he said something.

Should she take the chance, or should she just take her hat off? She knew it looked bad, and she didn't have any makeup to try covering it up. Not that it wouldn't have done any good because she didn't know anything about makeup or how to apply it.

"Can I please just go to work?" she softly asked. "I'm covering for Monty and it might be super busy tonight."

She needed to get in there because there could be several people in there waiting to get snackies and drinks but she wasn't there.

"I don't want you to worry about that. I have Lucy covering right now," Jaxson said.

A whine left her lips at the mention of her coworkers name. If Lucy found out she was covering for Sofia, it wasn't going to end well. Lucy already gave her dirty looks, and she didn't want to give her anything else to fuel the fire.

"What's wrong?" he asked. "You can talk to Daddy."

"Nothing," she said. "I am just tired, my hair is greasy, and I need to get to my shift."

She knew it wasn't right that she kept lying, but she really didn't want them to bother with this. Why were they worried since she wore a hat?

"I'm going to give you five seconds to take it off or I will," he said.

Sofia gasped and looked up. "You can't do that!"

Her eyes went wide as she realized she just looked fully

up, giving him sight of what her eye and face looked like. Before she could drop her head, he grabbed hold of her chin.

"What the fuck happened?"

CHAPTER FOURTEEN

SOFIA

Sofia stared at him with wide eyes. Shit. She should've thought about her actions before she looked up. How could she be so stupid to lift her head when she knew she was trying to hide her face?

"Shit, Tiny," Dominic said. "Who did that to you?"

She looked up at Dominic and saw his murderous expression. She didn't know why he was looking at her like that. Did Dominic care about her? Sofia didn't think there were many people that cared about her here in Missouri. Not many people knew her and she didn't have any friends.

"Little one," Jaxson softly said. "Can you look at Daddy for me?"

Her eyes wandered over to his. She didn't know what to say to Jaxson right now. What was she supposed to say?

"Can you tell me what happened?" he asked.

She felt a mix of being exhausted and having all the adrenaline pumping through her. She didn't want to let him know what happened because it would show all the lies she told him.

"I fell last night when I was walking to the bathroom and hit my bedpost," she whispered, cringing at how bad the lie was.

She should've thought about what she was going to say if anyone asked, but she hadn't. Lying on the spot wasn't a strong suit of hers and it was showing right now.

"Bullshit!" Dominic raised his voice. "What the fuck happened to your eye and cheek? Who hit you?"

She flinched at his loud voice and cowered away from him. Deep down she knew he wasn't going to hurt her, but right now her brain wasn't thinking. It heard his tone of voice and the volume and immediately thought it was dangerous.

"Dominic," Jaxson said. "Don't yell at my girl. And no using that language around her."

"Sorry," Dominic said. "Just please tell us Sofia. Who did this to you?"

Tears formed in her eyes as both of them looked at her and asked questions. She didn't know what to do in this situation and everything was becoming overwhelming. What was she supposed to do? She didn't know the guy who mugged her.

"Tiny," Dominic said. "It's okay. You can tell us."

"Dominic is right," Jaxson agreed with him. "You can tell us anything. You trust Daddy, right?"

She nodded her head but still didn't speak. If she told Jaxson what happened, he would know that she lied about all those times someone came to pick her up. She didn't know anyone in this city who would pick her up and she knew Jaxson would be disappointed in her when he found out.

"Little one," Jaxson said. "It's going to be okay. Can you tell Daddy what happened? Who hit you?"

A sob broke out of her mouth, and she flung herself at Jaxson. His arms wrapped around her and she continued to cry in his arms. Everything was so overwhelming and she just didn't want to talk right now.

"It's going to be okay," he whispered as he held her in his arms. "I'm going to take her to my office. Are you good?"

"I'm good. Just make sure you find out who did it," Dominic said.

"We will, don't worry."

Sofia felt Jaxson start to walk, but she didn't lift her head from his shoulder. She didn't want anyone to see her right now, especially with her bruised face. There would be too many questions and she was already feeling overwhelmed.

"Jaxson!" Lucy said. "Who are you holding?"

"Sofia," he replied and continued to walk.

"Leave her be. Could you help me with something?" she asked.

He stopped walking and turned around. "No. Find another Dom to help you. You can clearly see that I'm busy right now."

Sofia cringed into his shoulder. She knew Lucy would not like being dismissed like that, especially since it involved her. She honestly had no clue what Lucy had against her, and she hadn't had the chance or courage to ask her yet.

"But-," Lucy started.

"No buts," he said. "Find another Dom if you need something and please don't bother me."

Before Lucy could say anything else, Jaxson started to walk towards his office again. Sofia's whole body had gone stiff as Jaxon talked to Lucy.

"You're okay," he whispered. "You can relax."

She tried to, but it was so hard. She was overwhelmed, scared, and nervous about everything.

Jaxson sat her down on a couch while she clung to his shirt. She didn't want to let go of him yet, but he was releasing his hold. Why was he letting her go?

"I'm not going anywhere. I'm just putting you down so I can see your face," he softly said.

She let go of his shirt and snuggled into the couch. Her body started to shake as she thought about everything that had happened in the past day.

Jaxson crouched down in front of her, resting his hands on her thighs as he looked at her. "Can you tell me what happened? What really happened?"

Sofia opened her mouth, ready to tell him what happened, but her breathing picked up. Was he going to believe her? How was he going to react when she told him she walked home every night after her shift and lied?

Every Dom or Domme took lying very seriously. She knew what she did was wrong, but Sofia believed anyone would've done it if they were in her situation. She didn't want them to know where she lived because it wasn't the best place. And if she told them she didn't have enough money for a cab, they would have insisted on driving her.

Something she didn't want.

"Sofia?" he softly asked. "Can you take a deep breath for me?"

She hadn't realized that she had started to hyperventilate as her mind went all over the place. She took a slow breath in and let it out.

"Good girl," he said. "Now, can you tell me?"

"I," she took a breath in. "I. I got."

Tears were streaming down her face as she thought about getting mugged again. Everything was so fresh and she didn't really have time to process everything. Also, walking down the same street when she walked to work hadn't helped her at all.

"You're okay," he softly said. "You're safe now."

She knew she was safe right now, but what about later when she went home? What if the mugger ran but hid so he could see where she lived? Was she going to have to find a new place to live?

Sofia didn't know where that would be with her tiny budget. Maybe she could find a women's shelter she could stay at for a couple of nights until she figured something out. They have security, right?

She knew nothing about women's shelters in the United States and didn't even know if they were any here in Springfield.

"Deep breath in. Hold it. Let it out," Jaxson softly said as he placed her hand on his chest, right above his heart. "That's it. Such a good girl for Daddy."

Her heart fluttered as he called her a good girl and she felt herself slowly start to calm down.

"Daddy's so proud of you," he whispered. "Such a good girl."

Tears still ran down her face as she managed to calm herself down. She knew she was going to have to tell him and she needed to stay calm the whole time.

"Are you okay?" he asked.

She nodded her head. "I, I got m-mugged l-last night," she whispered, not looking him in the eyes.

Sofia didn't want to see his reaction when she told him that. What would he think? How was he going to react?

"When you walked from the car to your building?" he calmly asked.

More tears ran down her face as the mention of getting out of a car. She hadn't, and she felt so guilty for lying to him several times.

"I didn't have a ride," she wailed. "I walked to my apartment yesterday. I lied and then I got mugged."

"Shhh," he said. "It's going to be okay. We'll talk about you walking home later. Right now, I want to know everything about what happened and what you did afterward."

"I walked home last night and when I was close to my apartment building," she took a shuddering breath in. "He came out of nowhere. Told me to give him my purse, and I didn't. He punched me in my face, knocking me down on the ground, and then ran off."

Had he kicked her? She honestly couldn't remember and right now she didn't want to. Sofia just wanted to forget about what happened and go on with her day. She didn't want to have to think about it any more and bring it up in her mind.

Had the guy followed her to her apartment? She couldn't remember what she had in the purse besides the money. Did she have something valuable or that he could identify her with?

"You should've just let him take the purse," he said. "Your safety is important and we could have always gotten you another purse but we can't get another you."

She knew that now, but at the time, all she could think about was losing her last bit of cash. Jaxson didn't know that she was struggling for money, and she wanted to keep it that way. What would he think of her if he knew she could barely pay for rent and she didn't eat a lot?

"Was there anything valuable in your purse?" he asked. "Do we need to talk to the police? Did you get a good look at his face?"

"There was cash, but I can't remember if there was anything else," she started to cry again. That cash was super important to her and now she didn't know what she was going to do. "I didn't get a good look at him at all."

"Why didn't you call me?" he asked. "You know I would've been there in a heartbeat. You should've called me."

"I just wanted to get to my apartment and go to bed. I was scared and wasn't thinking straight."

And that was the truth. It may have briefly crossed her mind that she should call him, but her being scared took over and she didn't call him. Maybe he could've made things better.

"Did you put anything on your face?"

She shook her head. "I didn't have anything, and I just

wanted to lay in my bed, snuggle up to Trixie, and go to bed."

"Next time, you call me," he said. "Not that there will be a next time because I'm walking you to the car and watching you get in. No more walking to your apartment."

She nodded her head, not telling him she never had anyone picking her up. She'd been lying to him all along. Next time she worked, she needed to call a cab before her shift ended so it would be there for him to see.

"For the next couple of days, you're going to be staying with me so I can take care of you and make sure that your bruises are healing up nicely," he said. "You're going to have several days off so you can just focus on healing and nothing else. Understand?"

"I can't," she blurted out. Sofia didn't even have to think about that. "I need the money."

"You'll be taking sick leave. Everyone gets two weeks of sick leave."

"I can't."

Sofia didn't think Jaxson understood she couldn't take sick leave. She needed the money so she could pay her rent and the little food she could buy. There was no way she was going to be able to afford rent if she didn't work the next couple of days.

"Do you know what sick leave is?" he asked. "You get paid for it. What you would normally make in a shift, you'll make but instead of working, you'll be resting to recover from the mugging."

"I don't know," she whispered. "I'm okay working."

"You won't be working," he said. "You'll be taking a

couple days off, paid days off, to rest up, and let your body heal from everything. It's not up for discussion and my decision is final. You'll be staying with me for the next couple of days, so I know that you're actually resting and letting your body heal."

Sofia opened her mouth to argue, but Jaxson raised his eyebrow and looked at her, making her quickly shut her mouth.

"No arguing," he said. "You're overwhelmed, scared, and hurting. I'm taking over as your Daddy, so you don't have to worry about any of that."

She loved the sound of that, but she also didn't know. She was hesitant..

"Do you understand?" he asked.

Before Sofia could say anything, the door opened, and both of them looked at Leo who walked in.

"What the fuck happened?"

CHAPTER FIFTEEN

SOFIA

Sofia's eyes went wide as she stared at Leo. What was he doing here? She had only seen him a handful of times at the club, but never talked to him.

He was scary.

With how broad his shoulders were, his height, and the way he carried himself, she knew he meant business at any point. Sofia didn't know what he did before he became one of the owners for BTS. All she knew was he was terrifying.

He never smiled at people, never talked much, and never really interacted with anyone besides the owners.

Leo took a step towards them and Sofia shied away and got closer to Jaxson. She knew he wouldn't hurt her, but her mind wasn't in the best place right now. He was big, scary, and he could hurt her very easily.

"Sorry," he said as he slowly raised his hands. "I didn't mean to scare you. You don't have to be afraid of me. I'll never hurt you."

She continued to stare at him, watching his every move

as he took a couple steps closer. He turned his body towards Jaxson who was still in front of her, kneeling on the ground.

"What happened?" he asked, his voice growing cold. "Who did that to her?"

Jaxson turned towards Sofia and gave her a small smile. "Do you know the man who mugged you?"

She shook her head. She didn't get a good look at him and she was pretty sure the guy was wearing a mask. The man's voice was also unfamiliar, everything about him was unfamiliar.

"Where exactly was it?" Jaxson asked.

She took a breath. She just wanted to fall asleep and not talk about this, but she knew he wouldn't let her right now. He was asking questions, and he wanted to know the answers.

"Tired," she mumbled, closing her eyes.

She felt his hands cup her face.

"I know you're tired, but can you answer a couple more questions for me?" Jaxson softly asked.

Tears formed in her eyes. Everything was getting to be too much, and she just wanted to sleep and forget about everything.

"Sweetie," Leo said. "Can you please tell us where it was?"

She blinked and let the tears fall from her eyes and down her cheek. "Right in front of my apartment."

Leo pulled his phone out and brought it up to his ear. She heard him talk, but couldn't make out what exactly he was saying. What was he doing?

"Sofia," Jaxson said her name to gain her attention, but she continued to look at Leo.

He was still someone she didn't know very well and wanted to make sure he wasn't going to do anything.

"You're safe here," Jaxson whispered. "I'm going to keep you safe. No one is going to hurt you again."

She knew that what he was saying was true, but right now it was hard to believe. She had gotten mugged, and she didn't feel safe anywhere.

"Can you tell me anything else that happened?" Jaxson asked.

Nothing else had happened. She had gone home, exhausted, bruised, and in pain. Even now, she felt all of those things and just wanted to go to sleep.

"I heard there was a situation," Oliver said as he walked into the room.

Sofia's whole body went stiff as she saw him walk over to Leo. They were brothers and looked exactly alike. Both of them were scary, and she had never talked to them before.

"Shit," Oliver said as he looked over at her. "Who did that to you?"

She let out a sigh and closed her eyes. How many times was she going to have to say it was a mugger? How many times was she going to have to go through every single detail?

"It was a mugger outside her apartment," Jaxson said. "Happened last night when she walked home."

"What the fuck was she doing walking home?" Oliver asked. "We have rules in place so no one walks home."

She screwed her eyes shut even more. If they were upset

about her walking home last night, they were going to throw a fit when they found out she had been walking home every night she worked.

"We're going to have that discussion later," Jaxson said. "She isn't getting away with it."

"Sofia, honey?" Oliver said.

She opened her eyes and wearily looked at him. She didn't know him and didn't know if she could trust him. Yes, he was a Dom and one of the owners at the club, but he was scary looking. He had huge muscles and could definitely squash her if he wanted to.

"Can you tell me where you live?" he asked.

Sofia looked over at Jaxson. Maybe asking permission if she could answer the question, but right now she didn't know fully. She was exhausted and clearly wasn't thinking right.

"You can tell him," he softly said.

She looked back over at Oliver before looking at Leo. It was hard to tell them apart, but Oliver had a slightly fuller beard than Leo did. But if they shaved, she didn't know if she would be able to tell the difference.

"Honey?" he asked again. "Can you tell me where you live?"

"I didn't know the man who mugged me," she whispered. "His voice and his features weren't familiar. I think he was wearing a mask but I'm not sure. It was random because I don't know anyone outside the club."

She leaned forward and placed her head on Jaxson's shoulders. Closing her eyes, she took several deep breaths in.

Sleep was calling her, but she knew with everyone in the room, she wasn't going to get any sleep.

"Where do you live?" Oliver asked.

Sofia stayed silent. She was embarrassed at where she lived and didn't want them to know that she lived in that particular apartment building. What were they going to say when they found out?

She wanted to find a better place to live before they found out. Sofia would skip some more meals so she could put some in savings for a better place. It wasn't a lot, and she knew it was going to take her a while, but she was prepared.

When Sofia had filled out the paperwork, she had told Jaxson she was staying in a motel at the time. It wasn't a lie and said she would fill out where she lived when she found a place. For all she knew, they could still think she was staying at the motel.

"Is there a reason-" Oliver didn't finish his sentence.

She turned her head, peeking up at Oliver and Leo.

"Can you please tell us where you live?" Leo softly asked. "We just want to make sure you're okay."

"I'm fine," she tiredly whispered.

But she wasn't fine. How was she fine after she got mugged and traumatized like that?

Leo gave her a funny look, and she tried to smile. The more she laid her head on Jaxson's shoulder, the more she grew tired.

"I'm going to take the next couple of days off and take care of her," Jaxson said. "Make sure she is healing up nicely."

"Good idea," Leo said.

"Could one of you find a replacement for her while she's out the next couple of days?"

Sofia whined. She didn't like that she was taking the next couple of days off. She needed every penny she could get.

"Shush," Jaxson said, running his hand up and down her back. "You're my responsibility now and there will be no further arguments about this."

She was going to fight that battle later, she was just too tired to do it now. It wouldn't hurt to let him take care of her tonight and then leave tomorrow to go back to work. Maybe all she needed was one night of being taken care of and she would be all better.

"Honey, you let Jaxson take care of you," Oliver said. "If I hear you didn't, you won't be getting those cookies anymore."

Her eyes went wide. He was the one that put the cookies there every shift? She had assumed that it was Monty.

"Yeah, it was me, Little girl," he said. "You let your Daddy take care of you for the next couple of days. He just wants to make sure you're alright and healed."

"What is he talking about?" Jaxson asked. "Tell Daddy."

They kept referring to Jaxson as Daddy and he felt like her Daddy. Everything in her wanted to start calling him Daddy, but she wasn't sure. Would he still want her after he found out she had been walking home every night?

Sofia didn't think it would hurt to call him Daddy in her head right now. He didn't know, and he kept referring to himself as Daddy. It was okay, right? She didn't want to think about it much with the slight headache she was getting.

"Every time she had a shift, I would leave a little packet

of cookies on her locker where she kept her stuff," Oliver said. "I give Monty gummy bears. Thought after having an entire night of working, they should have a little treat."

Sofia pulled her head away from her Daddy's shoulders and looked at him. Was he mad Oliver had given her those? She didn't always eat them, but sometimes she did and they were delicious.

"I need to finish something up really quick and then we'll be on our way," Daddy said. "Can you two find someone to take Lucy's place? She was supposed to go home an hour ago."

"Sure," Leo said before he turned to Sofia. "You get better now. Follow Daddy's rules."

She blushed and looked away from them. She could hear the little chuckle Leo and Oliver gave before they headed out of the room.

"Now, let's get you all comfortable on the couch while I finish up my paperwork," Daddy said. "Take a little nap before we head home."

For once, she couldn't disagree with taking a nap. It sounded glorious.

Sofia watched as he walked over to his desk and pulled out a blanket before coming back to her.

"Do you want to lay down?" he asked.

She nodded her head and slowly positioned herself on the couch, resting her head on the throw pillow.

"Jaxson?" Dominic said.

Sofia's head shot up, and she watched Dominic walk into the room. What was he doing here?

"Can I help you with something?" Daddy asked.

"I thought it was weird, but as I stood out there, letting people in, I thought to myself. You didn't know," Dominic said.

She gave Dom a weird look. What did Daddy not know?

"What?" Daddy said, looking between Dom and Sofia. "What are you talking about?"

"Sofia walks home every night," Dom replied and her eyes went wide. "Lucas, Pete, and I were talking the other night about it and thought you knew but that wouldn't make sense. No Dom that's part of the club allows any of the employees or Littles to leave unless they have a ride or are driving."

"No!" She yelled.

Both of their heads snapped towards her. Her head was pounding at this point, but she didn't care. Dominic was telling Daddy her secret that she wasn't ready to share yet.

"Is this true?" Daddy asked.

But she didn't pay any attention to Daddy but looked at Dominic. "It wasn't your place to tell him!"

"Sofia," Daddy said. "Look at me *now*."

"You weren't supposed to say anything! It was all fine!" she raised her voice.

"You getting mugged is fine?" Dominic said. "Bullshit. It's not and you know it."

"Sofia," Daddy barked out her name.

She turned her head and glared before looking back at Dominic. She didn't care at the moment.

"It wasn't your place to tell him. You should just keep your mouth shut," she said.

Dominic stepped towards her and bent down a little so that they were on eye level.

"Tiny," he said. "I want what's best for you. You shouldn't have kept that from your Daddy and if I knew that he didn't know, I would've told him the first day. Hell, Pete or Lucas would've done the same thing."

She continued to glare at him, but it didn't seem to faze him at all.

"Sofia," Daddy said. "Look. At. Me."

Her gaze went towards him, and he did not look impressed.

"Don't you dare glare and get angry with him," he said.

"But Daddy," she started to say, but when his eyebrow went up, she went silent.

"But nothing. You knew the rule, and yet you decided to ignore it. Why?"

More guilt started to build up in the pit of her stomach. She knew it was wrong, but she didn't think it would be this bad. Nothing was supposed to happen to her.

"Sofia," Daddy said. "Why did you lie?"

"I didn't want to bother anyone," she whispered.

That was part of the truth, but the other part was because she didn't want them to see where she lived. It wasn't in the best part of town and she was a little embarrassed.

"That's unacceptable," Daddy crouched down next to her. "You knew better than to do that. When you're all better, you'll get your punishment."

Her eyes went wide as she stared at him. She was getting punished for that? She wasn't his at that point.

"I wasn't yours," she softly said.

"Doesn't matter, Tiny," Dominic said.

"He's right. You knew the rules we had for every employee and yet you decided to lie and break them," Daddy grabbed her hand and held it.

Sofia let out a sigh and nodded her head. She wasn't going to fight him on this.

"Now, lay your head down and get some rest while I finish up this paperwork," Daddy said as he pulled the blanket over top of her.

"I'll leave. I hope you get better soon, Tiny," Dominic said. "I know you might hate me at the moment, but later you'll thank me."

She huffed out a breath and didn't say anything. He had gotten her in trouble. How was she going to thank him later for that? Maybe he should get his bottom spanked for tattle-taling on her.

"Thank you for mentioning it," Daddy softly said.

Sofia closed her eyes and heard them speaking more, but didn't pay any attention to it. Putting her thumb in her mouth, she started to suck on it and fell asleep.

CHAPTER SIXTEEN

JAXSON

Jaxson let out a sigh as he sat down at his desk. He didn't expect today to go how it went. He was expecting a smooth afternoon.

But that wasn't what happened.

He didn't know what compelled him to walk downstairs and into the main room when he did, but he had gone anyway. He was thankful because he wouldn't have caught Sofia and Dominic arguing.

Jaxson had seen red when he saw Dominic grab her arm but as the situation unfolded, he was partially glad. He still didn't like that another man was touching her, but if he hadn't she would've gotten away.

Not that she could go very far. She had been coming in to cover for Monty and then she had her shift. He didn't like that she was working so much, but maybe she was in a tight position.

Jaxson didn't like the thought of that either. He wanted her to flourish and to live comfortably, not worrying about when she was going to eat next or if she would be able to pay her rent.

Granted, he had no clue if that was how she lived. He had wanted to ask several times, but he didn't want to make her uncomfortable or push her away from him. Leo and Oliver had asked several times where she lived and she never answered them.

Where could she possibly live?

He was trying to wrack his brain for places she wouldn't want either of them to know about. She could be staying at the apartments a couple blocks away but he highly doubted that. They were cheap places, and she was getting paid plenty more than that.

Jaxson opened his computer and pulled up her file. She had mentioned that she was going to update her application when she found a place and he wanted to see if she had done that. Maybe that could tell him where she was living.

When she first moved here, she had mentioned staying at the motel, but she said apartments earlier so she couldn't be staying there anymore. Jaxson had wanted to pay for a better place when she mentioned the run down motel, but she didn't know him and she was new to the country. He didn't want to scare her and run her off when he felt a connection with her.

He had bit his tongue several times when she would say something or he would see something. He needed to take it slow with her, but he didn't want to. Jaxson wanted her as his and he wanted to take care of her. Make sure that she was okay, getting enough food, sleep, and was safe.

It didn't seem like she was right now and that hurt him.

Every Dom wanted to make sure that any submissive was safe and taken care of. And knowing that she wasn't, broke him.

How could he have prevented this? Could he have pushed her a little more and gotten more information? Could he have followed her when she got off of her shift?

He let out a sigh when he realized that her residence was still blank on her application. He needed to remember to get her to fill it in and make sure it was an actual place.

The other night he had gotten a bad feeling when she said she had a ride, but he ignored it. She had said it several times and thought that if it wasn't true, that one of the bouncers would say something to him. He was so wrong, and he wished he could go back in time and insist on walking her out.

Maybe her getting mugged wouldn't have happened.

Jaxson looked over at Sofia sleeping on his couch. Her thumb was still in her mouth as she sucked on it. He needed to get her a pacifier, but he didn't want to leave her in his office alone. What if she woke up and panicked? What if someone walked into his office while he was gone?

That wasn't going to work.

He was going to stay here and finish up what he had left and then take her home, where he could watch over her and make sure she was okay. There he had pacifiers that were never used that she could have.

His office door opened and Leo and Oliver walked in. What were they doing back in his office? Normally they were out teaching people how Shibari worked or doing a scene with a sub.

"Please be quiet," he whispered. He didn't want Sofia to wake up. Jaxson wanted her to have as much rest as she could get because he didn't know when the last time she had slept.

"We can come back later if need be," Leo said.

Out of the two of them, Leo was the more talkative one. Oliver could be talkative, but he normally let his brother do most of the talking.

"No," Jaxson said. "It's okay. What can I help you with?"

They both sat down in front of his desk and he looked between both of them. For them to sit down, it must be serious and he was curious. The brothers normally kept to themselves.

"Advice," Oliver said.

"How we should deal with a situation," Leo said at the same time.

Jaxson's eyebrows raised at that. They wanted his advice on how to deal with a situation.

"Okay," he replied. "What is the situation?"

"There is a girl we are interested in," Leo said.

It didn't surprise Jaxson when he mentioned a girl. They had been glued to their phones for the past month and not doing as many scenes as they normally did at the club. It was odd, but he hadn't brought it up because it wasn't his place. If they wanted to bring something up, they would.

Oliver and Leo are secretive people and selective with whom they talked to. Both of them are retired military men, and they're great people. They just liked to keep some things to themselves which wasn't bad.

"We've been talking to her for over a month now, just

getting to know each other. She lived in New York with Monroe's brother," Leo explained. "I think they are best friends or something, but we aren't sure."

"And?" Jaxson found himself asking.

How was that important to what they were about to tell him? Not that he was complaining, but it was odd they brought up Monroe's brother, Miles. He had never met the man, but he had seen him from a distance when Monroe, Michael, and Miles met at the cafe. He wanted to make sure Monroe and Michael were safe.

"We were talking every day for over a month. We knew something was happening because she said a friend of hers got taken. They ended up getting her back and everything was tense," Leo said. "We were talking about meeting up when she just ghosted us."

Jaxson's eyes went wide. He was not expecting them to say that they got ghosted by a girl. They had subs lining up at their feet, waiting to scene with them or be their potential Little. It wasn't unknown that they were single and looking for someone, but a lot of the subs going to them just wanted one night and not forever.

Jaxson knew that wasn't what they were looking for. They wanted forever, but he suspected it was hard when they also wanted to share a girl.

"So, what's the problem?" Jaxson asked.

"We found out she's in town," Oliver said.

He was not expecting them to say that, either. What was she doing in town? Why hadn't she communicated with them?

"Where is she staying? Do you know where?" he asked.

"With Monroe and Michael," Leo said. "We just found out earlier today. She's been reading our text messages, but not responding."

"How was your relationship before she started to ghost you?"

Jaxson was intrigued at this point. Why was this girl ghosting them? Did they do something wrong? Did she finally realize that they wanted to share her, and she didn't want anything to do with them?

"Strong. We were talking about meeting up but any time we mentioned it, she would put it off or say she got busy and not answer the question," Leo said.

"Scared?" Jaxson asked.

He had heard of subs talking to Doms online and getting scared or nervous when they wanted to finally meet up.

"She's a spitfire," Oliver said. "Curses like a sailor, even when you try to correct her, but she didn't seem scared when we talked about it."

"Her breathing never picked up, voice never went higher," Leo added. "She seemed comfortable over text and video call."

"So what happened?" Jaxson asked. "Why do you think she's ghosted you and never wants to meet up? Do you think she just wanted to string you on? How did you guys even meet each other?"

"Monroe had introduced us. She was talking to her over video chat one time, and we were over at their house. She introduced us and then gave us her number because Hedda kept asking about us," Leo said.

"Hedda is an interesting name."

"She's interesting," Oliver said.

"We had talked about forming a dynamic and had already talked about safewords, hard limits, and everything. Then all of the sudden she just stopped responding to us about a month ago," Leo said.

Nothing added up.

"She would never string us on. That didn't seem like her nature. She seemed like she wanted something more in her life and we were prepared to give it to her," Leo said. "She showed us her Middle. I don't think she would've done that if she was just stringing us along."

He had a point, but it was still weird.

"Do you know what happened?" Jaxson asked. "Have you asked her?"

They both nodded their heads.

"We did, but she didn't respond. So, when we found out that she was staying with Monroe and Michael today, we asked Monroe what went on and why she wasn't responding to us," Leo said. "Monroe wouldn't give much detail, but she said something really bad happened, and that Hedda was dealing with it."

"So what are you going to do about it?" he asked.

They wanted his advice, but he felt like there was more to the story than what they were giving. He needed all of the information before he gave them any advice.

"Both of us have a gut feeling that we need to step in," Oliver said. "Monroe is worried about her and we are too."

Jaxson hadn't seen either of them worried about someone so much. He could see it written all over their faces as they talked about Hedda. Jaxson had never met her, but he knew she must mean a lot to Oliver and Leo.

"And you want my advice on if you should intervene or not?" he asked, trying to get the whole picture.

"Yes," Leo replied. "We want another opinion on this matter before we do anything. We don't want to overstep and make things worse."

They had a good point to a degree. It was probably great that they were wanting a second opinion in case they were in too deep and couldn't see the whole picture. But at the same time, he felt like they knew best what she would need since they had talked for so long before.

"You guys knew each other for a while?" he asked.

"Yes, we got to know each other really well. Knew a lot about her and she knew a lot about us," Leo replied.

"If you really think that you need to intervene, that it would be best for *her*, not for you guys, but for her, then I would go with it," Jaxson said. "But I wouldn't push her too hard. Trauma can be a difficult thing and you don't know what she went through."

"We understand," Leo said. "And we thought the same thing."

"Push her, but don't push her too much. There's a fine line and you need to know when that is. You don't want to push her too far and make everything worse. Make sure she knows she can say her safeword if things get to be too much but make sure you guys have a discussion."

They both nodded their heads.

"Not that you guys need the refresher, but be mindful," Jaxson chuckled before he got serious again. "Make her feel safe and that she can trust you. I wouldn't just go see her and ask all these questions. Gain her trust back and make her feel safe and maybe she'll come to you or maybe one of you guys will have to prompt her but be gentle."

"Gotcha," Leo said.

"See how fragile she is before you do anything. Assess her and where she is at. None of us know. You could also ask Monroe and Michael about it and get their opinion since she's living with them."

"Thank you," Oliver said as he stood up.

"Good luck with Sofia," Leo said. "If you need anything, and we mean anything, you let us know. We want to find the bastard who did that to her and make him pay for what he did."

"Thanks, but she said she didn't recognize the guy."

"Find out where she lives and I'll find security cameras. Or send it to Miles' guy and he can get all the info you need," Oliver said. "She may not recognize him, but he could've been watching her for a while. Need to be careful."

Jaxson nodded his head and watched as they left his office. He looked over at Sofia who was still sleeping on the couch. He wanted her to be comfortable and while the couch was comfortable, the crib at his house or his bed were much more comfortable.

He could finish the paperwork later when she was down for a nap at home. With that thought, he closed his computer, packed it away, and slung it over his shoulder before he walked over to her and gently picked her up.

Time to go home.

CHAPTER SEVENTEEN

SOFIA

Sofia slowly started to wake up and felt a gentle pressure on her chest. She gasped, opening her eyes wide as she stared in front of her.

She was in a car.

A car.

Why was she in a car?

She didn't own a car. Had the guy come back for her and shoved her in a car?

The last thing she remembered was falling asleep on the couch in her Daddy's office. Had someone taken her from there? Before she could do anything, she heard his voice.

"You're okay," he softly said as he grabbed her hand. "Daddy's here and you're safe."

She looked over and found her Daddy sitting in his seat, looking at her with worry. Why were they in a car? What had happened? How long had she been asleep?

So many questions went through her mind as they stared at each other. He had said she was okay, but that didn't answer any of her other questions. Not that she had asked him, but she didn't know what was going on.

"Sofia," he gently said. "Are you with me?"

She nodded her head, but she didn't know if that was the truth. She felt so out of it and like she couldn't focus on things. Why did she feel like this? Sofia knew that she had gotten mugged the night before, but that was last night and today was a whole new day.

"Sofia," he softly said. "It's going to be okay. Daddy's here."

She blinked several times. "W-where a-are we?"

She cringed at how she stuttered, but she couldn't help it. Sofia was still scared, even though her Daddy was here, and she knew he would take care of her. Something didn't feel right but she couldn't place what it was.

"We're at my house. We just pulled up, and I was about to get out and take you into the house," he said.

"Why?" she asked.

She wanted to go back to her apartment so she could get some sleep before she went to work the next day. She had already missed today and knew that it was going to bite her in the butt.

"I told you before you went to sleep that I was going to take you home and take care of you. And I meant it," he said. "I'm going to take care of you for the next several days so you can heal up."

Sofia didn't actually think that he was going to do it. She thought he was joking when he initially told her and the brothers, but maybe she shouldn't have underestimated him.

Deep down she should've known that he was serious. He's a Dom after all.

"Now," he said. "Have you had dinner yet?"

She opened her mouth to tell him she wasn't hungry, but he raised his eyebrows and she closed her mouth. Sofia didn't want him to waste food on her. He shouldn't have to feed her because she didn't have the money to feed herself. It wasn't his responsibility. She also didn't want him to spend any money on her. It was his money and he should save it for something he really wants to do.

He probably didn't want to feed her or pay for her food. Why would he?

"Don't you dare think about lying," he said. "You're hurt now, but that won't stop me from keeping track of punishments you've earned."

Her mouth fell open in shock. Was he serious? He had punished her before, but that was when they were at the playdate. They weren't now.

"I took responsibility for you and that includes punishing you when you're naughty," he said. "Just remember that if you're going to lie because I know when Little girls lie."

She took a deep breath. "No," she whispered.

Part of her felt ashamed that she hadn't eaten dinner yet but she couldn't. She was waiting for her shift so she could have a little snack when she took her break. That was the only time she was going to be able to eat. Well, until she got paid but she couldn't exactly remember when that was. Was it this up coming Friday or was it next Friday?

"I'll make you some food and then you can go to sleep and get some much needed rest," he said.

She wanted to argue that she didn't need anything and could go to sleep, but she stopped herself. Part of her realized it wasn't going to end well if she started to argue with him over this. He wanted to take care of her and he was going to do it, with her having a hot bottom or not.

"Do you want me to carry you inside?" he asked.

She shook her head. She didn't need to be carried, but would she like to be carried in? Sure. She craved to feel his hands around her again. Sofia felt comfortable and safe in his arms, but she didn't want to exhaust him.

"Sofia," he softly said her name. "I don't appreciate it when you lie to me."

Her eyes went wide, and she looked away. She didn't want him to see her facial expressions and give anything away. That was how he was reading her, right? She honestly didn't know, and it worried her. How was he reading her so well?

"Look at me," he commanded.

She moved her head so she could look at him. He didn't look mad but actually quite calm. Was he mad at her and just covering up his emotions?

"Do you want to be carried into the house?" he asked.

She was about to shake her head no again, but he stopped her.

"I didn't ask if you needed to be carried. I asked if you wanted," he said. "There is a difference."

Sofia really wanted to feel his arms around her again, but she didn't want to be a bother. She didn't want to be needy.

"Here's what's going to happen. I'm going to get out of the car and come around. I'll carry you into the house and then make you some dinner," he said. "We'll give you some pain medicine and then get ready for bed. Does that sound okay?"

She nodded her head.

"Words, Little one."

"Yes, Daddy," she whispered.

She was glad she didn't have to make the choice. It was like he knew she wanted to be carried and she couldn't verbalize it, so he just took over. Sofia waited for her Daddy to get out of the car and walk over to her side.

"Are you okay?" he asked. "If I ever do anything that makes you uncomfortable, let me know. I don't want to trigger you or make you uncomfortable."

She nodded her head, and Daddy picked her up. Letting out a sigh of contentment, she relaxed in his arms as he walked towards his house. She could get used to the feeling of his arms wrapped around her.

"Like that, don't ya?" he asked. "That's okay. Anytime you need some snuggles or to feel my arms wrapped around you, you just let me know. I'll gladly do it any time."

She was glad to hear that, but she didn't know if she would be able to ask him or not. It was weird to ask for a hug or to cuddle with him. It was a foreign concept for her and she didn't know if she would be able to ask him.

"If you can't ask, we could come up with a word that you say to let me know you need me," he said. "I know it can be hard for some people to say they need physical touch and if that's you, then we can come up with a word. You think on it, and when you figure it out, you let me know."

She nodded her head and relaxed even more into his

arms. Sofia didn't want him to let go, but she knew sooner or later he was going to. He said he was making her dinner, and she didn't think he could make it while she was in his arms. Or if he could, it would be extremely difficult.

"I'm going to set you down on the kitchen counter," he said.

A whine escaped past her lips at the thought of being away from him. She didn't want to be out of his embrace yet.

"I know, Little one," he softly said. "But I need to make you some food real quick and then you can be back in my arms. Is that okay?"

She let out a sigh and detached herself from him as he set her down on the counter. She knew he was right that he needed to make her food, but that still didn't mean she wanted to let go of him. She couldn't remember the last time she felt so safe and secure in someone's arms. Well, she couldn't really remember a time she felt like that at all.

In Chile, she was normally safe, but that didn't mean she felt safe. She was a single woman in Chile and she worked a lot to save up the money to come here.

This was truly the only time she ever felt so safe she could let her guard down and now she didn't want to have to put it back up. She wanted her Daddy to take care of everything, so she didn't have to think.

"I promise I won't be long," he said as he pulled back.

He cupped her face in his hands, and she leaned into his touch. She felt like she was starved for touch and any time he touched her, she wanted to soak it all in. Would he withhold touch whenever she was naughty? She had only been punished once by him and it was a spanking and corner time, and he gave her all the snuggles after.

But that didn't mean he wouldn't withhold them later.

"Will you w-withhold cuddles?" she whispered before she could stop herself.

She needed to know if he was going to. Sofia had to mentally prepare herself if he was ever to do that.

"No, baby," he softly said. "I'll never withhold cuddles. Those are too important."

A sigh of relief passed through her mouth at those words. She was glad he had said that because she didn't know how she would react if he had said yes. Sofia really liked him but withholding cuddles was something she didn't know if she could cope with.

"If you ever need cuddles or any physical touch, you let me know and I'll gladly give it to you," Daddy said. "Now, how do you like grilled cheese?"

A smile broke out across her face. "Yummy."

"Good. I would make you something else, but I know you must be tired and grilled cheese is something I can make super quick but it's still delicious."

She wasn't a complicated girl when it came to food. For the past several weeks, she's had bread with sometimes peanut butter and jelly and other times with ham but it wasn't much. Having grilled cheese was a treat and she couldn't wait to dive into it and fill her stomach up.

Sofia watched her Daddy start to put together the grilled cheese before putting it in the pan. She watched in fascination as he put a generous helping of butter in the pan before placing the bread onto it. It sizzled, and she saw the cheese slowly start to soften and melt onto the bread.

She couldn't wait to dig into this. It looks so good and she knew it was going to hit the spot. Sofia couldn't remember the time when she had a grilled cheese. It must have been years ago, and it probably wasn't that good.

"Do you want one or two?" he asked.

"One," she whispered.

"If you want more, I can make you more. Don't hold back if you're still hungry."

It was like he knew she was hesitant on telling him if she was hungry or not. She didn't want to waste any of his food. He worked hard to earn the money that he bought the food with. It wasn't her money but his.

"Alright," he said as he brought a plate over to the counter she was sitting on. "One delicious grilled cheese is up and ready to fill the monster in your tummy."

She giggled and reached for the grilled cheese, but Daddy slightly tapped her hand.

"Not yet, Little one," he said. "It's still hot and Daddy still has to cut it up. I don't want my baby burning her tongue or mouth."

She watched in fascination as he cut it into little square bites. He picked one up, slightly blowing on it before he touched it to his lips.

"Perfect."

She stared in awe. No one had ever fed her let alone checked to see if the food was too hot. It warmed her heart that he was taking care of her like that.

"Let Daddy feed you," he said.

Sofia's cheeks went bright red as he brought the piece of grilled cheese up to her mouth. She wasn't embarrassed that he was feeding her, but she wasn't used to it. It was a foreign concept, but she found herself enjoying it.

She sat there while he fed her the rest of the grilled cheese. It was absolutely delicious but by the last piece, her stomach was full and she knew she wouldn't be able to eat any more. What a bummer. She had wanted to eat a whole nother one, but she didn't want to puke.

"Do you want another one?" he asked.

She shook her head. "No, thank you. Tummy full."

"You let me know if your tummy gets hungry again. Now, let's get some medicine in you."

He held up her sippy cup and some pills in his other hand. "Ready?"

She nodded her head, opened her mouth, and waited for him to put the pills in her mouth.

"Such a good girl," Daddy said as he held the cup up to her.

She took several sips of water to drown the pills down her throat.

"Yucky," she said, shaking her head.

"Sorry, Little one. I'll get some liquid stuff next time."

Daddy picked her up and walked towards who knows where. She didn't know the house, but she suspected he was bringing her to a room. Exhaustion weighed down on her body as she snuggled up to his embrace.

"No falling asleep on Daddy," he said as he rubbed her back.

"Daddddyyyy," she whined. All she wanted to do was fall

asleep in his arms. She was so comfortable and knew it wouldn't take her long to fall asleep or stay asleep.

"No whining. We need to get you ready for bed and then I'll tuck you in."

She let out a sigh and tried to stay awake. It got harder and harder as the seconds went by but right as she was about to, he placed her on the counter.

The cold counter.

"Cold," she said.

"Sorry, Little one. It'll warm up in a second," he replied. "Let's get your teethers brushed and you can go potty."

Her face went red at the mention of going to the bathroom. Hopefully, he wasn't going to be in the bathroom when she went. That would be super embarrassing.

"Open up," he said.

She opened her mouth and let Daddy brush her teeth. Sofia felt so Little and taken care of right now.

"Such a good girl," Daddy whispered. "Spit into the sink."

She spat and he helped her off the counter.

"Go to the bathroom. I'll be out in the room ready to tuck you in," he said.

Sofia quickly did her business before she walked out of the bathroom. Daddy was sitting on the bed, looking absolutely handsome.

"Ready to go to beddy?" he asked.

A gasp fell from her lips as she stared at the empty bed. Her stuffy.

"I can't!" she wailed.

His eyes went wide, and he stood up quickly, walking towards her, and grabbing her hands.

"What's wrong?" he asked. "Does your head hurt? Are you feeling faint? Do you need to puke?"

"No!"

"What's wrong then? Are you feeling light headed? Do you need to go to the bathroom again? Are you thirsty?"

"I don't have Trixie!"

Tears welled up in her eyes at the thought of leaving Trixie in her apartment. She normally brought her to work with her, but she had decided to leave her stuffed animal at her apartment this time. How was she going to sleep without her friend tonight?

"Oh Little one," he softly said as he knelt to the ground. He grabbed her face with his hands. "It's going to be okay."

"N-no," she stuttered. "No sleeps."

Trixie was going to be so scared tonight sleeping all alone in her apartment. They hadn't parted ways since she bought the stuffed animal and that was years ago.

"Give me one second," he said. "Let's get you in bed and then I need to go grab something."

Daddy helped Sofia get into bed, but she didn't lay down. How was she going to be able to fall asleep without Trixie? She didn't think it was going to be possible. Who was going to protect her while she slept tonight?

Sofia had decided while her Daddy was gone that she wasn't going to sleep tonight. She couldn't because someone had to fight off the monsters that were coming.

"I know this isn't Trixie, but I hope this will do for

tonight until we can get Trixie," Daddy said as he walked back into the room.

His hands were behind his back and her eyes stared at his arms, wanting to see what he could possibly be holding.

"Are you ready to see what I have?" he asked.

She nodded her head and wiped away the tears that had fallen down her cheek. She was still sad she left Trixie, but she was also intrigued by what her Daddy could have behind his back.

He brought a white cow with blue spots from behind his back, and she let out a gasp. It was gorgeous.

"I've had this stuffie for several years now," he said. "Do you want to sleep with it?"

"Can I?" she whispered, sounding so unsure.

She wanted to hug it and never let it go, but she didn't know if she was allowed to.

"Of course you can," he said. "What do you think the name should be?"

"Mattie," she said as she made grabby hands towards it.

"Mattie it is."

She hugged the soft plush cow against her body, loving the feeling the soft fur had against her cheek and arms. This was amazing.

"Happy?" he softly asked.

Sofia nodded her head and looked at him. She was so happy.

"Now, do you want a story before you go to bed or do you want to just go to sleep?" he asked.

"Story!" she yelled.

His eyebrow raised. "Inside voices."

She laid down in bed and gave him a sheepish look. "Sorry, Daddy."

She knew she should use her inside voice, but it was so hard when she was excited. She got a new stuffie, and he was going to tell her a story.

"Alright," he said, sitting down in the chair next to the bed. "Once upon a time in a land far, far away was a Little who wanted to rule the world."

Sofia giggled and turned to her side. She wanted to be able to look at Daddy while he told the story. But she knew she wasn't going to last long, her eyes were already starting to droop.

"The Little was named Miss Rosemary, and she wanted all the Littles in the world to be loved and cherished," he continued to tell the story. "She had a heart made of gold, but some very bad people wanted to take advantage of that."

"Oh no," she whispered, feeling herself slipping off to sleep.

Sofia heard a chuckle, but she ignored it and snuggled into her pillow and stuffie.

"The bad people wanted to rule over the Littles and make them all miserable. They didn't want them to thrive, but they wanted the Littles to suffer," Daddy said. "But Miss Rosemary wouldn't allow that."

She let out a sigh of contentment and fell asleep.

CHAPTER EIGHTEEN

SOFIA

The next morning wasn't any different from last night. Daddy had insisted on taking care of her from when she woke up. It was a sweet gesture, but she wasn't used to it at all and she felt like she was just mooching off of him.

Who wanted to be a moocher?

Maybe somebody in the world wanted to be, but Sofia didn't. She had worked so hard in her life and now it felt weird to let someone take care of her. Yes, it had been her dream to have a Daddy who would take care of her, but she was also an independent person. It was still uncomfortable getting used to another person being this involved in her life.

"Little one?" Daddy asked. "Are you okay?"

She blinked and looked at her Daddy. He was currently making French toast for her and she was super excited. That was another thing she hadn't had in a while and she couldn't wait to eat it.

"Sofia," he said.

"Sorry, Daddy," she softly said. "What did you say?"

"Are you okay?"

She nodded her head. She was okay, well for the most part. Her face had started hurting a little, and she was just waiting for the medicine to kick in but Daddy already knew that. That was one of the first questions he had asked her when she woke up. Well, when he woke her up.

Daddy had let her sleep in until ten in the morning. It was kind of weird to wake up that late, but Sofia wasn't complaining today. She had been exhausted and knew she needed sleep. If she had been back at her apartment, she probably would've slept in as well.

"What's on your mind, Little one?" he asked.

She sighed and watched him make her breakfast. He was currently cutting up the French toast before putting syrup on it.

"I need to go to work," she whispered, afraid of what he was going to say.

He had mentioned she wasn't going to work yesterday, but she didn't know if he was being serious or not. She wasn't hurt that bad, and she knew she could work, but she didn't know if he would allow her to work. He was her Daddy, but he was also her boss.

Daddy placed her plate in front of her and gripped her chin with his fingers. "You aren't going into work for a couple of days."

She pouted, and worry started to churn in her stomach. How was she going to pay for her rent? How was she going to feed herself? There were so many questions and she didn't know how to ask or answer them.

"What's worrying you?" Daddy asked. "Is it money?"

She shyly nodded her head when he let go of her chin.

"Little one," he said. "You remember I talked about sick days and PTO?"

"Yes," she whispered.

"We give employees plenty of PTO and sick days in case things happen. Littles get sick very often and we know it can be hard. Granted, we don't like people just taking them to take them. When they genuinely have a sickness for sick days and PTO, if you ask us far enough in advance, we give it to you," he said. "When emergencies happen, we normally always let the person take the time off."

"Okay?" She honestly didn't know where he was going with that. She wasn't sick, and she didn't have an emergency.

"You're taking a couple days off and using sick days."

She continued to stare at him in confusion. Was he able to do that?

"I know you aren't sick, but you are hurt, and that falls under sick days. You have a bruised face and I have no doubt you have other bruises on your body," Daddy said. "I want you healed before you go back to work so you aren't in any pain. We don't know if you broke anything in your face or anywhere else. Do you have a high pain tolerance?"

She guessed she did have a high pain tolerance. Most of the time she had to ignore the pain because she needed the money. No one else was working to earn the money for her. It was all her and she couldn't rely on anyone else.

Even if she wanted to, she couldn't because she didn't have anyone.

"Answer Daddy," he said.

"Yes, Daddy. I do," she grumbled.

"So, you're taking the next couple of days off so you can heal properly. You don't have to work through all this pain anymore. You can relax and heal while you still get paid."

She still didn't understand the concept of PTO and sick days.

"Do you trust Daddy?" he asked.

She nodded her head. "Yes."

"Can you trust Daddy on this? Give me two days to show you I'll take good care of you while you heal up."

Sofia thought about it for a second. Maybe this would show her what it was like to have a Daddy before she committed to anything long term. What if they didn't work out? What if they didn't mesh well together? She didn't want to start something without knowing how it was going to end or work.

"Okay," she hesitantly said.

"Thank you, Little one," he said, kissing her forehead. "Now, are you hungry?"

"Yes!" Her stomach chose the perfect moment to grumble. Her face went red, and she wrapped her arms around her stomach. "Shhh stomachy. Foods comings."

"We better feed the monster before it takes over the world."

She giggled and looked up at Daddy. "Tummy won't take over world. Only tummy."

He booped her nose. "It could take over the world if we

don't feed it. It'll go around scourging for food, not caring if anyone gets hurt. We wouldn't want that, would we?"

Her eyes went wide as she stared at him. Was that true? She couldn't believe it, but Daddy said it so it had to be true.

"Really?" she asked in wonder.

"Oh yes," he replied. "It could be five minutes before your tummy decides to take over or it could be in a couple of seconds. We have to hurry and satisfy it before that happens."

Sofia opened her mouth, waiting for food. She didn't want her tummy to take over.

"Daddy! Foodie please," she said. "Needs foodies. Tummy no takes overs."

Daddy forked some of the French toast and fed it to her. Cinnamon and syrup bursted in her mouth and a little moan escaped. It was so delicious and she couldn't wait for the next bite.

That continued for several minutes until Sofia was so stuffed, she couldn't move.

"No mores Daddy. I is full," she whined as he held another bite up to her lips.

"Okay, Little one," he said. "No more food."

She relaxed in her chair. Thankfully, she was wearing shorts that were elastic, so her stomach got to breathe. She didn't know what she would do if she was wearing a pair of jeans. Unbutton them? Sofia had done that before, but never in front of anyone and it had been ages since she did that.

"Sofia," Daddy said.

She froze and looked up at him. He normally called her

Little one or baby and only said her name when he had something serious to talk about or she was in trouble.

"Yes, Daddy?" she asked.

"I want to call Michael and ask him to come here to check you over," he said.

Sofia shook her head. She didn't need a doctor to come here. She was perfectly fine.

"Sofia," he said. "You're hurt and I want to make sure that you're okay."

"No, thank you," she replied, remembering to use her manners. Maybe if she was nice to him, he would say she was okay to not see the doctor.

"No. It's either Michael or I can take you to the ER."

She stilled and shook her head. "I don't like either option."

"Tough luck. Pick one. Michael or ER."

Sofia let out a sigh. "Michael," she whispered, not liking the idea at all. But if she had to pick one, she would rather have Michael than some random person.

Though, would she? She knew Michael but would that make it weird between her and Monroe?

"Wait!" she yelled as he brought out his phone. Did she want Michael to look at her?

"What's wrong?" he asked.

"I don't know," she whispered. "Michael is Monroe's Daddy."

"That won't be a problem. She knows he looks over the other Littles and makes sure they are healthy and she's okay with that. Michael asked Monroe before he started doing it. It won't make anything different between you and Monroe."

She let out a breath before she nodded her head. She still didn't like this and when Michael came, she was going to say something.

"Let me call Michael and then we can snuggle up on the couch until he gets here," Daddy said.

Sofia tried to relax in the chair as Daddy talked on the phone but it was hard. She knew the doctor was coming, and she didn't like that. She didn't want that.

"Come on," Daddy said, and he picked her up. "Let's go snuggle."

She stayed silent as he walked them into the living room and sat down on the couch. Sofia immediately snuggled into his side and closed her eyes. Maybe she could somehow convince Michael that she didn't need to be looked over. She didn't know how she was going to convince him, but she could figure it out by the time he got here.

The doorbell rang, and Sofia's whole body stiffened. That was quick.

"Michael was nearby when I called," Daddy said. "Let me go get the door. Be a good girl and stay on the couch."

Daddy got up and Sofia tried to think of something she could do to get out of this, but couldn't think of anything.

"Hello Sofia," Michael said as he walked into the living room.

CHAPTER NINETEEN

SOFIA

Sofia stared at Michael as he walked into the living room. She wasn't prepared for him to come here so soon. She thought she had a couple more minutes to think of a way to get out of this situation, but she was wrong.

He was here now, and she hadn't come up with anything.

"I heard there was a special Little girl who is hurt and needs me to check her over," Michael said. "Do you know who that could be?"

"Not I," she whispered.

Daddy stood behind Michael and shook his head. "Naughty girl. You know it's you."

She shook her head. It wasn't her and she didn't know who Daddy was talking about.

"I is goods," she said.

"I think by the bruise on your face that it's you," Michael softly said. "I know doctors can be scary, but if you're a good girl, I have some candy in my bag that you can have."

She perked up at the thought of getting some candy. Sofia hadn't been able to splurge on candy in a while and she had missed it. Her sweet tooth was calling out to her at the mention of candy.

"Ah," Daddy said. "You caught her attention with candy."

"I thought I would. It normally helps Littles let me examine them without a fuss if they know they are getting candy," Michael said. "Now, can I come and look you over?"

She thought about it for a second. Did she want him to come over and examine her? She really didn't, but the thought of getting some candy was sounding pretty good.

"You can either be a good girl while he examines you and you'll get some candy or he'll examine you and you won't get any candy," Daddy said. "And if after everything, Michael says you're okay, then we can go play tomorrow at the club."

Her lip pushed out after he spoke. Either way, she was going to be examined by the doctor, whether she liked it or not.

But the idea of going through the examination and possibly going to the club with Daddy filled her with excitement. She wanted to go play with him, in Littlespace or not.

"No pouting," Daddy said. "So, what's it going to be?"

"I'll be a good girl," she whispered.

She didn't like it, but she would rather get some candy out of it than get nothing.

"Can you tell me what happened?" Michael asked.

Sofia went to answer him, but she realized he was talking to her Daddy and not to her. Part of her liked that she didn't have to answer the question and her Daddy was taking care of it, but the other part, the independent part of herself, was upset that Michael hadn't asked her. She was her own person.

"She got mugged two nights ago and apparently the guy hit her in the face and she fell," Daddy said. "She has the bruise on her face, but I suspect that she also has some bruises on her body. Sofia also had some cuts on her hands, but I took care of those. I just wanted you to come and check her over and make sure that there wasn't anything sinister that I couldn't see or wouldn't know to look for."

"It was a good idea to call me," Michael said. "I'm going to be careful when I touch your cheek and around your eye. Let me know if anything hurts."

Sofia watched as Michael knelt in front of her and placed his bag down next to him. She didn't want him touching her, but she knew it was inevitable and if she didn't complain, it would be over faster.

"The bruising is going to get worse before it gets better," Michael said as he gently started to touch around her bruise.

She winced as pain shot across her face and tried to pull away from his hands.

"Sorry, sweetie," Michael said.

He moved his hands to start feeling around again, but a whimper escaped past her mouth and she pulled her head back. She didn't want him touching her face again. It hurt a lot, and it was only going to hurt more when he touched her.

"I've got a pacifier for her. Do you think that'll be okay for her to suck on?" Daddy asked. "I think it would distract her and also calm her down while you look at her."

"I don't think anything is broken, just bruised so it

should be fine for her to suck on it," Michael replied. "But I still need to feel around her eyes to make sure. I don't want to leave anything and it be bad."

Tears filled her eyes as she watched her Daddy leave the room. She didn't want him to leave her and yet he was.

"You're going to be okay," Michael whispered. "Your Daddy is coming right back."

Sofia sniffled and tried to get up, but Michael blocked her way.

"Daddy," she whimpered.

He had been gone too long, and she didn't like it. Why had he left her here with Michael? She trusted Michael, but he wasn't her Daddy.

"I know, sweetie," he said. "Daddy is coming right back. Can you be a brave girl for me until he does?"

She stared at him, and before she could respond, her Daddy walked back into the room.

"What's wrong?" he asked as he walked over towards her.

"Someone missed her Daddy," Michael said. "Didn't like that you left the room."

"Sorry, Little one," Daddy said. "I was just getting a pacifier for you."

She shook her head. She didn't want a pacifier. All she wanted was for Michael to leave and to snuggle back in her Daddy's embrace. But her Daddy didn't pay attention as he plopped the pacifier into her mouth. She tried to spit it out, but he kept his hand there, holding it in place.

"Be a good girl and suck on it while Michael looks over the rest of your face and body," Daddy said.

Sofia whined but eventually started to suck on the pacifier. She felt herself starting to calm down a little bit as she continued to suck on it.

"Such a good girl for Daddy," he praised her.

She blushed and let Michael continue to look over her face. He touched several parts of her face and she winced each time, but it wasn't as bad of pain as it was before.

"If she complains about headaches or her vision changing, I would take her to the ER," Michael said as he flashed a light in her eyes. "It doesn't look like she has a concussion but I would watch out for that as well."

"Thank you," Daddy said.

"You mentioned her having bruises in other places?"

Sofia looked at her Daddy. She had never mentioned having other bruises on her body, but she didn't doubt that she did. Somehow she still hadn't looked at her body to see if she had any other owies.

"Did she tell you how she landed?" Michael asked. "I'm assuming from the owies on her hand that she fell when she got punched?"

"She didn't tell us," Daddy replied.

They both looked at her and Daddy started to pull her pacifier, but she didn't want to let it go now. She was comfortable and relaxed, well for the most part she was.

"Let go of it, Little one," Daddy said. "We need to ask you a couple questions."

A whine escaped her lips as her Daddy pulled the pacifier out of her mouth.

"Can you tell us how you fell two nights ago?" Michael asked.

"On my hands and bottom," she whispered before she opened her mouth again, wanting the pacifier.

"I'll give it to you in a second," Daddy said. "I think Michael has a couple more questions to ask you."

She didn't want him to ask her any more questions. She wanted to be left alone, but she knew her Daddy was going to make her answer the questions or she would get into trouble.

Sofia looked at Michael and waited for him to ask her some questions. She didn't know what he was going to ask, and she was slightly worried. What if he asked her some really personal questions, and she didn't want to answer them in front of either of them? Yes, Michael was a doctor, but she had to see him at the club when she worked or when she hung out with Monroe. It would be awkward for him to know that stuff.

"Have you been feeling any pain anywhere else?" Michael asked.

"Just a reminder, if you lie there will be consequences," Daddy said. "Sorry Michael, I had to say that again. She likes to tell half the truth when it comes to her pain."

She grimaced, but he was right. Sofia didn't like to tell people when she was hurting because they tended to make it bigger than it was and she didn't want that. Especially if it was at work and they wanted her to take the day off because she had a bruise. Who took off work because they had a bruise?

No one.

It was ridiculous but her Daddy, Leo, and Oliver didn't see that. Shouldn't they, though, since Daddy was a retired police officer and Leo and Oliver were retired from the military. They went through worse than her no doubt and they wanted her to take a day off when she had a bruise. It didn't make sense.

"My hands are a little sore," she softly said.

All morning yesterday she had been careful when she picked things up. She didn't want to aggravate the tiny little cuts on her hands and make them worse. For something so small, it hurt a lot more than she remembered it would.

"Is there anywhere else? Your bottom where you fell on it? Your legs? Stomach?" Michael asked.

She shook her head. Sure, her bottom was sore when she initially fell on it and a couple hours after, but it wasn't bothering her anymore. It was like she didn't even fall on it two days ago.

"Are you sure?" he asked.

"Yes, Sir," she replied. "Nothing else hurts or aches."

Well, her head was about to if he didn't stop doubting her and asking all the questions. Shouldn't he take her for her word? She knew she tended to lie sometimes, but Daddy made it clear that she wasn't allowed to do that unless she wanted to get in trouble.

And she didn't want that.

Sofia wanted to get the candy, but she was also hoping to go to the club tomorrow with her Daddy to play. They hadn't had a day or time where they could be Little and Daddy together and she craved that. She wanted it so much and she would do anything to be able to do it with him.

"Alright, my next questions aren't about pain," Michael said. "Do you eat three meals a day?"

She opened her mouth to lie, but the thought of getting into trouble and not being able to go to the club stopped her. Sofia didn't want to tell them that she didn't eat three meals a day, but she wanted to go to the club. She knew Daddy would be disappointed she wasn't eating all the food she needed for her body. How was she supposed to when she could barely pay rent each month?

"No," she whispered, looking down at her lap.

She felt embarrassed that she couldn't eat three meals a day. Yes, she was hungry, but her body had gotten used to not eating a lot because it had to. She didn't want that for herself, but she also couldn't do anything about it.

Well, she could've said something to one of the Doms, but she didn't want to be a charity case. Who wanted that?

"What do you normally eat in a day?" Michael asked as he wrote something down on a piece of paper.

She hadn't seen him get the paper, but she suspected it came from the bag he had. Who knows what all he had in there.

"Some snacks at work and a sandwich," she barely whispered, hoping either of them didn't hear her. "I also drink water and some milk."

Part of her hoped that adding those on would help, but she suspected it wouldn't.

"Just while you're working?" Daddy asked.

She shook her head. "All day."

Tears filled her eyes, and she looked away from both of them. She didn't want to see the disappointed faces when she said that.

"Why didn't you tell me?" Daddy asked. "I would've brought you food."

"I'm still figuring out what I like?" she whispered. It was partially true because things were different here and she couldn't walk down to the store and get fresh bread like she could in Chile. Things were different in the United States, and she was still trying to learn everything.

"Do you not have enough money to buy food?" Michael softly asked.

She shook her head. "I'm trying to save to get a different place."

Sofia closed her eyes and wished she could take that back. She didn't need Daddy asking her more questions about her living condition.

"I don't like that you're only eating so little each day," Michael said. "Definitely underweight and you're working a lot."

"That's why I lie so I don't disappoint people."

Her hand flew to her mouth when she said that. She didn't mean to say it and yet she couldn't help herself. What did they expect?

"Never lie about that stuff," Daddy said. "I need to know if you aren't getting enough food so I can take care of you."

She didn't look at her Daddy as he spoke. What if he didn't want her after this? What if he decided that he wanted someone else who didn't have so much baggage?

"I want you to watch her diet closely. She's already tiny as is and not eating enough will cause her to lose weight with how much she's working," Michael said. "And make sure she's also drinking enough liquids."

"I will," Daddy said.

"I've got some cream for her bruises that you can put on for the next couple of days. If her head starts to hurt, she gets lightheaded, her vision goes out, or she gets sick, take her to the ER immediately."

"Thank you so much for coming."

She let out a sigh and relaxed on the couch. Doctor visits always took so much out of her, and she was glad it was over now.

"Now, I need to give a Little girl her candy since she was such a good girl while I asked her questions and looked over her bruises," Michael said. "Do you want a lollipop, KitKats, or some skittles?"

"KitKats!" Sofia raised her voice and looked at Michael.

He chuckled and grabbed two bars from his bag and handed it to her Daddy. She pouted and made grabby hands towards the candy. Why did he give it to her Daddy?

"I don't want you eating it all at once and I don't think your Daddy will like it either," Michael said.

She pouted even more. That wasn't fair. it was her KitKats because she was a good girl, not her Daddy's.

"No pouting or you won't get any tonight," Daddy said.

Sofia stopped pouting immediately.

"I'll see myself out," Michael said. "It was nice seeing you both. And Sofia can go and play tomorrow as long as she doesn't feel sick or any of the other symptoms I gave you."

She looked at her Daddy, and he gave her a smile.

"You were such a good girl for Daddy. So brave when it was scary," he said. "I think you should get a reward."

Her brain immediately went to him giving her an

orgasm. She had been wanting one from him for a while, but didn't know how to ask. Especially since they were so new in their dynamic. Would he want to give her one?

"Why are your cheeks getting red?" Daddy asked as he sat down next to her.

She shook her head and looked away. She didn't want to tell him what she was thinking in case he didn't want to do it.

"Does my Little girl want an orgasm?" he asked.

Sofia whipped her head over towards him with wide eyes. How did he know? Could he read minds?

"Do you?"

She nodded her head.

"Ah, remember words."

Her face got even redder. He wanted her to say she wanted to orgasm?

"Yes, Daddy," she whispered.

"Yes, what?"

"Yes, I want to have an orgasm."

She looked away from him, embarrassed.

"Your wish is my command," he said. "Lay on the couch and take off your pants and panties."

She quickly did as he said but covered herself when he just stared at her.

"Did Daddy say you could cover yourself?" he asked.

Sofia shook her head and slowly pulled her hands away from herself. She didn't have time to think before Daddy pushed her legs apart and started to run his fingers through her folds. She moaned as pleasure coursed through her body.

"Ooo," she whispered as her back arched.

"Like that?" he said as he gently eased his finger into her tight channel.

"Daddy," she whimpered as the pressure started to build inside of her.

His other hand moved, his fingers connecting with her clit. Her hips moved as she tried to create more friction. She needed him to go faster.

It was like he knew because his finger started to pump into her faster as his other finger moved in a circular motion.

"Daddy," she moaned.

"Come when you like."

Daddy continued to pump his finger into her, and she felt the pleasure coursing through her body like her blood did. She felt so close.

"Daaadddyyy."

He pinched her clit, and she found herself screaming as she rode her release.

"Such a good girl," he whispered as he pulled his finger out of her. "Daddy's good girl."

CHAPTER TWENTY

SOFIA

Today was the day Sofia and her Daddy were going to play at the club. Nerves ran through her body as she thought about it. They were sitting in the car about to head into the club.

Tonight was also the night she was going back to her apartment. Daddy wasn't happy about it, but she had said she needed to go back, that she needed to do things around there and needed to go back to work. He didn't like that, but he told her they would talk about this later.

She hoped it wasn't going to be soon, but she had a feeling it was. Daddy didn't know where she lived, and she knew it bothered him. Oliver and Leo had asked her, and she hadn't answered them. Then she slipped up yesterday when Michael came over to check on her. Sofia didn't know if Daddy caught on to that, but she was pretty sure he did.

Nothing got by him.

He had his eyes on her, and he wasn't letting her get away with anything.

"Are you ready?" Daddy asked.

She looked over at him, and he gave her a smile. Was tonight going to be okay? She hadn't really played with other Daddies before, and she didn't want to mess up.

"Sofia," he softly said as he cupped her face in his hands. "Everything's going to be okay. We'll do what you want and if you don't want to continue to play, we can figure something else out."

She nodded her head, but she was still worried. Sofia wanted to go in and be Little with her Daddy.

"You can't mess up," he said as if he could read her mind. "Just be you."

"Easier said than done," she whispered more to herself, but her Daddy heard.

"Talk to me, Little one."

She turned away from him. She wanted to, but she also didn't want him to think she was second guessing going into the club and playing. Because she wanted to, but she was just nervous.

Everyone got nervous, right?

Maybe she should ask Monroe and Charlotte that. They had been coming to BTS for a while now and maybe at some point they felt the same way.

"Sofia," he softly said her name. "Can you look at me?"

She let out a sigh and looked back towards him. She needed to tell him that she was nervous but still wanted to go in.

"Talk to me, please," he said.

"I'm nervous," she whispered. "But I still want to go in and play."

Daddy grabbed her hand and gave it a little squeeze. "Why are you nervous?"

"I work here."

That was part of it.

"Why else?"

"I don't want to mess up," she looked down at her hands as she said that.

It was a real fear that she thought would come true. What was stopping it from coming true?

"Oh Little one," he softly said. "You aren't going to mess up. Can you look at Daddy?"

Sofia felt his hand grip her chin and bring her face up. He smiled at her.

"It's going to be okay," he said. "Just be you and you won't mess up."

She nodded her head and let out a breath. It was still a worry, but she knew she could believe him and that it was going to be okay. It had to be.

"Ready to go inside?" he asked and she nodded her head again. "Wait for Daddy to help you out of the car."

She waited for Daddy to walk around the car and to her side. Sofia was still getting used to the idea of waiting for him to help her out of the car. Not that she needed help, but he wanted to be a gentleman and she liked it. It was weird at first, but she was starting to enjoy it.

She felt taken care of.

"Ready to go in?" he asked.

"Yes, Daddy," she replied.

They started to walk towards the front door and saw Pete standing at the door.

"Hello there, Little miss," Pete said. "I heard what happened the other night. Sorry you got mugged, but we'll find out who did it to you and make them pay."

"Thanks," she whispered but didn't believe that they were going to find the person.

It was a random person so how were they going to find him? She didn't have anything identifying in her purse besides the money and maybe a little note. There was no way they were going to find this random person.

"I also want to say that I don't like you walking home and thought Jaxson here knew. Now that I know you weren't supposed to, don't expect me to let you do it," Pete said. "That was naughty of you."

She moved on her feet, not liking that she was getting scolded again but also because he sounded disappointed. She hated disappointing people.

"We'll see you later," Daddy said and started to walk into the club.

"Bye Little miss. Have some fun!" Pete called after them.

They continued to walk into the club and heard little squeals coming from Littles running around the room.

"Do you want to color first?" Daddy asked.

Sofia nodded her head, not wanting to talk just yet. She always got overwhelmed with how many people were there when she first walked in, and it took her a couple of minutes to get used to it.

They walked over towards the coloring corner and sat down on the ground. Daddy brought her a coloring book and some markers, setting them down in front of her.

"Thank you," she whispered. "Daddy."

"You're welcome, Little one."

Sofia started to color the cow on the front page a nice purple color.

"Purple?" Daddy asked. "Is that your favorite color?"

"Yes, Daddy," she replied. "Purple is prettys."

She looked up at her Daddy, and he smiled down at her. She was currently laying on her stomach while he was sitting on his bottom. It made her feel smaller when she was below him and she loved that feeling. Sofia knew he was going to take care of her, and she got to let go of her worries.

"Are you ready?" Leo said.

Sofia looked up to see him a couple feet away, in front of Janie. Her nose wrinkled at that. Why was Leo talking to Janie and asking her if she was ready when Mac was interested in her? Did he not know?

"What's wrong, Little one?" Daddy asked.

"Nofing," she whispered but continued to look at Leo and Janie.

She watched as Janie nodded her head and held out her arms and Leo started to wrap rope around her. What did that feel like? Did it hurt? Did it make them feel different things?

"Are you interested in Shibari?" Daddy asked.

"I don't know," she replied.

It was new to her, and she had no clue what it was about or how it felt.

"I've heard some subs say it makes them relax," Daddy said. "There are lots of different reasons why Doms and Subs like Shibari."

Sofia couldn't keep her eyes off of Leo and Janie. She could see how Janie was relaxing as Leo tied the knots and wrapped more around her. She wanted to feel how it felt to have the ropes against her skin.

"Do you want to see what it would feel like?" Daddy asked. "I know just a little basic Shibari that I can show you."

She didn't respond right away.

"Sofia," Daddy said. "Look at me."

Sofia didn't want to look away from Leo and Janie.

"Now."

Her eyes snapped towards him.

"Good girl. Now, can you answer my question?"

"Yes, Daddy," she whispered. "Just a little."

"Good girl for answering. Let me go grab my rope and I'll be right back."

She nodded her head and looked back at Leo and Janie. Her arms were bound together with the rope and Leo had started to wrap it around her torso. As if he could tell she was looking at them, he looked up and gave her a smile. She blushed and looked away, embarrassed that she got caught.

She didn't know if it was okay or not to stare at them. Sofia figured since they were in the big room that they didn't mind, but she wanted to be respectful.

"Ready, Little one?" Daddy asked as he kneeled onto the floor.

She sat up and nodded her head. She didn't know what to do, so she just stared at her Daddy waiting for him to say something.

"I'm just going to put it on your arm," Daddy said. "If you start to panic, don't like it, or feel uncomfortable, you yell out your safeword and I'll take it off."

"Okay," she whispered, nerves running through her body.

"I have scissors here that can cut through the rope in case anything happens. Can you tell me what your safeword is?"

"Pina."

"You say that or red and I'll get the rope off of you immediately. Okay?"

She nodded her head.

"I need words, Little one," he said, booping her nose.

"Yes, Daddy. I understand."

"Good girl."

She blushed when he called her that. Sofia didn't know if she would ever be able to get used to him calling her a good girl.

"Can you stick your arm out?" he asked.

She held her right arm out and watched as he slowly started to wrap the rope around her arm, tying a knot here and there. It was like he had done it thousands of times before and it was just muscle memory for him.

"Are you feeling okay?" he asked.

"Yes, Daddy," she whispered.

She loved the feeling of the soft rope around her skin. It was snug against her skin, but not too tight.

It was just right.

A sigh of relief fell past her mouth as she relaxed into the feeling of having the rope around her skin. It almost grounded her in a way, but she couldn't exactly explain it.

"How are you feeling?" Daddy asked. "Do you need me to stop?"

"No!" she raised her voice, her heartbeat speeding up at the thought of it being taken off.

"Okay, Little one. I won't take it off," he said, chuckling a little.

Sofia felt her Daddy stop moving, and she looked down at her right arm that was covered in a pretty little design.

"So pretty," she whispered and relaxed even more.

She closed her eyes and took several deep breaths. She had no clue she would love the feeling this much, but she never wanted it to come off now.

"Other arm?" she whispered, opening her eyes and looking at him.

"Are you sure?" he asked.

She nodded and held out her other arm for him to do. Maybe the next time they did this, he could do her torso like Leo did for Janie.

"Such a good girl," he whispered. "Tell Daddy if you need me to stop or need me to take it off."

"Yes, Daddy," she replied and felt him start wrapping the rope around her other arm.

She didn't know how long it took him to do the other arm or how long they sat there, but she didn't mind. She loved feeling the rope on her skin.

"Okay, Little one," Daddy said. "It's getting late and we both have work tomorrow. I'm going to start taking the ropes off slowly."

Sofia whined and opened her eyes. She didn't want them to come off.

"We'll do this again," he said. "I promise. Maybe we can put it around your torso before you work the next time.

Remind you that Daddy is always with you and ground you. What do you think about that?"

"Yes, Daddy," she replied. "I would love that."

Sofia couldn't wait for the next time they did this. She was looking forward to it.

Daddy handed her a water bottle when he freed her left arm from the ropes.

"I want you to drink all of this tonight," Daddy said. "Can you do that for Daddy?"

"Yes," she whispered and started to drink the water.

She didn't realize how thirsty she was until she was actually drinking. By the time Daddy got her right arm free from the ropes, she had drunk half the water bottle already. There would be no problem with her finishing this by the time she went to bed.

"Can I drop you off?" Daddy asked.

"I've got a taxi waiting for me outside," she softly said.

Sofia had made sure to order a taxi before they started playing so he didn't have to worry.

A look of disappointment flew across his face and she knew he didn't like the idea of her taking a taxi. They weren't always safe, but she didn't have a car and she didn't want him to take her to her apartment.

Not yet.

"Alright," he sighed. "Let's get you to your taxi."

She didn't like that he was disappointed in her. Sofia wanted him to be proud of her and it seemed like she was just making things worse the more they hung out and were together.

They walked towards the entrance, passing Pete, and to the taxi.

"This is the last time you're taking a taxi," Daddy said. "Next time, I'm taking you home. I don't like you taking a taxi when I'm not there. What if something happens? They aren't safe."

"I don't want to waste my money," she whispered.

"Next time I'm taking you. No arguments."

She nodded her head. That meant she was just going to have to figure out a way for him to not take her the next time.

"I'll see you tomorrow for your shift," he said, kissing her forehead.

Sofia got into the taxi and smiled at him. "See you tomorrow."

"Text me when you get home."

"I will."

Daddy closed the door, and she rattled off her address to the driver. She didn't want to leave him, but at the same time, she couldn't wait to get back to her apartment and sleep.

"Thank you," she whispered as she got out of the car.

Sofia quickly made her way into the apartment building and up to her apartment. She didn't want to stay out there too long and possibly get mugged. That wasn't going to happen again.

She sighed as she put her stuff down and made her way towards her room. Sending a quick message to Daddy, she laid down in bed and closed her eyes, content with the past couple of hours.

Sofia slowly woke up with a groan. Her body was shaking, and she was so cold. Why was she so cold?

She slowly drew out her arm and grabbed her phone, checking the time. She had to leave soon to make it to her shift, but she didn't have the energy to go. It was like someone had zapped her of all her energy.

Tears filled in her eyes as all the emotions got to her. She was exhausted, had no energy, was shaky, cold, and sad. But nothing made sense. She didn't have a reason to feel all of those.

Grabbing the blanket, she held on tightly to it and snuggled into her pillow and Trixie. Maybe if she fell back asleep, everything would be okay when she woke up. But part of her knew it wasn't going to help and she started to cry.

Sofia clenched her eyes shut and squeezed Trixie in her arms.

Ring.

Her phone went off, but she didn't have any motivation to check it. No one needed to contact her. She didn't need to respond. It was probably some sales person calling her to tell her she needed to get insurance for her car.

A car she didn't have.

Crying even more, she buried her head into her blanket as her phone went off again.

CHAPTER TWENTY-ONE

JAXSON

*S*hit.

That was all Jaxson thought as he waited for Sofia to pick up. She should've been here forty minutes ago for her shift, but she didn't arrive. Did she not get home safely? Did something happen to her? Why wasn't she here?

Jaxson tried to call her again.

He didn't understand why she wasn't responding or at work. Worry gnawed at him as the phone went to voicemail again. This wasn't like her and he was worried that something had happened.

"Everything okay?" Leo asked.

"No," he replied and walked off. He needed to find Monty and ask her if she had heard from Sofia.

He knew they were close, and he was glad they had each other. They were both shy and newer employees at the club.

"Monty," he called her name as he saw her walking across the bar.

She turned around, her eyes wide and face went pale.

Shit. He didn't mean to make her feel like she was in trouble, but he was in a rush.

Something didn't feel right, and he needed to get to Sofia as soon as possible.

"Have you heard from Sofia?" he asked.

Monty shook her head. "Sorry, I haven't. Isn't she supposed to be here?"

He nodded his head and turned around, heading towards Michael's office. Even though Jaxson was a retired police officer, he didn't know what type of phone Sofia had and he didn't know how to hack into it.

He needed to figure out where she was.

"I'm busy," Michael said.

"Give me Miles' number," Jaxson said.

Michael stopped doing what he was doing on his computer and looked up, his eyebrows raised.

"Why do you need his number?" Michael asked.

"Sofia isn't answering her phone, and she was supposed to come in almost an hour ago for her shift. Something is wrong," Jaxson said. "I need his guy to track down her phone."

Michael rattled off his phone number, and Jaxson walked out of his office, calling Miles. He hoped that he would be willing to help him out.

"What?" Miles growled into the phone. "What could you possibly want?"

"It's Jaxson," he replied. "I need your guy to track down a phone number for me. Tell me where she is."

"Give me the phone number. Who's this for anyway?"

"Sofia," he replied and then told him the phone number.

It wasn't his business to know, but Jaxson didn't want to deal with him bantering back and forth. He just wanted to find out where Sofia was so he could figure out what was wrong and take care of it.

"Monroe mentioned a Sofia," Miles said. "Something about a playdate that happened recently."

"That's her, and she's mine," Jaxson said.

Miles chuckled through the phone. "Don't worry. I've got my own Little."

Jaxson didn't know what came over him when Miles said that. He just needed to make sure that he knew Sofia was his and no one else was going to take her.

"Sorry," Jaxson said. "I just need to find her."

"My guy will be in contact with you soon," Miles said and hung up.

Jaxson let out a sigh and leaned up against the wall. He felt useless right now, waiting for Miles' guy to contact him with her address. Was it going to take him a while? Should he start to look at nearby apartments?

"What's going on?" Leo asked as Jaxson started to walk towards the entrance of the club.

He needed to get to his car so when the text came through, he could quickly get there. Has Sofia fallen and hurt herself? Had she passed out on her floor?

"Sofia isn't answering her phone," Jaxson said. "I've got to go."

"Text me when you find her!" Leo yelled as Jaxson got into his car.

Right as he sat down, he got a text message with the address on it and the guy's name. Kirk.

Jaxson looked at the address and cursed. He didn't like that neighborhood at all. What was she doing living there? Why had she decided to walk from work to her apartment? He would've given her a ride to and from work every day if he knew she lived there.

His phone started to ring as he drove to her apartment. It wasn't going to take him long to get there.

"Yes?" he answered the phone.

"You got the address?" Miles' voice filled the car.

"Yes."

"Good. If she really is your girl, then you get her out of that location."

Jaxson couldn't agree more with him. He didn't want anyone living here.

"You got me?" Miles said. "If I find out she's still living there, I'll have Rogan send people."

"I heard you," Jaxson replied. "She won't be living here any longer. Shouldn't have been living here in the first place."

"Damn straight," he said and hung up.

Jaxson had never met Miles in person and hoped he never had to. He still couldn't believe that Monroe was related to him. They were polar opposite, but Jaxson had to remind himself that Monroe didn't grow up with him.

He quickly pulled into a parking spot and got out of his car, making his way into the building and up to her apartment. He hoped and prayed that Sofia was okay in there and that she just slept through her alarm.

"Sofia," Jaxson said as he knocked on the door.

Please answer. But she didn't.

"Sofia," he said louder, hoping that she would hear him.

His hand wrapped around the door handle and twisted. Worry went through him as the door opened. Why wasn't the door locked? Did she know how dangerous that was? Anyone could have come into her apartment and done anything to her.

"Sofia!" He raised his voice as he walked into her apartment. "I'm in your apartment. Can you tell me where you are?"

Silence.

Was she being held against her will in her apartment?

Jaxson carefully made his way through her apartment and to her room. As he walked past the living room, worry gnawed at him as he saw how bare it was in her apartment. Had she been living like that since she got here?

He figured she was starting from scratch on living, but he didn't think it was this bad. She didn't have a couch or a TV. The living room was bare except for an old armchair, and he didn't like that. Sofia should have everything she wanted. She should be spoiled and shown that someone cares for her.

Jaxson didn't want to look in the kitchen and see what she didn't have but at the same time, he did. Maybe he could sneak a little peek before they left. He wanted to see how he failed her and how to make it up to her.

Why hadn't she said anything?

He was going to have a serious talk with her on what she should be telling him. She shouldn't be living like this, and he wished he had made that clear earlier on. He should've asked where she lived, demanded to know so that he could get her out of here.

Jaxson thought they paid well for their employees to live comfortably. He was going to have to reevaluate the club's pay scale. If Sofia is living like this, that means some other people might be living like this.

And that wasn't acceptable.

"Sofia?" he called out again as he walked towards the only open door leading from the living room.

He didn't want to startle her if she didn't hear him before. A scared Little was never good and he would feel guilty if he scared her.

The first thing Jaxson saw when he walked into her room was a mattress on the ground. He clenched his jaw. She should have a proper bed to sleep on. Not a fucking mattress on the ground.

The closer he got to her, the more he realized. She was shaking and whimpering as she clutched her covers and Trixie in her arms.

What the fuck was going on?

He had let her out of his sights for less than twenty four hours and she was shaking and whimpering.

"Sofia?" he softly said. "Little one?"

She moved slightly in her bed, but her shaking still continued. Was she cold? It wasn't cold in her apartment.

"D-Daddy," she whimpered.

"Yes, Little one?" he asked as he knelt on the floor beside her.

Jaxson could see the tears streaming down her face when he got closer. What could possibly be wrong? He felt her forehead, but she didn't feel hot. She wasn't sick, so what else could it be?

"I d-don't know what's wrong," she whispered, clutching her stuffed animal tighter.

Realization hit him as he thought about all of the symptoms he could see.

Sub drop.

That was the only explanation he could think of. Has she been feeling like this since she got home last night? Why hadn't she called him or picked up when he called her?

"Daddy," she whimpered again.

He touched her cheek with his hand.

"Shhh," he whispered. "It's going to be okay. Daddy's here."

She cried harder, and it broke his heart. He should've kept a better eye on her after they went to the club yesterday. He had no doubt that the ropes were part of the cause. Jaxson was going to kick himself in the ass for a while. He knew better and yet he hadn't checked in with her last night or made sure she knew she might experience this.

"Daddy's going to take care of you," he whispered.

CHAPTER TWENTY-TWO

SOFIA

Sofia didn't know what was happening or how Daddy managed to get into her apartment. Why was he here? Why was she shaking so much? She was so cold, and it didn't make any sense because she had the covers wrapped around herself. When she fell asleep last night, it wasn't cold but now she was freezing and couldn't stop shaking.

"You're okay, Little one," Daddy whispered as he helped her sit up.

She shivered as the air hit her skin, and she whined.

"C-cold," she whimpered. "Daddy."

"I know, Little one," he replied. "Let me go get a thicker blanket."

In the back of her mind, she knew he wasn't going to find a thicker blanket in her apartment unless he brought one. She hadn't gone out yet and purchased one, but it was on her list whenever she had the money or until she moved out of this apartment.

She heard him cursing and closed her eyes, snuggling into Trixie as her upper body started to sway.

"Shit, Little one," Daddy said. "You shouldn't be living like this."

"No choice," she whimpered.

Sofia didn't realize how expensive it was to live in the United States. She thought it would be cheaper than Chile, but she was so wrong. There were so many taxes that came out of nowhere. Rent was more expensive and the cheapest place was in a bad part of town.

"I wish you would've told me," he whispered. "I would've taken you in."

She didn't want to be a charity case to him. Sofia wanted to prove to herself that she could do this but with each passing day, she was realizing that she couldn't.

"I couldn't find a blanket," he said. "Here's my jacket. Can you let go of Trixie for a second so I can help you put it on?"

She didn't want to let go of Trixie but she knew she would be warmer if she had his jacket on. Or she hoped she would. She let go of Trixie and felt Daddy put his jacket on her. It was so warm and she could smell him.

It reminded her of Thieves and it smelt delicious.

"I'm taking you home," he softly said. "I'm going to take care of you there."

She wasn't going to argue with him right now. She remembered his house, and she loved it. It felt like a home and so safe.

"Do you need anything?" he asked.

Sofia grabbed Trixie and held her close. She didn't know

what she would need and right now she didn't want to think about anything.

"I d-don't know," she whispered.

"Sit here for a couple of minutes while I grab some of your onesies," he said.

She let go of Trixie, crying out and grabbing onto his arm. She didn't want him to leave her alone.

"Daddy," she whimpered and held tighter onto his arm.

"It's okay, Little one," he softly said. "I'm right here. I'm just going to grab a couple of your onesies."

She shook her head. She didn't want him to leave.

"No."

"Do you want Daddy to hold you?" he asked.

She let go of his arm, grabbed Trixie before she made grabby hands at him. Her hands were shaking in the air as she held them there, but she didn't care.

"Oh baby," he said as he picked her up. "Daddy's got you."

She snuggled into his embrace, putting her face into his neck. She wanted to feel his skin against hers. Sofia tugged at his shirt with her free hand.

"Off?"

"Not yet, Little one," he said. "I need to grab your onesie and go home before I can take my shirt off."

Sofia didn't like that but stayed silent as Daddy started to walk around the room.

"Do you want to pick your onesie?" he asked.

Sofia managed to shake her head a little bit. She didn't want to make any decisions.

"Alright, Little one," he softly said. "Daddy will make the decisions. You just hold on and relax."

She loved the sound of that. There wasn't a time in her life that she hadn't made the decisions for everything and it was nice to be able to relax and not have to think about it.

"You're doing so amazing," Daddy said. "Do you have any candy? Chocolate?"

Sofia shook her head. It hadn't been on her list of things to get when she went to the grocery store. She had needed things that would sustain her and candy didn't, even if she wanted it. Her sweet tooth was huge, but she had to put it on hold when she moved to the United States.

"That's okay. I've got some in the car you can snack on while we go home," he said as he started to walk. "Do you need anything before we leave?"

"No," she whispered.

She had Trixie, and that's all she wanted. Well, and Daddy but he was coming with her.

"Alright, Little one," Daddy said. "Let's go home."

She loved it when he called his house 'home' because that's what it felt like. She felt safe and comfortable when she went to his house.

"When we get to the car, I'm going to need to put you down," he softly said.

Sofia whined and held on tighter to him. She didn't want to let him go. She wasn't going to let him go.

"I know, baby," he rubbed her back. "But I promise you once we get home you can have all the snuggles you want."

It made her feel better knowing she could still get more

snuggles, but it also meant she was going to have to let go for who knows how long. She knew he didn't live far, but she still didn't want to let him go, not when she just got him.

"I'm going to set you down now," Daddy said.

Her grip tightened around his shirt as he set her down on the car seat. She hadn't heard him open the door, but she also hadn't realized they walked out of her apartment and down to his car. Was she that out of it? It wasn't normal for her and it was starting to worry her.

"You've got to let me go, Little one," he gently said. "It's going to be okay."

She reluctantly let go of his shirt and leaned into the seat. She still felt so out of it, shaking, and cold. Daddy buckled her in before grabbing something out of the center console.

"You start nibbling on this while I drive home," he said as he handed her a piece of chocolate.

Sofia started to slowly eat it as he walked around the car and got in.

"You doing okay?" he asked. "Do you need anything before I start driving?"

She grabbed his hand, wanting that skin to skin contact with him.

"Okay, Little one," he said. "You hold my arm for the whole drive."

She wished this was a truck so she could sit in the middle and snuggle up against him. That was all she wanted, but she knew it wasn't safe, especially in his car. The car started moving, and she closed her eyes for a second, just wanting to go back to sleep. She felt exhausted.

"Can you eat a bit more of the chocolate?" Daddy asked.

"No hungry," she mumbled.

"I know but I need you to eat a little more for me. Get the sugar in your body so you stop shaking as much."

She grumbled but brought the piece of chocolate up to her lips and started to eat it. She didn't want to eat it, but she also didn't want to continue to shake.

"Such a good girl," Daddy said. "My good girl."

She melted hearing him call her that. The more she ate the chocolate, the more she felt herself slowly starting to shake less.

"You're doing so good," he continued to speak as they pulled into the garage. "Daddy's going to come around and get you."

He held her hand for a second before he carefully pulled it off of his arm and got out of the car. She waited patiently for him to walk around and open her door.

"I may need to get you a booster seat," he mumbled. "Are you ready to go inside?"

She held out her arms, waiting to be picked up. Once in his arms, she put her face in his neck and felt herself slowly starting to relax.

"My baby," he softly said.

She absolutely loved hearing him call her that. He had so many different nicknames that it just made her feel so loved and cherished. It made her feel like he cared for her which she knew he did.

"Let's get you comfortable," he said. "Do you need anything?"

Sofia didn't know what she would need. This had never happened before and she was out of her depth. What could she possibly need besides him?

"You," she whispered. "Skin."

She wanted to feel his skin, his warmth. It seemed to make her feel better, and she just wanted more of that. She wanted his arms wrapped around her so she felt safe and could just relax.

"Okay, Little one," he softly said. "I'll take my shirt off and we can just snuggle. If you need anything, you let me know."

She nodded her head and felt him walk towards the living room.

"Do you want to watch something or just snuggle?"

"Snuggle."

Exhaustion weighed down on her as the seconds went by. She had already been exhausted and the drive from her apartment to his house just seemed to make things even worse.

"We'll go snuggle in my bed."

She felt him walk further into the house and towards his bedroom.

"I'm going to set you down on the bed so I can take my shirt off," he said before he placed her on the bed.

A whine escaped her mouth, and she watched him like a hawk. She didn't want him to go and leave her. She wanted him with her. Part of her knew he wasn't going to leave her, but the other part was worried.

"I'm right here," he softly said. "I'm not going anywhere."

Daddy got into bed, and she snuggled up into his side, placing her head on his chest. She could feel and hear his heartbeat and felt herself slowly starting to calm down.

"Daddy's got you," he softly said.

CHAPTER TWENTY-THREE

JAXSON

Jaxson didn't know how long they laid in bed for but he didn't care. He would give her anything she needed right now. She deserved that. He had been so stupid to not check in with her after they went to the club. He had thought she would've been okay until he saw her the next day, but he was wrong.

So wrong.

How could he be so stupid? It was something he knew he should've done and yet he hadn't. How long had she been like that before he came?

Every part of him hoped it wasn't long. He didn't like knowing that she had been suffering without him. Did she even know what was going on? Jaxson needed to talk to her about it, but he knew it could wait until she was in a better mind set.

Jaxson didn't know how much she knew about BDSM but from what he saw, she didn't know what sub drop was.

He let out a sigh and held her closely. Every once in a

while he would run his hand up and down her back to comfort her.

He was feeling guilty about everything that had happened. How could he have let this happen? Was he good enough to be her Daddy? Jaxson knew that Michael or Finn would've taken better care of her if it happened while she was on their watch. Heck, even Leo and Oliver would've known.

Doubt started to fill him as he looked down at Sofia in his arms. She was snuggled up tightly to him, almost like she was afraid he was going to leave her. Maybe he should. Maybe he should find someone that would take better care of her and know to communicate better about the risks.

He hadn't taken proper care of her, and it was showing. He should've insisted that he take care of her after he had put the ropes on her. What was he thinking when he didn't?

Sofia snuggled into him more. "Thank you," she whispered.

Jaxson was confused. Why was she thanking him? He hadn't done much of anything.

"What for, Little one?" he asked, genuinely curious.

"For taking care of me," she softly said, keeping her head in the exact same place.

His heart warmed as she said those words, but he couldn't help but also feel the guilt come back even more. He had let her suffer alone for who knows how long and she was thanking him.

"I need to do a better job," he gently said. And it was the truth. He needed to make sure he was taking better care of her and watching for signs and symptoms for anything.

Sofia moved her head off of his chest and looked into his eyes.

"How were you supposed to know that whatever this was, was going to happen to me?" she asked.

He took a deep breath in. "I should have checked up on you. I should have made sure you were okay and taken care of. I should've insisted that you come home with me in case this happened. I introduced you to something new and I was aware that there was a possibility of this happening and yet I didn't do anything."

She placed her hand on his chest and ran her finger up and down, almost in a soothing motion.

"It's going to be okay," she whispered. "You're here now and you can take care of me."

Part of him felt like that was hard for her to say. Before she hadn't wanted him to take care of her fully, but she was giving him permission to now.

He let out a sigh and kissed her forehead. She was so precious and even though he messed up; she said it was okay. But it wasn't. He was going to make up for it.

"Do you need anything?" he asks. "We can continue to snuggle in the bed or if you need a drink or food, we can get anything you need."

Jaxson didn't know what all he had in his kitchen, but he knew he could find something that would fill her tummy. May not be the best nutrition wise, but something was better than nothing in her stomach right now, if she was hungry.

"Just snuggles," she softly said, laying her head back down on his chest. "I'm not hungry."

Right as she said that, her stomach grumbled, and she went taut in his arms. Someone wasn't hungry but her stomach was definitely disagreeing with her.

"When was the last time you ate?" he asked.

She shrugged her shoulders as much as she could on top of him, not looking him in the eyes. He would chuckle with how cute she was right now, trying to avoid eye contact, but he didn't want to encourage this. She needed to eat since Michael thought she was underweight. He wanted to make sure she was healthy.

"Let's go get food in your stomach," he said as he slowly sat up.

Sofia held onto him, but he didn't mind. He knew she probably still needed to be close to him and he wasn't going to complain.

"I'm okay," she softly said.

"Nope," he replied. "Not going to work. Your stomach grumbled and I have a feeling you haven't eaten since yesterday, which isn't okay. You need food to nourish your body and help you do the things you want to do. If you skip meals, it isn't good and your body is going to start taking what it needs from itself. I won't allow that to happen."

"You won't allow it?"

"Nope," Jaxson said, booping her nose.

He tried to get off of the bed, but her grip around his torso tightened.

"Little one," he said. "I need to get out of bed and then I can pick you up."

She let go of him, and he quickly got out of bed before pulling her into his arms. Sofia held onto him like a Koala, but he didn't mind. He loved that she felt safe enough to latch onto him like this. Though, Jaxson didn't know if it was because of the sub drop or if she actually felt comfortable enough to do it.

"Do you need to go potty?" he asked.

"No," she whispered.

He wasn't surprised that she didn't need to go. He had a feeling she didn't drink much at all today. Jaxson was going to have to change that. It wasn't healthy. A lot of things that Sofia did were not healthy. Did she not have enough money for food? Or did she choose to not eat a lot? He hoped it was because of money but he couldn't rule the other one out.

"Alright. If you do, you let me know," He said as he started to walk towards the kitchen. "I have grilled cheese, toast, or I can make you a fruit smoothie. Which one do you want?"

"Smoothie."

Jaxson had vanilla protein powder he was going to put into the smoothie so she could get some of the protein she needed. He wanted her to be healthy and gain some weight.

"Alright, Little one," he said. "I'm going to set you down on the counter so I can make the smoothie."

A whine escaped her lips, and she held tighter onto him. Okay, maybe she wasn't going to let him go.

"I'll be right here. You'll be able to see me the whole time."

That didn't help one bit. How was he going to make it with her in his arms?

"No, let's go," she whispered.

"Alright," he replied. "Hang onto me so I can make your smoothie."

Jaxson made quick work of cutting the fruit and putting it into the blender. Thankfully, he had put them in the freezer before he went to work yesterday so they were already cold, and he didn't need to add any ice in it.

"You doing okay?" he gently asked as he turned the blender on.

He felt her nod her head ever so slightly before putting it back in his neck. Jaxson added the protein powder in before quickly blending everything together and pouring it into a cup.

"Alright. Smoothie is ready for you to eat," he said as he walked into the living room.

He figured she wasn't going to let him go and he wasn't even going to try. Jaxson sat down on the couch carefully.

"Can you look at Daddy?"

Sofia pulled away from him and let him start to feed her the smoothie. He held the cup, tilting it back when she drank some and resting his arm when she wasn't. Jaxson could get used to this. He absolutely loved taking care of her and showing her that she mattered to him.

"Is it good?" he asked.

"Yep," she replied, giving him a smile.

He put that information away for later. This would be a good snack or breakfast meal for her if she didn't want to eat a full breakfast. It had enough protein, fat, and carbs to help sustain her body.

"Good. If you ever want one, you let Daddy know and I'll

make you one," he gently said as he fed her some more of the smoothie.

She quickly finished the rest of the smoothie. Jaxson was about to get up, but Sofia snuggled into his chest and closed her eyes.

I guess we're not moving, he thought to himself.

That was fine with him. He had made sure before he started to feed her that he was comfortable because he didn't know how long they were going to sit there.

"Such a good girl," he whispered and kissed the top of her head.

Sofia gripped onto his shirt and his heart strings got tugged on. She was so cute and precious.

CHAPTER TWENTY-FOUR

SOFIA

Two days had passed since Daddy found Sofia in her apartment and took her to his house. Two days since he told Sofia that she had hit sub drop.

Sofia had heard about sub drop but didn't know the symptoms or what could bring it on. Not until she had experienced it herself and she never wanted to do that again.

Daddy had told her he was going to keep an extra careful eye on her the next several days and she honestly didn't mind. It was weird, but she also didn't want to experience that again and if that meant him watching her closely, then that was it.

He had made sure to ask her several times throughout the day if she was alright and how she was feeling. He could tell when she was lying, so she had been honest whenever he asked. It also didn't benefit her to lie to him in this situation. Not that any lying she did to him benefited her.

They were currently walking up to her apartment. Daddy

told her she wasn't going to live here anymore because it wasn't in the safe part of town. She understood, but at the same time, she told him she didn't want to get rid of it just yet. What if they didn't work out, and she didn't have an apartment to go back to?

So they had compromised, and he told her he was going to pay for one more month of rent. At the end of that, if they were still together, which he claimed they would be, she would move all of her stuff into his house. She figured they would be because she loved being around him and him being her Daddy, but she just wanted to be safe.

Everything was new and what if he figured out he didn't want her anymore?

"Where is your key, Little one?" he asked.

Sofia handed him the key, and he unlocked the door. Not that it did much because she didn't have a deadbolt so anyone could get in if they really wanted to.

"We're going to talk about how you didn't lock the door the other day when I came over," Daddy said. "When we get home."

She had thought she locked it when she got home, but apparently she didn't. Sofia knew either way she was going to get a lecture about it. She couldn't blame Daddy for wanting to give her one, but he also had to know that it being locked may not have helped keep a person out at all. She was pretty sure if someone ran into the door with their shoulder, they would open it.

She hadn't really liked that about the apartment, but she couldn't complain because it was what she could afford, which wasn't a lot. Even if someone broke into her apartment, they wouldn't find much at all because she didn't have a lot. There was nothing valuable in her apartment.

"Come on, Little one," Daddy said as he held the door open for her.

Sofia spotted something on the ground behind the door. What could that be? She bent down to pick it up and saw U.S. Citizenship and Immigration Services. Her eyes went wide, and she quickly stuffed it in her pants and put her shirt over it.

She had no clue what it was about, but she didn't want Daddy to see it. What if they were trying to deport her? She hadn't had time to fill out the application to get her Green Card yet. Sofia hadn't saved enough money up for that yet. She hadn't thought it would be so expensive, but it was and she was trying to save up for it.

There were several things she was trying to save up for and she didn't know which one was more important. Her Green Card or a new apartment in a better location.

"Sofia?" Daddy asked. "What's wrong? What was that on the ground?"

She turned around and gave him a smile, trying to hide her panic welling up inside of her. "It was just a bill I have to pay, Daddy."

Daddy held out his hand. "Give it to Daddy and he'll take care of it."

She stared at him, blinking several times before she shook her head. She had lied to him about it, and she knew it was wrong, but she didn't want him to worry about it. He was always worrying about her, and she didn't want him to do that anymore.

"No," she softly said. "You don't need to do that. It's my bill and not yours."

"But you're mine," he said. "I want to take care of you. Let me take care of you."

Before she could stop herself, she continued to lie. "It's something feminine and I would really like to just take care of it myself."

Sofia closed her eyes and took several deep breaths. She didn't enjoy lying to him. It made her feel guilty every time, but she couldn't stop. She knew Daddy would do anything to help her, and she wanted to be a little independent.

"Nothing comes between us," he said. "There aren't any secrets."

Guilt continued to build up inside of her. She had several secrets he didn't know about. What if when he found out all of them, he didn't want her anymore? She didn't know how he was going to react, and Sofia didn't want to lose him.

That would devastate her.

"I don't know," she whispered, feeling bad about everything now.

"Don't know about what?"

"About having no secrets. It's something I'll have to get used to, telling you everything."

"We obviously have to build up trust. I know you may not be able to tell me everything now, but soon we won't be keeping things from each other."

She nodded her head. Maybe in several months she would get to that point with him. She hoped she would.

"I do hope you tell me sometime soon what the bill is," he softly said. "Do I need to be worried?"

"No," she whispered, not looking into his eyes. She didn't know if she needed to be worried or not, but she hoped she wouldn't.

"Alright," he said. "If it changes you let me know."

"Okay, Daddy."

"Let's go pack up some of your stuff."

He grabbed her hand and led her into her room. She didn't have a lot to pack up in her apartment because she didn't own a lot. So it didn't take them long to put her few clothes into a bag she had and head out the door.

Daddy had mentioned that he would just buy her all new things, but she didn't want that. She couldn't let him do that. That would have been a lot of money, and she knew he had money, but she didn't want him to spend it on her.

He didn't like that and said at some point he was going to buy things for her if she liked it or not. She huffed and was silent the rest of the drive to her apartment.

"Ready to go home?" Daddy asked.

"Yes," she whispered.

It didn't take them long to get back to his house.

"I've gots to pee," she hurriedly said.

She really didn't but she wanted to read what the letter said. The anticipation was killing her, and she didn't know how much longer she could last.

"Okay, Little one," he said. "I'll start unpacking your clothes."

She nodded her head and dashed towards the bathroom.

"No running!" Daddy yelled. "You know the rules."

Sofia slowed down and walked into the bathroom, shutting the door and locking it. She pulled the envelope out of her pants and opened it.

Tears started to stream down her face as she read the words.

CHAPTER TWENTY-FIVE

SOFIA

Sofia continued to look at the letter, reading over the words again and again. She couldn't believe what she was reading. She had thought she had several more months until she had to reapply for her work visa.

But she was wrong.

So wrong.

The letter said it would expire in the next month and a half and she needed to reply or else she would be deported. Sofia didn't want that, and she knew if she got deported, it would be harder for her to get her Green Card in the end.

How was she going to come up with the money to renew her work visa? Sofia felt like she was drowning, at this point, because she didn't know what to do. How much longer would she be able to hold her head barely above water?

The only thing Sofia felt right now was being scared and overwhelmed. There were so many things she needed to do and get into order to be able to renew her work visa. Did she have enough money? Would Monty be able to lend her some if she didn't?

Sofia didn't want to leave the country. She had just started to love it here and she didn't want to leave. She was starting to make friends and she had a Daddy right now.

Things she didn't think she would have but she did.

She finally did.

And she didn't want to give that up. Even though she lived in a bad part of town, she loved her work and the people she got to hang out with. She had made friends with some other Littles and loved every bit of it. They were planning on having another playdate soon and she was excited for it.

Maybe at some point she could have a sleepover with some of them. Would they want that? Sofia had never been to a sleepover, but she so badly wanted to host one or go to one.

"Sofia?" Daddy said as he knocked on the door. "Are you okay?"

She looked at herself in the mirror and cringed when she saw how red her face was. Sofia was not a pretty crier and her face always got bright red.

"I'm almost done," she said. "Gots to wash my hands."

Sofia flushed the toilet and turned on the water. She carefully splashed some cold water on her face to get rid of some of the red, but it didn't do much. She would just have to keep her head down.

She opened the door, keeping her head down, and stepped out.

"Little one?" Daddy asked.

She continued to look down at her feet, not wanting him to see her red, splotchy, face.

"Can you look at Daddy?" he asked and she shook her head. "What's wrong?"

Sofia burst into tears. She quickly felt her Daddy wrap his arms around her and pick her up. He held her close as she continued to sob into his arms.

She could feel him starting to walk and before she knew it, he was sitting down and just held her. Sofia continued to cry in his arms, letting all her emotions out.

"Can you tell Daddy what's wrong?" he asked as he pulled away.

Sofia looked at him, tears still streaming down her face. She snuffled several times as she tried to think about what to say. She so badly wanted to tell him that she needed to fill the form out again, but she didn't know how.

How would he react to it? How would she tell him that? Would he be disappointed in her?

"Sofia," he softly said, cupping her face with his hand. "Are you alright?"

She shook her head and sucked in a breath. She was going to start sobbing again and she had just stopped.

"Can you tell Daddy?" he asked.

"C-can I t-tell you in a c-couple of days?" she stuttered her way through.

Maybe, in a couple of days, she could wrap her head around everything while also figuring out how to tell him. That was if he remembered she needed to tell him something. Part of her hoped he would forget all about it.

Daddy sighed and rubbed his thumb across her cheek.

"I don't like it," he said, and she held her breath.

Was he not going to let her do it? She didn't know if she could tell him right now.

"But this once, I'll allow it. I really don't like it," he said. "If I see in the next day that it's hurting you more, then you will tell me. No arguments. Understood?"

She nodded her head.

"Words, Little one," he reminded her.

"Yes, Daddy. I understand."

"Good girl." Daddy kissed her forehead and she melted into his body.

CHAPTER TWENTY-SIX

SOFIA

Sofia walked up to Monty's door and stood there for a second. Should she do this right now or should she wait? She didn't want to bother Monty, but she also needed to talk to her about what she should do.

She needed to tell Daddy what was going on, but she was worried about what he would say or react.

"Are you going to stand there all day or are you going to come in?" Monty asked.

Sofia looked up and gave her a smile.

"How did you know I was here?" she asked as she stepped into the apartment.

She only had thirty minutes before she needed to leave for work. Daddy didn't know she was here, and she was worried about that. They had driven together to the club, and he had gone to work while she just hung around. Then she decided to come visit Monty and get her opinion. She wasn't scheduled to work tonight and today was the day that Sofia was supposed to tell her Daddy.

"My little brother saw your shadow and told me someone was at the door," Monty said. "Peepholes are amazing for situations like this. Not that the door would do anything."

Sofia nodded her head in agreement. This door was just like hers and there was no argument against it not being safe. Everyone in the building knew that it was a shit door.

"So, what did you need?" Monty asked.

"I need advice," Sofia softly said, nervous about telling Monty. "It's about me and Jaxson."

"Sit down and spill the beans."

She couldn't help but chuckle. Monty was trying to make her feel comfortable.

"I got a letter the other day."

"From who? You didn't give your friend your address."

"The government about my work visa expiring in less than two months."

Monty gasped and stared at her. "W-what?"

"Yeah, I thought I had more time, but I don't. So, I need to get the money and reapply."

Sofia closed her eyes and took a deep breath. She had been stressing over this ever since she read the letter. She was short of money, and she didn't know where she was going to get it. Maybe she could get paid a little earlier.

"Have you told Jaxson?" Monty asked.

"No," Sofia replied. "I don't know how, and I don't know if I should. I've been saving to apply for a Green Card but it's so expensive."

"Why haven't you told him? I know he would be happy to help you."

She sighed. "He's my Daddy now and I just don't want him to worry about it. This isn't his problem, and I don't want to become a burden for him. Especially when everything is so new."

Monty shook her head. "You don't get to make that decision for him. You need to tell him and let him decide if he wants to still be with you and help out."

"I don't know," Sofia whispered.

She had tossed and turned last night, not getting much sleep at all. Daddy had held her after a while and she laid there, awake and feeling alone with her thoughts. Waking up this morning had been a struggle and Daddy put her down for a nap several hours later.

Her first nap at his house. He had been so sweet and put pillows around her to make her feel safe, comfortable, and stayed with her until she fell asleep.

"You need to tell him. I know that he loves you and will do anything to be with you. Before you came, he never came down to the main floor unless it was an absolute necessity. Then when you started, he was coming down for every one of your shifts."

"No," Sofia whispered but she knew it was a lie. He had come down for every one of her shifts.

"Don't bullshit me," Monty said. "You know I'm right. Tell your Daddy about it. He would love to help you and you know it."

"He also doesn't love me," Sofia said, finally realizing what Monty had said.

"You're a fool if you don't see it. You have him wrapped

around your pinky. That man, your Daddy, would do anything for you."

Sofia was silent as she processed the words. He had said multiple times that he wanted to take care of her and spoil her a lot, but she didn't understand and said she didn't want it. But it did sound nice. Sofia wasn't used to it, and she didn't know if she would like it or not.

Did that mean he loved her?

Whenever she caught her Daddy looking at her, he had this look in his eyes. But she had never thought about that look and what it meant.

She couldn't remember a time when her parents looked at her with love. Maybe that was the reason she found it hard to decipher if he was looking at her with love.

"Promise me that you'll tell him," Monty said. "He should know since you guys are in a dynamic together."

Sofia sighed but nodded her head. She didn't know when she would tell him, but maybe it would be soon. She had promised her Daddy that she would tell him sooner than later, and she didn't want to break her promise.

She already felt so guilty about lying to him several times and keeping it from him. She had done it so many times and it was starting to get to her. The guilt sat in her stomach as the days went on. It was like a huge ball that weighed hundreds of pounds.

Always there to remind her that she had lied to him.

"I'll see you when we work together?" Monty said as they stood up.

"Yeah, I'll see you then," Sofia replied. "Just to let you

know, I'm staying at Jaxson's house for a little while. I got mugged recently and he didn't like that."

It was weird for her to call her Daddy by his name now. She was so used to calling him Daddy and it sounded almost wrong to call him anything else.

"Well, I have your number if I need anything," Monty said. "Have a good shift at the club."

Sofia made it quick to get to the club. She didn't want to stay outside long enough to get mugged again. Her heartbeat was racing as she walked up to the entrance of the club.

"Did you just walk here, Tiny?" Dominic asked.

"Nope," Sofia replied, lying. "I got dropped off a little ways off because the parking lot was so busy."

He looked at her and shook his head. She hoped he wouldn't say anything to her Daddy about walking, but for some reason she felt like he was going to tell him anyway.

She made her way towards the employee room to put her stuff away. When she arrived, a little folded up piece of paper was sitting in front of her locker.

What was that doing there?

Sofia picked it up and opened it, her eyes going wide as she read what was on the paper.

Die, bitch. Go back to your country or else you'll find yourself dead.

Chills ran up and down her body as she continued to read it. She looked around the room, trying to see if anyone was in the room but no one was. Who left this for her?

She felt shaky as she stuffed it into her pocket and put her things away. Who would want her to go back to her country? She didn't know a lot of people here. There was Lucy, who didn't like her, but Sofia didn't think she would give her this note.

Sofia thought Lucy just wanted her gone because she had started working more hours than her. Had she taken Lucy's hours? Maybe she could talk to Jaxson about her hours being cut a little so Lucy could get hers back.

But that would hurt Sofia because she needed all the money she could get. If she cut her hours any more, she would be out of a house and be living on the streets.

A shiver ran through Sofia as she walked out of the employees room, in a daze. What was she going to do?

"Are you okay?" Leo asked.

Sofia looked at him and gave him a small smile. It didn't reach her eyes and she felt like he knew that.

"I'm okay," she whispered."

"What's wrong?" he asked as he stepped in front of her.

She looked down at the ground, not wanting him to see her face. She had no doubt it was giving a lot away and she didn't want that. All the Daddy Doms around here just seemed to be able to read her really well.

"Nothing," she responded.

"Bullshit," he said.

Sofia shook her head. "I just ate something bad and feel a little nauseous."

She hoped that lie would work, especially since he couldn't see her face.

"Then go take a break or better yet, go home."

"Cold water will fix it," she said as she took a step to the side. "Besides, I just got here so I can't take my break yet."

"You shouldn't be working here if you're feeling sick. Your Daddy wouldn't like that."

Sofia started to walk towards the bar, nervous that he was going to say something to Daddy. Should she go and tell him that she wasn't feeling good before Leo did? She shook her head at her thought and walked behind the bar.

She looked around the place, trying to see if she could find anyone that would give her the note. Maybe they were in the club watching her. The thought of that made Sofia feel even more ill than she already did.

Placing a hand on her stomach, she took several deep breaths in to try and calm herself down. She didn't need to work herself up over this right now. The person wouldn't be here, would they?

Why would they be? They were risking being caught. Unless they were a regular and no one ever thought it would be them.

Sofia's eyes went wide at the thought, her hand flying to her mouth. She was going to be sick.

Out of the corner of her eye, she saw her Daddy walk into the room right as she was dashing towards the bathroom.

She didn't care who was watching her at this point, all she wanted was to make it to the bathroom before she puked. Sofia dropped to her knees in front of the toilet and started to puke.

Sofia felt someone grab onto her hair and hold it back as she continued to expel her guts. Tears were streaming down her face as this continued. She hated puking.

"It's okay," Daddy whispered as he rubbed her back.

She slumped back, leaning into his body as she finished. Her body felt weak as she relaxed some.

"What's wrong?" Daddy asked. "What has you all worked up that you made yourself sick?"

The thought of the person being here right now had Sofia leaning over the toilet again.

"Shhhhhh, you're alright," he softly said as she started to cry harder.

Everything was getting so overwhelming, and she didn't like it. She just wanted life to be simple and it was anything but that.

Daddy picked Sofia up and held her against him as he started to walk. She snuggled into his embrace, feeling awful about everything. Why did this have to happen to her?

"Sofia," he gently said as he placed her down on his office couch.

She was getting used to sitting and laying down on this couch. It was quite comfortable, especially with a blanket wrapped around her. Definitely a good napping place. Not that she took naps, but if she did, it would be a perfect spot. With her size, it was almost like a bed.

"Can you tell me what's wrong?" he asked.

"I feel better," she softly said. "I just ate something bad before work and it didn't agree with my stomach."

"Why didn't you tell me or take your shift off? I don't want you or anyone working when they don't feel good."

More guilt built up in her stomach as she lied, and he believed her. Why was she doing this? Why did she have to lie? She needed to tell him the truth, but it was just another thing for him to worry about.

Sofia started to cry even harder. She couldn't take this anymore.

"Oh baby," he cooed at her as he pulled her into his lap. "I thought you were lying to me, but I wanted to believe you weren't. Now, tell me the truth."

She snuggled into his embrace and cried. He knew she was lying but still gave her the benefit of the doubt. What did she do to deserve that?

Nothing.

That's what. There was nothing she did to deserve all his goodness. Not when she lied to him for weeks on end. Sofia didn't deserve her Daddy.

"Little one," Daddy said. "I need you to tell me what's wrong. You've been so stressed since we went to your apartment and I don't like it. I gave you a couple of days to wrap your head around it, but maybe I was wrong in doing that."

Part of her agreed with him. Maybe if he had pressured her into telling him at the apartment this all would've been better. But the other part of her didn't think so. This was different than the government saying she needed to reapply for her work visa. This was a threatening note in the club, and she didn't know who it was from or who would want to get rid of her.

What had she done to deserve this? She was nice to everyone she met.

Sofia pulled away from her Daddy and looked him in the eyes. Tears were slowly stopping, but her eyes were still damp from them.

"Can," she started off. "Can I tell you after my shift?"

"I don't know," he replied.

"Please," she begged. "I promise I'll tell you after my shift ends."

Sofia wanted to work her shift. She wanted to have a little normalcy for once in the past few weeks.

"Please, Daddy," she asked.

"Not your whole shift," Daddy said. "One hour."

She opened her mouth to argue, but stopped when he raised his eyebrow.

"A minute late and you'll be in worse trouble," he said. "I don't like this, but I'm giving you one hour."

"Thank you," she said, letting out a sigh of relief. She could wrap her mind around everything that had happened and figure out the best way to tell him. So, hopefully, he doesn't get really mad.

"No matter how tired you are, after an hour, you're going to tell me," Daddy said. "Do you understand?"

"Yes, Daddy."

He helped her stand before she started to walk out. She had no clue what she could do in an hour. There wasn't much, but maybe she could restock some of the fridges. There were other bartenders at the bar and, even though it was busy, it looked like they had it under control.

Did they even need her here tonight?

With a sigh, she got to filling the fridges with things the bartenders needed. She was tired and knew that she would be sleeping well tonight, or she hoped. The past couple of nights she hadn't been sleeping well, since she got the letter from the government.

As she passed the employees locker room to grab some more applesauce packages, Monty appeared.

"What are you doing here?" Sofia asked, her eyes wide.

Monty wasn't supposed to work tonight, but here she was.

"Leo called me in. Said someone was sick and asked if I could cover for them," Monty said. "My little brother is having a sleepover at a friend's house, so I thought it was a good time to grab an extra shift and then Leo called. Do you know who was sick?"

Sofia raised her hand. "It was me."

"Oh my goodness. Are you okay?"

She nodded her head. "Just threw up a little."

Monty looked at her and shook her head. "Have you told Jaxson yet?"

"Not yet. I'm going to tell him in about thirty minutes."

The more time passed, the more nervous she became. What was she going to do? How was she going to tell him?

"You need to tell him," Monty said. "You can't keep it from him. He deserves to know."

"I know," she whispered. "He already talked to me and said, after I finish up, he wants to hear what I've been holding back."

Maybe Sofia could get away with just telling him about the letter she received the other day and not the threatening note from today. He didn't know there were two different things going on that could make her sick, because he didn't know about the note.

But as Sofia thought about that, the guilt started to return with a vengeance. She couldn't live with herself if she let this guilt build up even more. She needed to come clean with everything she had done and lied about. It was going to be tough, but she needed to get it all out and then she needed to get a spanking.

She needed this guilt to go away.

"How about you go get your stuff and head to him," Monty suggested. "I know you said you have thirty minutes left until you were going, but maybe you could head there early and tell him. I've got you covered."

Sofia let out a sigh and knew she was right. She just needed to get this over with. There was no point in putting it off for another thirty minutes.

"Okay," Sofia said. "I'll grab my stuff and go tell him. Thank you for being such an amazing friend."

"Anytime, Sof," Monty replied as she walked away.

Sofia made her way to the employees room to grab her things. She was so nervous to tell Daddy about what had been going on and what she had been keeping from him. Part of her was worried that he was going to say he didn't want her anymore after this.

Would he say that?

She didn't think he would, but she wouldn't know until she told him. The sooner she told him, the better. Or at least, that's what she thought.

As Sofia made her way closer to her locker, she noticed another note placed in front of it. Her heart started to beat faster as she slowly made her way towards it. Looking around, she tried to spot if any one was in the employees room with her, but there wasn't.

Shit.

Was this another threatening note? Maybe it was just a simple empty piece of paper that landed in front of her locker. But deep down, she knew that wasn't it.

Sofia carefully picked up the paper, her breathing coming in short pants. She sat down on the little bench and opened the note.

Stay away from Leo and Jaxson. If you don't, you're dead.

She gripped onto the note as she started to get light headed. Shit. This was so much worse than she thought. The person was here in the club and had seen her interact with Leo and her Daddy. What was she going to do?

The more she thought about it, the more her breathing started to pick up and the dizzier she got. Before she knew it, the edges of her vision were going black, and she felt herself passing out.

CHAPTER TWENTY-SEVEN

JAXSON

Jaxson knew Sofia should be coming up to his office any minute now. It had killed him inside to let her go and work for another hour. He didn't want to, but he had a feeling that she probably needed the hour to get her brain wrapped around everything.

He didn't think it was part of what happened the other day. It was a different reaction, a *very* different reaction. Which made him think this was completely unrelated to what happened at her apartment.

He was hoping she would tell him first what had happened tonight and then he could ask about the other day. That was his hope. However, he had a feeling she would try to tell him what happened the other day and ignore today.

But he was *not* going to let that happen.

If she tried to play it off as if it was the same thing as the other day, he was going to call her out for it. He didn't like that it made her so ill she threw up. Something small wouldn't have done that. Not to Sofia, his precious Sofia.

Jaxson stood up from his chair and made his way towards the main room. He didn't want to wait any longer to talk to Sofia. He had given her plenty of time and she was out of it now.

Right as he stepped onto the main floor, Monty was at his side, yelling.

"Jaxson!" She yelled. "It's Sofia!"

He was alarmed when Monty said Sofia's name. What was wrong? Was she in the bathroom again?

"What's wrong?" Jaxson asked as he jogged over to Monty.

"She's unconscious on the floor in the employees lounge."

His heart stopped beating for a second. She had passed out? Had someone hurt her?

"Get Michael to the employee room," Jaxson said before he hurried over there.

So many things were going through his mind as he jogged over there. What had made her go unconscious? He didn't like not being in the know, especially when it came to Sofia. She was precious to him. So precious.

He loved her.

Jaxson stopped in front of the employee room, peering in. He loved her, but he didn't have time to think about that right now. Sofia needed him and he needed to be there for her.

"Everyone, please go back to work," Jaxson said. "I'll take it from here."

As the people started to leave, he took in Sofia. She was laying on her side on the bench, her feet dangling awkwardly. He hoped no one had harmed her, and she had just passed out. None of the options were good, but he just hoped that no one hit her to make her go unconscious.

Had she been surprised? Did she see it coming? What had made her pass out like this?

Jaxson stepped forward and carefully placed his hand on her neck, trying to find a pulse. He could see her chest rising and falling as she breathed, but he wanted to see if her pulse was strong or weak.

Please be strong. He thought to himself.

Her pulse was strong against his fingers, and he let out a sigh of relief. He didn't know much above the basic first aid and, right now, he wished he knew more. He didn't want to move her in case something was wrong that he didn't know about.

"What's wrong?" Michael asked as he walked into the room.

"Took you long enough," Jaxson snapped and then sighed. "Sorry. I'm just worried about her and I shouldn't have taken it out on you."

"No worries. What happened? Monty didn't give me much besides you needed me in the employee room."

"I don't know much besides Sofia was found unconscious on this bench in front of her locker," Jaxson said. "I felt her pulse and it's strong. Not too fast and not too slow. She's breathing. I didn't want to move her in case there was something wrong with her neck or spine."

"Good. I'll take a look at her and see if I can find anything wrong."

Jaxson took a step back and watched as Michael checked

her over. It was agony watching him look her over and not being able to do anything. Had she been scared when she passed out?

"Everything looks to be okay. Let's move her up to your office so we don't have prying eyes," Michael said as he stood.

"I'm good to carefully pick her up?" Jaxson asked.

He knew Michael just said everything looked to be okay, but he wanted to make sure. Was there a special way he was supposed to carry her?

"Yeah," Michael said. "We'll take the stairs back here, so people don't stare at her."

Jaxson had already decided he was going to do that. Sofia didn't like to bring attention to herself and yet she had by passing out in the employee room. No doubt people were going to be talking about it, asking her if she was alright.

He carefully picked her up. They made their way towards the stairs, walking up them, to get to his office. He gently placed her down on the couch and looked at her.

"What do you think caused it?" Jaxson asked.

"I don't know," Michael said. "There could be several factors, but I don't think anyone did it to her."

Relief slightly filled Jaxson as he heard those words. He had hoped it wasn't caused physically by someone else but that didn't mean someone didn't scare her into passing out. What could have happened?

"When do you think she'll wake up?" Jaxson asked as he put a blanket over Sofia. His office was colder than downstairs, and he didn't want her to be cold.

"I don't know. It could be any second or it could be several minutes," Michael said.

Jaxson sighed and knelt down in front of her. He gently ran his fingers through her hair while looking at her. She looked exhausted and he didn't like that. It was his job to make sure she was getting enough sleep, eating enough, and taking care of herself. He hadn't been doing his job. Well, the past couple of nights he had made sure she went to bed at a reasonable time and woke her up in the morning.

How long had she gone without getting good sleep and full meals?

Too long and it was catching up with her as she was finally starting to get the sleep her body needs. He was going to keep a close eye on her for the next several months.

Heck. He was kidding himself. He was going to keep a close eye on her for the rest of their lives. She didn't have a choice because she obviously needed someone to look over her.

Jaxson looked down and saw her hand peeking from the blanket. Something in her hand caught his attention. A piece of paper. What was that doing in there?

"If she doesn't wake up in the next ten minutes, then we're taking her to the ER," Michael said. "I may be overdramatic, but I don't know what happened before and I would rather be safe than sorry."

"I completely agree," Jaxson replied. "Money isn't an issue. She gets insurance through the club, if that doesn't cover it, then I'll cover the rest."

He took the piece of paper out of her hand and opened it. "Shit!"

"What's wrong?" Michael asked.

"Fucking shit!" Jaxson said as he stood up.

He could feel himself starting to get angry. How could she not have told him about this? It was a fucking threatening note, and she didn't mention it one time. Is that why she was throwing up earlier? Because she got the note?

"This is fucking stupid," he growled. "Shit! This is bad."

"Jaxson, get a hold of yourself," Michael said. "What's wrong?"

Jaxson handed him the piece of paper and right as he did, Sofia's eyes opened, and she gasped.

CHAPTER TWENTY-EIGHT

SOFIA

Her eyes opened and she let out a gasp. Where was she? Why was she laying down? Why was there a blanket over her?

"Shhh," Daddy said. "You're okay. You're in my office."

She moved her head around and found her Daddy standing a couple feet away. Why was she in his office laying on his couch?

"You're okay," Daddy took a step forward. "Daddy's going to keep you safe."

Her eyes went wide as she remembered what had happened before she passed out. Sofia sat up, clenching her hands but didn't find the piece of paper she was clutching before. Did it slip out of her hand? She needed to go to the employee room and find the piece of paper before anyone else did. No one could find out about it.

"Are you looking for this?" Michael asked as he waved a little piece of paper in the air.

She felt the color drain from her face. Shit. He had the

piece of paper from her hand. This wasn't good. Why hadn't she had better control over her body? Why did she have to pass out?

"Take a couple deep breaths in for me," Daddy said. "Can you do that for Daddy?"

She continued to look at Michael, but more specifically the piece of paper in his hand. Had he read it? She hoped he hadn't, but were the odds of that?

"Sofia," Daddy said. "Look at me."

She continued to look at the note. Maybe she could play it off that it wasn't important, and he would give it back to her.

"Now," Daddy commanded.

Her eyes went to him, and he didn't look happy.

"Breathe," he said. "In. Hold it. And out. Good girl. Can you do that again? No, don't look over at him again. Look at me."

She hadn't even realized her eyes were moving back to Michael, until Daddy said something.

"Good girl," Daddy said. "*My* good girl."

She blushed and continued to look at him.

"Now, can you tell Daddy if that was the first note you received?"

Sofia opened her mouth, ready to tell him yes, but he started to speak before she could.

"Don't you think about lying. You're already owed your punishment from walking home alone when I told you at the interview not to. You don't want to add more to your punishment," Daddy said.

Her eyes went wide. How did he know she was going to

lie? Sofia also didn't think he was actually going to punish her but maybe she was wrong. It had been several days since he had caught her walking home and he had said she would get punished, but never did anything.

For a second, she thought he was all bark and no bite, but he just proved her wrong. Or well, he was about to. He had brought up the punishment again and she could just see it in his eyes that he was going to follow through.

"No," she softly said.

"No, what?" Michael asked.

"No, it wasn't the first note."

She looked down at her hands, not wanting to see either of their reactions. What were they going to say?

"When did you get your first one?" Daddy asked.

"Before my shift started," she whispered.

"And why didn't you come to tell me?"

She clasped her hands together and took a deep breath. Why hadn't she come to her Daddy? She didn't want to bother him or make him worry about things. He already worried about her enough and she didn't want to add onto it.

"Sofia," Daddy said. "Tell Daddy."

"I didn't want to make you worry about me," she barely managed to get out.

It was stupid, but it was so true. Ever since she started to work here, he had asked her questions about her taking her breaks on time and now worrying about her in general.

"Baby," Daddy said. "Look at me."

She slightly lifted her head and looked at his chin.

"In my eyes," he said and she did. "No matter what it is, you come to me."

Sofia nodded her head. It was going to be tough to do, and no doubt she was going to mess up, but she was going to try for him.

"Can I see the other note?" Michael asked.

She reached into her pocket and handed him the note. She waited for their reactions, but both of them just took a deep breath and looked back at her.

"I should just go back to Chile," she softly said. "Then no one will leave me threatening notes. I should've never come here."

"No," Daddy said. "You're not going back."

If only that was true. There was no guarantee that she was staying. She needed to reapply for her work visa and save up money for the application to get her Green Card. But reapplying and applying for them didn't guarantee that she would be able to stay. That was what worried her. Why had she gotten involved with Jaxson when she wasn't guaranteed to stay in the United States?

"We're going to figure this out," Daddy said. "No matter what, we're going to figure this out. I'm not letting you go."

Her heart warmed at that. What did she do to deserve this? He was so good to her and she didn't deserve that.

"Leo is on his way," Michael said.

She had completely forgotten that Michael was in the room with them.

"I'm sorry," she whispered, looking down at her hands again. She felt so bad about everything that was happening.

"Why are you sorry, Little one?" Daddy asked.

He sat down right next to her and brought her closer to him. She loved the feeling of having his arms around her, but did she deserve it right now? She had been naughty, but she also was a lot more trouble than she was worth.

"I'm a mess. I'm bringing this up and I should just leave," she said, tears welling up in her eyes.

"I don't want any of that," Daddy said. "Do you hear me?"

"But it's true."

"No."

Sofia looked at her Daddy. How did he not think it was true?

"You shouldn't leave because then I would be missing the person I love in my life," he said. "I know that it's not the best way to tell you, but I need you to know. I love you and I'm going to do whatever I can to figure out everything."

The tears she tried so hard to keep in her eyes fell down her face. He loved her?

"I didn't mean to make you cry," Daddy said. "That wasn't my intention. I just wanted you to know that you are loved and have people who care about you. You aren't alone here. You have a family."

"That's right, Little girl. We're your family here. Well, that's if you'll have us," Michael said.

Sofia gasped and looked at him. "If I'll have you? More like if you guys will have me."

"It's settled then. We're family and this family helps each other out in time of need. So whenever something like this happens again, and you need help, you let us know," Daddy said. "Hopefully, you don't get any more threatening messages and it's less dangerous things."

She giggled and leaned into his side. She was exhausted after everything, but she was also relieved that she could count on him. Sofia knew she could before, but it was different when he verbally said it. He was reaffirming it.

"What's wrong?" Leo asked as he stepped into the office. "Sofia."

She didn't look up at him because the last time she did, he told her to take a break after she found the first note.

"You tell your Daddy you weren't feeling well?" Leo asked.

"Not exactly. I saw her dash towards the bathroom, and she was throwing up," Daddy said.

"You should've told your Daddy that you ate something bad. He would've made you feel better."

She flinched at the mention of her lie. She knew she shouldn't have done it, but she couldn't help herself.

"She didn't eat anything bad," Daddy said. "Do you know anyone who would want either one of us or both of us?"

Sofia looked at Leo and he was giving her a disapproving look. She knew she shouldn't have lied, but it was the only thing she thought about doing so he didn't get involved. Now that his name was mentioned in the threatening note, he couldn't stay out of it.

"I hope you give her a spanking for lying," Leo said. "It's unacceptable. But no, I can't think of anyone who would want either one of us or both of us. We aren't really out much."

"It would have to be someone that is here right now. She

got one before her shift started and after," Michael said. "Maybe one of the employees?"

"What's going on?" Leo asked.

"Sofia got two threatening notes today," Daddy said. "The last one mentioned to stay away from you and me."

Sofia leaned into her Daddy's embrace and closed her eyes.

"I'm going to call This We'll Defend Security and get them to look into it. I'll also have them get a bodyguard here to keep Sofia safe," Daddy explained.

"Don't you have a friend there?" Leo asked.

"Yeah, he does. He helped with Monroe when she was in danger," Michael said. "I suggest asking for Ezra, if he can come. He seemed to get along with Monroe and I have no doubt he'll get along with Sofia."

She wanted to argue that she didn't need a bodyguard, but that would be a lie. She probably did need one and should keep her mouth shut. The sooner they figured out who this person was, the sooner things could go back to normal.

"Sofia, can you look at Daddy?" he asked.

She opened her eyes and looked up.

"I want you to answer honestly," he said. "Can you do that for me?"

"Yes, Daddy," she replied.

Anything to do with this person threatening her, she would try to answer to her best ability. She didn't know much, but she could tell them what she did know.

"Is that all you've been keeping from me?"

CHAPTER TWENTY-NINE

SOFIA

Sofia stared at her Daddy for a little bit, trying to comprehend if he really asked that question.

"Was that everything you've been keeping from me or is there more?" Daddy asked more directly. "It doesn't have to be related to the threatening notes."

She closed her eyes for a brief second before looking back at him. How did he know she was keeping something else from him? She had tried to keep it a secret that she had something else she was keeping from him, but apparently, she didn't do a good job of that.

"What happened the other day at your apartment?" Daddy asked. "Was it another threatening note?"

She shook her head. "No," she whispered.

"Then what was it?"

She thought about keeping up the lie she told him about it being a feminine thing, but she knew that was wrong and he deserved to know. Sofia also promised Monty that she would let Daddy know about it. He had a right to know since he was involved with her.

"I got a letter from the government," She softly said.

"Why?" Daddy asked. "What did they want?"

"They were reminding me that I need to reapply for my work visa or else I was going to get deported."

She didn't like the thought about getting deported, not when she was finally getting comfortable here. Michael and Daddy had said she had a family here and she didn't want to leave here yet.

All three of them stared at her with their eyes wide. She didn't like how they were all just staring at her. Why were they just staring at her?

Sofia started to fidget on the couch as their eyes bore into her.

"What do you mean?" Daddy asked. "Don't you have a year? You haven't been here a year yet or even close to it."

That was true that a person had a year for their work visa, but that didn't mean her year wasn't almost up.

"I did," she replied.

"When did you apply and get accepted?" Micheal asked as he sat down on the chair in front of her.

"When I originally applied, I thought I was going to get denied but I didn't. So, then I had to work more to be able to get a plane ticket but several months had already passed."

Sofia hadn't realized how much time had actually passed since she applied and got accepted. How has almost a year already happened? It felt like yesterday that she had a whole year for her work visa. She wanted to cry with how overwhelming this was. Could her life possibly get any harder?

"I thought I had more time," she whispered, feeling so defeated.

She didn't know if she had enough money to send in the application again. What was she going to do if she didn't? Daddy had said he was going to take care of her, but she didn't want him paying for the application. It was a lot of money, and she didn't want him to waste it on her.

"I'm going to take care of it," Daddy said.

Sofia shook her head. "I can't ask you to do that. It's a lot of money."

"Good thing you didn't ask. I'm going to take care of it. You just fill out the information and I'll cover the cost."

Before she could say anything, Michael started to speak.

"Have you thought about applying for a Green Card?" he asked.

"Yes," she softly said.

"But?" Leo asked.

"But I couldn't yet because it's so expensive and I didn't have the money saved up."

She was so embarrassed that she didn't have enough money to do a lot of things. She was sitting in front of people that had a lot of money and didn't have to worry about things. She wasn't that lucky.

"I'll be taking care of that too," Daddy said.

"No," Sofia replied. "You aren't doing that. It's a lot of money."

She knew he had money, but that didn't mean he needed to spend it on her. Especially for her Green Card. She needed to do this herself.

Daddy gripped her chin and brought her head to look at him. "You are mine and I take care of what is mine."

She opened her mouth to argue, but he raised his eyebrow at her, and she closed her mouth. He meant business.

"I'll look into the Green Card things and see your options," Leo said. "Give me a day and I'll get back to you."

"Thank you," Daddy replied.

Sofia wanted to argue and tell Leo that she had already done her research, but she knew that it would fall on deaf ears. When these men said they were going to do something, there was no changing their mind. And Sofia was starting to realize that.

"Little girl, you get some rest, eat, and drink enough," Michael said as he got up from his chair. "And stay safe. Listen to your Daddy and don't get into trouble."

"She's already in trouble for lying to me and I have no doubt she also lied to her Daddy," Leo added. "You won't be able to sit for a week, Little girl."

She took in a shaky breath as it all sunk in. She was in trouble. Not only had she lied to him about what was wrong earlier, she had also kept important information from him. She had lied countless times and knew that her punishment was going to be severe.

"Is it okay to spank her?" Daddy asked Michael.

Her mouth hung open at the question but she quickly looked at Michael, shaking her head. She wasn't ready for a spanking.

Michael looked at her and smiled. "She certainly deserves a spanking and is okay to get one."

"No fair," she mumbled, slouching in her chair.

They were all ganging up on her and she didn't like it. She knew that she deserved the punishment, but she had just gone through something traumatic. Shouldn't Daddy wait a couple of days for her to feel better?

But Sofia didn't know if she would like that. It was just going to prolong it but maybe she could prolong it long enough that he didn't actually do it.

"I think it would be good for her. No doubt she has guilt about lying and being naughty. It'll help her release all the emotions she needs to," Michael said. "If anything is concerning, you know to call me."

"Thank you," Daddy said.

Sofia watched as Michael and Leo left the office. When was Daddy going to do her punishment? Maybe he would wait until they got home and were in the comfort of his house.

"Little one," Daddy said. "Punishment time."

Shit, she thought, too soon. How was she going to get out of this?

Her poor bottom.

CHAPTER THIRTY

SOFIA

"I don't think I need a spanking, Daddy," Sofia tried to reason with him.

There was no way she wanted this punishment. She knew it was going to be a hard punishment and she didn't think she was going to be ready for it.

Sofia had lied to her Daddy, been in danger, and kept important information from him.

"I think you do," Daddy replied.

"But those things happened before we were together," she said.

Maybe she could get him with that. He wouldn't punish her for something that happened before they got together, would he?

"I laid out the rules about walking home at the interview when I hired you," Daddy said. "And yet you ignored them and got hurt."

Her shoulders sagged at the mention of that. She did remember him telling her that no employee, male or female, walked home. If they didn't have a ride, they were supposed to tell one of the owners. Then the owners would get them a taxi or would drive them to their house. But Sofia didn't want them to know where she lived.

"But," she started to say.

"No buts."

"I learned my lesson after I got mugged," she said really quickly.

His eyes narrowed in on her, but she held her ground. She did learn her lesson after she got mugged. Well, sort of. She had walked to the club today from the apartment, but he didn't have to know that.

"Did you?" he asked as he raised his eyebrow.

"Yes, Daddy," she replied. "I think I would know if I did or not. I'm the one that got mugged."

"For some reason, I don't believe you."

She gasped as she looked at him. He didn't believe her?

"That's rude," she said. "You should believe me."

"A little birdie told me that you left the club today and were seen walking back," Daddy said.

"Someone needs to have a talking with Dominic about tattletaling on people," she grumbled. "He's done it twice now and it's not very nice."

Sofia crossed her arms and leaned back into the couch.

"Maybe I'll have a stern talk with him. Show him who's boss," Sofia continued to talk. "He needs to know that telling on other people isn't nice and shouldn't be acceptable."

"Little one," Daddy said.

"I mean, what does he expect?"

"Sofia."

"Has no one ever told on him? Maybe I should find something and go tell people."

"Sofia," Daddy said as he grabbed her chin with his hand. "Shush."

She blinked several times as she stared at her Daddy.

"What?" She asked.

"Shush and listen to me," he said

She huffed out a breath of air and looked at him. What did he want? She was trying to plan what to do to Dominic. How to get back to him.

"You aren't going to mess with Dominic. What he did was what he should've done. He wants to keep you safe," Daddy said.

"He doesn't have to be mean," she whispered. "He's a meanie."

"No, he isn't and you know that. He cares about you and wants you safe."

"He doesn't have to be mean about it."

"End of discussion. You need to know that if you do something wrong, against the rules, that I will follow through and punish you."

Sofia sighed and looked at him. A tiny part of her thought he wouldn't follow through, but that was squashed very quickly at Daddy's words. A huge part of her was relieved that he was following through. She loved having structure and rules, but that didn't mean it wasn't scary. She didn't get nervous at the thought of getting punished.

"Let's take your clothes off and then you can lie over my lap," Daddy said.

She stood up from the couch and let her Daddy undress her.

"Just my pants?" she softly asked.

"I think, this time, everything is coming off," Daddy said.

Sofia pouted but let her Daddy take everything off of her. She didn't like being so exposed, but maybe that was what he was trying to do. Make her uncomfortable so she really thought about everything.

"Over my lap," Daddy said. "Can you tell me your safe word?"

"Pina," she whispered as she got over his lap.

"If at any point it gets to be too much, you say your safe word and we'll discuss everything, okay?"

"Okay, Daddy."

She laid on his lap for who knows how long, waiting for him to start spanking her, but he never did. She relaxed onto his lap. Maybe he wasn't going to spank her. Maybe he decided that it wasn't the best option.

Smack.

Sofia yelped as the pain spread across her cheek. Shit. The hurt.

"You were thinking too much. Trying to anticipate when the first one was going to come," Daddy said as he rubbed her bottom for a second. "But you don't get to know when they come down. Only Daddy does."

Before she could say anything, Daddy peppered several down on to her bottom, getting harder as he went.

"Dadddddyyyy!" she yelled as she tried to move her body away from his hands.

It hurt so much and Sofia didn't want anymore.

"Lay still for Daddy," he said. "Or else you'll get a couple more added on."

Sofia continued to move for a second before she stopped.

"Good girl," Daddy said.

"H-how m-many more?" she stuttered out.

She didn't know how much more she could take of this. He wasn't hitting the same spot as he normally did. He was spanking all over her bottom and onto her thighs where she sat.

There was no way Sofia was going to be able to sit comfortably for the next hour or two, maybe even all day.

"Daddy isn't going to tell you," he said, landing a couple more on her bottom.

She whimpered and bit into her hand, trying so hard to stop herself from reaching back there.

"No biting your hand," Daddy said as he stopped. "Wrap it around my leg."

Letting go of her hand, she wrapped it around his leg and waited for him to start again.

"Do you know why you're getting spanked?" Daddy asked.

"I was naughty," she sniffled.

"Yes, you were naughty. Can you tell Daddy why?"

"I walked home when I shouldn't have, and I kept important details from you."

The guilt had been eating at her since she lied to him about having a ride home. She didn't think it was going to bother her that much, but as the time went on and she kept lying, it got worse and worse. Then lying about the letter and getting a threatening message, it was too much, and she just wanted it to go away.

"That's right and Daddy is spanking you for that," he said. "But after this, all is forgiven. Understand?"

She nodded her head.

"Words, Little one," Daddy reminded her.

"Yes, Daddy. I understand."

"And you know now to come to me for *anything*, right?"

"Yes, Daddy."

And she did. Sofia never wanted to feel this guilt again. It made her nauseous just thinking about it.

"Good girl. Let's finish this spanking and then we can cuddle."

"H-how many more?" she softly asked, hoping he would tell her this time.

"Nice try," Daddy said. "I'm not telling you."

She pouted but quickly stopped when Daddy started to spank her again. It was like his hand was made of steel because it hurt so bad. Tears formed in her eyes again as her bottom throbbed in pain.

"Daddddyyyy," she whimpered.

"I know, Little one. We're almost done," he said as he continued to pepper her bottom with spankings.

The swats got harder, and she felt herself sob and go limp over his lap. Daddy stopped and rubbed her bottom for a second.

"Such a good girl, taking the punishment so well," Daddy said as he helped her up.

She clung onto him as she sat on his lap, his legs apart so

her bottom wasn't touching anything. She sagged into his embrace as he held her tightly against him.

"Your hand is made of steel," Sofia said into his shirt.

She felt her Daddy's chest moving. "Every Daddy has a hand of steel. Helps keep the Littles in line."

"No fair. Maybe I should make my hand steel so I can spank your butt butt."

"Littles don't spank Daddies. That's Daddy's job to spank the Little's bottom."

Sofia pouted and snuggled into his chest.

"We're going to sit here for a couple of minutes and just snuggle," Daddy said. "Then we can go home."

CHAPTER THIRTY-ONE

JAXSON

Two days had passed since Jaxson found out about the threatening notes and Sofia's punishment. It had been long overdue and she had started to get anxious about it. He didn't like seeing her in pain, but he also needed to show her that she couldn't get away with naughty behavior.

She had been reckless, and he needed to help guide her back and be conscious about her decisions. He needed to help her understand that she mattered and it wasn't okay for her to put herself in danger.

It would never be okay for her to do that.

"Do you have a minute to talk?" Leo asked as he stepped into Jaxson's office.

Jaxson pushed away from his desk and looked up. "What do you need?"

It wasn't unusual for some of the other co-owners to walk into his office. They all liked to keep each other in the loop about things happening in the club. No one wanted to have a surprise land in their lap.

"I did some research and have found some options for Sofia and the whole Green Card situation," Leo said. "Is now a good time to talk about them?"

"Yeah," Jaxson replied.

He was interested to know what Leo had found. He hadn't had any time to look into things and that was probably why Leo offered to research it for him. Jaxson thought he would've had a couple of minutes to briefly look at things, but by the time night had come, he was exhausted and would fall asleep right next to Sofia.

He absolutely loved sleeping next to her. She was a cuddler at night and he loved it. No matter how he turned, she would always find herself right next to him. He had woken up a couple of times and she was sucking her thumb while holding his arm.

Fucking adorable.

Jaxson could watch her sleep for hours. Well, even if she wasn't asleep he could watch her for hours.

"First, I need to ask if you love her," Leo said.

"You heard me say that I do," Jaxson grumbled. "I love her and will continue to love her."

"Do you think she feels the same about you?"

He thought about it for a second. Did Sofia feel the same about him? He didn't have to think long because her actions spoke louder than words.

"Yes," he replied. "I do believe she feels the same or is pretty close to it. She hasn't said the words, but her actions are speaking pretty loudly, and I feel like if she isn't there already, she's going to be soon."

"Good," Leo said. "That's good."

"Do you want to tell me what's going on? Why are you asking all of these questions?"

Jaxson was starting to get impatient and he just wanted Leo to get straight to the point.

"Are you doubting that I love her?" Jaxson asked.

"No!" Leo said. "There are two options that I could really see you guys taking."

"Well?"

"The first one is the most obvious one. She reapplies for her work visa and, if she gets accepted again, then she applies for her Green Card. This could take several years for her to obtain or it could take a couple of months. I can't exactly tell you the timeline for how long it's going to take," Leo said as he sat down in the chair. "She could also get denied which means she'll have to reapply. There is no guarantee for anything."

"And the other option?"

"You guys get married."

Jaxson stared at him, blinking several times as he tried to understand what he just heard.

"Did you just say we get married?" Jaxson asked.

While he loved the idea, they had only been together a short while, and he didn't know if Sofia would go for that. Jaxson was all for it because he knew he was going to spend the rest of his life with her, but Sofia was a different story.

"Yes, I did say for you guys to get married," Leo said. "After you guys are married, and she applies, it isn't guaranteed that she'll get it. But it seems more likely they'll give her one if you guys *are* married."

Jaxson was speechless. What was he supposed to say to that? He didn't think he was ever going to get married. When he was young, he was married to his career and never gave any girl the time of day. But that was also because he hadn't found his perfect Little girl and he thought he never would.

Until Sofia walked in for the interview.

That had all changed, but even then he didn't think that she would want to get married to him. Marriage was a big deal, and it wasn't something to make quick decisions about. He didn't want to rush her into it but the thought of marrying her got him excited. To be able to call her his wife, his Little, his girl. There were so many names and even though he already called her his Little and his girl, there was something about calling her his wife.

"I don't know what to say," Jaxson whispered.

"I just wanted to give you your options. You think about it and if you think she's the one then you can bring it up to her," Leo said.

"Thank you for looking into that."

"Anytime."

They sat in silence for a second, alone to their thoughts. There was a lot that Jaxson needed to think about and have a conversation about with Sofia. There was so much, and he didn't know what to start with.

The most important things first. The lesser things can come later when things have cooled down.

"Have you heard anything from This We'll Defend Security?" Leo asked.

"They are sending two people down here," Jaxson replied. "A bodyguard and then a computer wiz to look into things around here."

That put Leo on alarm, and it had done the same thing when Jaxson had looked over the camera footage.

"What's wrong?" he asked.

"I was looking over the security camera footage but couldn't find anything. I looked thirty minutes before her shift started, during that time, and around when she got off," Jaxson said. "Nothing. Absolutely nothing."

"What do you mean nothing?"

"Exactly what I mean. No one walked into the employees room around that time. How could the note have gotten there? It can't just magically appear there."

Realization flew across Leo's face. "You think someone tampered with the security footage?"

He nodded his head. "Yes, I do. It was weird to not see anyone enter, especially when people are getting off shifts and coming to start their shift. It was almost like the camera was on a loop around those times."

"But you could see Sofia entering the room?"

"Yes, and leaving when she started her shift. Caught her whole reaction to her reading the letters on camera. It was like they didn't want us to see who placed them but purposefully wanted us to see her reaction. Almost taunting us that they messed things up."

Leo shook his head. "That's not good."

"I sent the footage to the computer wiz, so he could look over it while he is on the plane. They should be here soon. I had your brother go pick them up from the airport."

Everything was messed up. Why would someone want to do this to Sofia? Why was she the target? She had mentioned she didn't know many people and he believed her. She was shy and didn't talk to a lot of people.

Leo stood up from his seat. "If you need anything, you let me know."

"I will. Thank you," Jaxson replied.

"Also, think about what I told you about the Green Card. But also talk with Sofia about it. She is a part of this and needs to be informed but I know you already know that."

He nodded his head. He just needed to figure out how to tell her, get her to listen, and not react.

"How's it going with your mysterious girl?" Jaxson asked before Leo could leave his office.

They had come to him about this girl and he wanted to know if anything had progressed. It wasn't his place to know, but he was curious if Leo would give anything away. Both of them tended to keep to themselves, which was fine, but sometimes it is good for people to talk to other people about it.

"Oliver and I talked and we're going to pursue her. She has no clue yet. We're trying to come up with a game plan. She's fragile. We don't want to damage her any further and send her further into herself."

"Is she safe?" Jaxson asked.

"Yes, she's staying with Michael and Monroe. But she's apparently not doing too well so we may speed up our rough timeline on things."

Jaxson did not envy Leo and Oliver in this situation. It

was hard to know what to do in a situation like this, what was the right thing to do.

"If you need anything, let me know," Jaxson said. "I'm here for you guys."

"Thanks. We may need to take a couple days off and it might be short notice," Leo said. "We'll try and plan in advance, but just to let you know."

"No worries. All of us have racked up a good amount of PTO so you take off when you need to, and we'll figure everything out."

"Thank you. Well, I'll see you."

Leo left his office and he relaxed into his chair. There was so much going on, but he had meant what he said to Leo. They looked after each other and made things work in emergency situations, no matter how tough it was.

"Daddy?" Sofia whispered and he looked up to see her standing in his doorway.

"Hi, Little one," he replied. "Come here."

CHAPTER THIRTY-TWO

SOFIA

"Hi Daddy," she whispered as she took a step closer to his desk.

Leo had just come out of his office, and she was done with her shift. Well, she had been done for fifteen minutes. Monty had talked to her for a little while. Then someone told her that Leo was in her Daddy's office.

She knew she could enter his office if people were in there, but she wanted to be respectful. What if Leo didn't want her to hear what he had to say? She didn't want to be in there just because her Daddy said so and not pay attention to the other person's needs.

"Come here," he said as he patted his lap.

Sofia loved that he allowed her to sit in his lap a lot. She loved the feeling of having his arms wrapped around her, but she also loved feeling his chest to her back. It made her feel connected to him in a way. It was stupid how she felt, but she loved it and that was all that mattered to her at that point.

"Little one," Daddy said. "I'm not going to ask again."

She rolled her eyes and walked towards him. He hadn't asked the first or second time, but she wasn't going to tell him that. That was one way for her bottom to get spanked and she didn't need that. Not when her bottom was still a little sore from the previous spanking.

"Good girl," he said and she shivered.

Her insides melted each time her called her good girl or his good girl. It was hard not to and she didn't think she was ever going to lose the feeling.

"How was your shift?" he asked. "Uneventful?"

"Yes, Daddy. No rude customers and Monty was with me the whole time."

"Good."

She had begged him to still allow her to work. He didn't like the idea, especially since she got the threatening note here. But she said she would get bored if she just sat in his office and said there were several people who could help her if she was working. Dominic, Lucas, and Pete no doubt would have an eye on her any time she worked. She knew there were other Doms in the club, owners and members, who always had an eye on people.

It was comforting and didn't take long for her to persuade her Daddy to let her work.

"I wanted to tell you something," Daddy said.

But before he could say anything, two people walked into his office, people she had never seen before.

"Ah," Daddy said. "You must be Ezra and Antonio."

She looked at her Daddy, waiting for him to explain who they were. She had heard about an Ezra from Monroe, but she never said who he was, and he didn't stay long. Well, that was before Sofia was in the United States, but Monroe had told her about it one night when she was working.

"Nice to meet you Jaxson," said the guy on the right.

Who were these people? Sofia had no clue her Daddy was about to meet someone. If she did, she would've stayed outside with Monty and not come upstairs.

"I can leave, Daddy," she whispered. "I'll go hang out with Monty."

"Stay right there, Little one," Daddy said. "I want you to meet Ezra and Antonio."

Why did he want her to meet them? What was so important about them?

"Ezra is the man on the right. He's your bodyguard until we find the person who is threatening you," Daddy said. "Antonio is on the left and he's a computer genius who is looking into the security to see if he can figure out who the person is."

She stared at her Daddy for a couple of seconds before she looked over at the men. She had a bodyguard now? Was that absolutely necessary?

Her eyes went wide as she stared at them. Did they know that Jaxson was her Daddy? Did they know about the lifestyle? Should she have called Daddy by his name? What if she messed up?

Sofia hadn't even thought about them not knowing about their dynamic. Would they find her weird? Was Daddy going to have to find new guards for her?

"Don't worry, Little one," Daddy said. "They know about us. In fact they are also Daddy Doms."

Her eyes went even more wide as she stared at them. They were also Daddy Doms? That was cool but at the same time nerve-wracking. She was going to have another Daddy Dom as a bodyguard until the threat was gone? She knew that she wouldn't call him Daddy, but that didn't mean his Daddy side wasn't going to come out if she did something wrong.

"I know it's hard to believe, all these Daddy Doms around you, but it's true. So you don't have to be worried about calling me Daddy in front of them," Daddy said. "Understood?"

She nodded her head but still stared at them. She understood that she needed a bodyguard, but if she stayed with her Daddy then she didn't need him, right?

"Now, I don't want any objections about this. It's final and Ezra will be with you when I can't and while I can."

"Okay," she whispered.

There was no point in arguing about this, even if she didn't think she needed him.

Daddy put his hand on her forehead. "Are you feeling okay?"

"Yes, Daddy," she sighed. "I am just tired and want this person found."

It had only been a couple of days, but it was exhausting. Sofia felt like even with her Daddy around, she had to be on guard in case something happened. The bad person had to be a member of the club and it worried her. Who would want to do this to her?

Sofia watched as Ezra walked over towards them and knelt down in front of her.

"We're going to try our hardest and our best to find this person as quickly and safely as possible," he softly said to her.

She nodded her head and leaned into her Daddy's embrace. Sofia believed every word Ezra said and she just hoped it would be sooner than later when they found the person. She didn't want this to go on forever. She wanted to live her life, but she couldn't do that when someone was after her.

Well, she probably could but she would be too worried about if the person was coming after her at any moment. That was no way to live.

"Do you want Trixie?" Daddy asked.

She nodded her head, too shy to speak in front of the other people. Even though she knew they were Daddies, it was still weird to call him Daddy in front of them or have him take care of her. Would she ever get used to it?

It was different around Michael or Leo because she knew them before and was comfortable around them, but with Ezra and Antonio, it was weird.

Daddy grabbed Trixie from the top of his desk and handed it to her. She had left Trixie with Daddy when she started her shift because she didn't want anything to happen to her. What if the person came into the employees' room and destroyed her stuff? She wasn't going to have that.

"Thank you, Daddy," she whispered.

Ezra had gone back to standing next to Antonio. Both of them were tall, like Daddy, with broad shoulders. Ezra was bigger than Antonio, but Sofia could tell that Antonio worked out.

"Antonio will be working on trying to figure out who did this. I'll be doing perimeter checks at the house and in the club every once in a while," Ezra said. "You mentioned the person has to be a member or works here, correct?"

"That's right," Daddy said.

Unease filled her as they started to talk about this. She didn't like that the person was still out there, a member of the club or an employee, because it meant they had access to things. And they didn't have a clue who this person could be.

What did she do to deserve this?

"I don't want to put any of the other members in an uncomfortable position. But I would like to walk around every once in a while, and see if I see anything suspicious," Ezra said. "I also want to watch people, so I get to know how they act. I'll do this as discreetly as I can, but I just wanted to let you know. Do people in the club know?"

"Only people we know and trust. So basically just the owners and the bouncers," Daddy replied.

Sofia had wanted to tell Monty, but Daddy told her it was best not to, so she didn't feel uncomfortable at work. She understood and knew that Monty wasn't in any danger because she wasn't a foreigner like her.

"I'll be looking over the security feed again, but I see what you mean about it being tampered with," Antonio said. "I'll also be looking at the cameras to see if I can find anything."

"Just let me know if you need anything," Daddy said.

Daddy and Ezra started to talk again, but Sofia drowned it out. It was boring listening to them talk about this. She knew it was important, but she also didn't understand all of it.

"Do you have a name for your stuffy?" Antonio asked, pulling her out of her thoughts.

"Trixie," she softly said, looking at him.

He had taken several steps towards her and bent down.

"Do you have any other stuffies?" he asked.

She shook her head. She wanted to buy more, but it wasn't in her budget right now.

"Ah, well lucky for you, I always carry around a stuffed animal when I meet someone new," he said and her eyes grew wide, holding onto every word he said. "We can't have Trixie being all alone, can we?"

"No," she said as she shook her head fast.

It wasn't nice to keep stuffies all alone. Even though Trixie wasn't alone because she had Sofia and Mattie, she wasn't always there, and she wanted Trixie to have a forever friend.

"Would you like another stuffie?" he asked and she nodded her head.

Who wouldn't want another stuffie? That was the real question.

"I got lucky this time. I had no clue you liked cows and yet, I brought a mini cow," he said as he pulled a mini white and black cow from behind his back.

A squeal of joy flowed out of her as she grabbed the mini cow. It was so cute and she knew Trixie would be great friends with her.

"What do you say?" Daddy asked as he tapped her nose.

She looked up at him before looking at Antonio.

"Thanks yous!" she said as she hugged Trixie and Paz to her chest.

"You're welcome," Antonio said as he stood up.

"We're going to be headed home now. I don't have anything else to do," Daddy said. "You'll be staying with us?"

"Yes, sir," Ezra said.

"Good. Follow me."

Sofia turned around and snuggled into her Daddy's embrace as he stood up, holding her tightly against him. He was super strong, and she loved that about him. Though, even if he wasn't, she was pretty sure she would still love him.

CHAPTER THIRTY-THREE

SOFIA

*I*t was weird having Antonio and Ezra in the house with her and her Daddy. It was hard to act normal when there were two strangers in her house. Daddy had told her last night before they went to bed that she should be herself, but that was easier said than done.

Not many people had seen her Little side or heard her call Jaxson Daddy. She wasn't ashamed, but it was weird or uncomfortable for her. What if they judged her? She was trying to get better about not caring, but she was a caring person and it was hard. She wanted people to like her and she wanted to make friends.

Thankfully, most of the Littles she knew were people from the club who were super nice. Well, most of the people she knew were from the club. She saw the occasional person at the grocery store that she saw each time, but that had been a while. Daddy had been taking care of the groceries and making sure that she was eating enough.

Sofia was pretty sure she was gaining some weight.

And it wasn't a bad thing. She had lost weight when she moved to the United States because she didn't have enough money to eat three meals a day but now, she doesn't have to worry about that. Daddy was taking care of her.

Breakfast had passed without much of anything. Ezra and Antonio had joined them. When Antonio finished, he went back to his guest room to get to work on trying to figure out who this person was. Ezra had stayed and sat in the living room with her.

Daddy had been weird the past twenty-four hours. Ever since she walked into his office yesterday, something had been off, but she brushed it off yesterday. Maybe all this stress was getting to him? She didn't want to worry him about anything, but she was worried about him.

Was he okay?

He kept looking over at her every once in a while and just staring. Not that she minded, but it was different than normal. The look in his eye was different and she wanted to know why, but she didn't know how to ask him. Did she just flat out ask him or did she put more skill into it?

He was also quieter than normal and hadn't reminded her nearly as often as he normally did to drink her water. It was still quite a lot, but not as much and it worried her. What was on his mind? Did something go wrong?

"Play with me, Daddy?" she asked as he looked at her once again.

He was currently walking towards the kitchen, no doubt to fill her water bottle. He had been obsessed with her drinking water since she said yes to him being her Daddy.

She understood his obsession, but at the same time he took it to a whole new level.

"Maybe in a little bit. I need to make you a snack to eat and fill up your sippy cup," he said.

Sofia pouted and looked down at her stuffies, Trixie and Mattie. She had hoped he would say yes so she could ask him if he was alright, but maybe she should go into the kitchen and ask him.

"I'll play with you," Ezra said. "Is that alright?"

She shrugged her shoulders and handed over Mattie to him. He sat down on the floor and positioned himself so he could look out the window. She found it weird that they had the blinds open, but maybe it was to see if anyone was trying to look in.

The thought of someone trying to spy on them made her have goosebumps. She didn't like that she wasn't even safe in her own home but hopefully the threat would be over soon.

"What do you want to play?" Ezra asked.

She sighed and shrugged her shoulders once again. She didn't know what she wanted to play or if she even wanted to play. Part of her wanted Daddy close and she knew he was, but he was also in the kitchen, and she was in the living room.

Would she ever have alone time with him again? Would he be less stressed after this or would he always be watchful in case something like this happened again?

Sofia placed Trixie down on the ground and closed her eyes. Everything was getting to be too much, and she just wanted her Daddy back. She didn't want him stressed or whatever was on his mind. He had been quieter, and she didn't like that.

It was never a good sign.

Did he want to get rid of her? Was he thinking after all of this was over that he was going to tell her he didn't want her as his Little girl anymore? Sofia didn't know if she would be able to take it and maybe she needed to take it into her own hands.

She sighed again and opened her eyes, grabbing Trixie and holding her tight. She didn't want to play anymore, and Sofia knew that Ezra figured that out.

"What's wrong?" he asked and he briefly looked at her.

"Nofing," she whispered, but it was a lie.

"There's obviously something wrong. You have sighed several times and look to be deep in thought."

He had her there and she knew she couldn't get out of this. Sofia looked behind her to see her Daddy still getting her snack ready in the kitchen.

"Something is differents with Daddy," she softly said, sounding so unsure about herself. "I don't knows what but he's acting weirds. I'm worried."

She was teetering in and out of Littlespace because it worried her so much. What was he hiding? Why was he acting so different than normal?

"I didn't know you felt that way, Little one," Daddy said and she froze. "Why didn't you come to me?"

She shrugged her shoulders, but she knew exactly why.

"Little girl," Daddy said. "You know the reason."

"I didn't want to bother you because of everything going

on," she whispered. "I didn't want to add onto any more stress."

She could hear her Daddy walking over towards her, but she closed her eyes before she could see him. What was he going to do or say about that?

"I'm going to go do a perimeter check while you guys talk," Ezra said. "If you need anything just holler."

Part of her didn't want Ezra to leave but the other part knew that having him here would make things awkward. She had wanted some alone time with her Daddy and now she was getting it. Maybe not how she wanted it, but she was getting it nonetheless.

So she should be thankful.

Daddy placed a plate with cut up apples and peanut butter next to her with her sippy cup before he sat down in front of her. "Eat and drink your water."

She waited for him to say something to her. She didn't know what to say to him after she told him she was worried about him. What else was there to say besides explaining why?

"Little one," Daddy said. "You know I love you and care for you, right?"

She nodded her head and took a bite of the apple. It was one of her favorite snacks, apples and peanut butter. There was something about it, even though it was simple, that always made her hungry. Maybe it was the juiciness of the apples her Daddy got and the richness of the peanut butter. He had told her that he got the apples from the guy who delivered them to the club, Gene.

He was such a nice person and his produce was the best.

Sofia had heard that the workers there were Daddies and Mommies. She had also heard they owned a little property for people in the lifestyle that needed a safe place to stay for a while or go on a little vacation. She thought it was a neat idea and loved that they were doing what they loved but also helping people out.

"I would do anything for you," Daddy continued to speak. "I hope you know that."

"I do, Daddy," she whispered.

"I want you to know that no matter how stressed I am or whatever is going on, even if I'm super busy, that you can come to me for things," he said. "You can come to me for anything and everything. I mean it."

She nodded her head, but she knew that she would feel guilty if she came to him when he was super busy or stressed just because she needed something or was worried about something. It didn't seem right to do that to him.

"It's my job as your Daddy to take care of you and to make sure that you're alright," he said. "I want you to come to me for your worries and your stresses. I don't care how small they are, I want you to come to me so I can help you."

Sofia nodded her head again, understanding what he said. Maybe she could come to him for some of the bigger things. Well, she knew she was going to come to him for the bigger worries, but she didn't know about the smaller ones. She didn't want to inconvenience him.

"What are you thinking?" Daddy asked. "And please don't lie to me or filter your thoughts. I want all the unfiltered thoughts and words."

She let out a sigh and then took a deep breath. She owed

it to him, always did, to tell him the truth and let him know what was going through her head. Communication was key to everything and she didn't want to fault on that.

Not anymore.

"I don't want you to think of me as a burden if I come to you for everything," she softly said. "I don't want to add on to your stresses or worries by telling you mine. That doesn't seem very fair."

"You will never be a burden," Daddy said. "Do you understand?"

Sofia nodded her head, but he raised his eyebrow. "Yes, Daddy. I understand."

"I'll have to remember to remind you about that. I don't want you to ever think that you are a burden to me because you aren't. You are a blessing and I want to cherish you and help you with everything. I'm your Daddy and I love being your Daddy."

Tears filled her eyes and he continued to talk. He knew exactly what to say to her to get his point across.

"I'm going to worry about you more if you don't come to me for things. I'm going to worry that you're trying to be a big girl all the time and take on the world by yourself. But you don't have to because you have me, your Daddy, who will help you and be your rock. You don't have to carry everything on your shoulders because you can give me some of the load, a lot of the load."

Those tears fell down her face, but she didn't try to hide it.

"So, I want you to come to me with every little worry you have," he said. "No matter how silly you think they are, I want you to come to me for it and we'll figure it out together."

She nodded her head and wiped away the tears from her face.

"Now, do you have anything to ask me? Why were you worried about me?" he asked.

"What's wrong? You've been acting weird," she softly asked, afraid of what he was going to say.

Would he tell her what was worrying him or would he keep it a secret? She knew he wasn't going to say he didn't want her anymore because of his whole speech he just gave but that didn't help her worry any less.

"Marry me," he said.

CHAPTER THIRTY-FOUR

SOFIA

Sofia stared at her Daddy in shock. Did he just say what she thought he said? Was he alright?

"What?" she whispered, not believing what he just asked her.

"Marry me," he said again. "Walk down an aisle in a pretty white dress, say our vows, and get married."

She continued to stare at him, trying to process his words. She couldn't believe what she just heard. Had he really just asked that again?

"I love you and I know you haven't said it back, but your actions speak louder than words. I know you feel the same way about me, or if you don't fully love me yet, I know that you will soon," he explained. "If you marry me, it could be easier for you to get your Green Card and I want you with me until we grow old. I'm not just asking because it benefits you with getting a Green Card. I'm asking because I love you and I want to spend the rest of my life with you. And I hope you feel the same."

Sofia's eyes watered again. "I do love you," she whispered. He had shown her just how much he loved her the past several days and she wanted to spend the rest of her life with him.

"Will you marry me?" he asked. "If you don't want to marry me then it's okay. I understand but I want you to know that I love you. Spending the rest of my life with you as my woman, my Little girl, would make me a damn proud Daddy and husband. I would cherish you for the rest of your life and you'll never want for anything. It won't be easy, but together we'll make it work and it's going to be amazing."

So many emotions were going through Sofia as she comprehended everything her Daddy just said. But the most prominent one was happiness. She felt so happy.

"Yes!" she squealed and launched herself at him.

Wrapping her arms around him, she felt him do the same and hold her tight. She couldn't believe that she was going to get married to him. She was going to marry her Daddy, her partner, and she couldn't be any happier.

Sofia didn't think she was ever going to get married and had decided a couple years ago that she was fine with that. Even though it hurt to come to the realization, she was so happy that it wasn't true anymore.

"I love you," he said.

"I love you too," she whispered, holding on to him even tighter.

She had always imagined that if she ever did get married the proposal would be in a forest with twinkle lights, but this was better. She was with the person she loved and she wouldn't want it any other way.

"I don't have a ring yet, because I wasn't planning on proposing tonight," Daddy said as he pulled away. "But I do have a necklace that I've been wanting to give you for a week. I think it's appropriate to give it to you now."

Daddy got up and walked over towards the dining room table, grabbed something and came back.

"I didn't know how I was going to give this to you, but when I saw it, I knew I was going to figure it out. It is small and dainty, but gorgeous," Daddy said as he pulled a necklace out of the box.

A soft gasp fell from her mouth as she stared at the little pendant of a cow in front of her. It was so beautiful and she couldn't believe that Daddy had gotten it for her.

"It's so pretty," she whispered as she continued to stare at it. She didn't ever want to take her eyes off of it.

"Can I put it on you?" Daddy asked.

She nodded her head, turned around, pulled her hair out of the way, and let him put the necklace on her.

Excitement filled her as she felt it lay on her neck. This was real.

She looked down, saw the cute cow pendant laying on her chest, and a happy squeal left her lips.

"I love it, Daddy!" she said, turning around and jumping into his arms.

He wrapped his arms around her, and she snuggled into his embrace. Her Daddy was the best and she couldn't believe this was actually real.

"I'm glad. I don't want you to take it off until I get the ring," he said. "Understand? It shows people that you're mine. While it's a cow pendant, it also has a J right next to it, to show people that you belong to me."

Sofia looked back down and just like he said, there was a J right next to it. She was so excited that she didn't even notice that it was there.

"Just people at the club?" she asked.

How would other people know she was his if they didn't know him?

"Yes, and some people out of the club may know that you belong to someone. Not everyone in the town is a member of the club," Daddy said. "I bet there are people out there that are into BDSM who aren't part of the club."

She nodded her head. That made sense and she didn't know why she didn't think of it. It was just like in Chile. She had seen several people with collars on and, while not everyone with a collar had a Dom, there were some she just knew. It was a vibe.

"We can go ring shopping in the next couple of days," he said. "Hopefully the guys will have figured out who this is, and we can then go without any stress so you can enjoy it."

She beamed up at him before snuggling back into his chest. She was the happiest she had ever been.

"Thank you, Daddy," she whispered. "Thank you for everything."

"Thank you for giving me a chance," he said.

Sofia completely relaxed and closed her eyes. Such a perfect moment with the perfect person for her.

She heard the door open and footsteps coming closer to them.

"Everything okay?" Daddy asked.

"We saw some activity around the perimeter. We don't know if it was the person who wrote the notes, but that's our guess," Ezra said.

Sofia let out a soft gasp, her whole body going rigid as she opened her eyes and looked at Ezra. Shit. Why couldn't they just have a moment without something bad happening?

She held on tighter to Daddy as everything sunk in.

"Shhhh," Daddy softly said. "I've got you. You're safe."

But she felt anything but safe at this moment.

CHAPTER THIRTY-FIVE

JAXSON

Jaxson stared at Ezra as he took in the information. There was activity near his house, and it could have been the person who wanted Sofia, his Little girl, to be gone. Who would go through this much to get Sofia to leave? Who would want Sofia to leave?

He had watched her several times interacting with people while she worked and while she was off the clock. She was never mean to anyone. She always treated people with respect and like they were her friend.

Sofia's grip tightened on his shirt, and he held her tighter.

"Shhh," he softly said. "I've got you. You're safe."

He had no clue if she believed him that she was safe, but he was trying his best to make her feel that way. He felt like he was failing in a way. How had he not been able to protect her from this? How had he not noticed that someone didn't like her and was trying to get rid of her? Jaxson thought he was protecting her and keeping her safe, but he wasn't.

And that was going to change.

"How?" Jaxson asked. "Did you see them?"

He hoped Ezra had seen the person and that this could be all over.

"Some of the cameras we placed around the house went off. They caught a person walking around, looking at the house," Ezra said.

But nothing was ever that easy. Why would it be?

"And their face was showing?" Jaxson asked.

He ran his hand up and down Sofia's back, trying to ease her worries as they talked. Maybe it was best if she was in a different room while they talked about this. He could feel her shaking against him, and he didn't like that. She was working herself up, no doubt thinking bad things.

"Antonio is looking more into it, but it looks like they were covered up, so the camera didn't catch anything," Ezra said and sighed.

Sofia started to shake more in his arms, and he held on tighter, trying to bring her a little comfort, ground her of sorts. Jaxson wondered if having something tightly around her would help her, comfort her in a way. He would have to try swaddling her the next time he put her down for a nap.

"Shhh," he said again. "You're okay. I've got you and nothing is going to happen."

She just held on tighter to him and he didn't mind one bit. He would rather her have a death grip on him than her puking and running away.

"Ezra and Antonio are doing everything they can to find this person," Jaxson softly said to Sofia.

He had no clue if she was even hearing any of this, but he

hoped that she was. Sofia snuggled deeper into him if that was even possible, and he held her tight. Maybe she was listening.

"I've got you," he whispered again.

"I'll be doing another perimeter check in an hour to make sure everything is okay," Ezra said. "I'll also be making sure they didn't place anything down. Antonio said it didn't look like it, but I want to make sure."

"You didn't check while you were out there?" Jaxson asked, slightly alarmed.

He knew that the workers at This We'll Defend Security were the best of the best and what Ezra said didn't make sense. Jaxson knew that Justin, the owner and his friend, wouldn't put up with his workers being lazy. Which made what Ezra said not make sense. It was dumb for him not to check if there was anything planted while he was out there.

"I did, but I want to check again to make sure that I didn't miss anything," he replied.

Relief washed over Jaxson as he heard those words. It hadn't made sense, and he didn't know why he second guessed what Ezra was doing.

Well, that was a lie. Jaxson was a retired cop and it was Sofia, his girl, they were trying to protect. He was going to be wary about what other people did, because it was Sofia's life on the line. It wasn't someone he didn't know, it was his Little, the woman he loved. He needed to make sure she was safe, and nothing was going to harm her.

"Can I help with anything? Do I need to do anything?" Jaxson asked.

He didn't like just sitting around and doing nothing. That

wasn't how he was wired. Working on the police force for years made him want to be out there, helping in any way possible.

"No," he said. "Nothing that I can't handle. What I need you to do is make sure Sofia is comfortable, be her Daddy. And also make sure she doesn't leave the house without one of us with her. I don't want to take any chances so, if she wants to go outside or go somewhere, she needs to either have Antonio or me with her."

"So I'm not allowed to take her outside alone?" he asked.

Ezra shook his head. "Right now, no. I want to be cautious, since we don't know who this person is. While in the house, you two can go wherever you want, but outside you need to have one of us with you."

"Thanks."

Jaxson knew what Ezra was talking about. They had a couple cases when he was still working as a police officer that, even though the person in danger had someone who could handle themselves and them, they wanted a police officer with them. It was protocol.

"If you need me, I'll be in Antonio's room talking and going over things," Ezra said. "Sofia, can you look at me?"

He felt her move her head.

"We're doing our best to find out who this person is. I need you to be safe so stay with one of us if you want to go out anywhere. Your Daddy can come, but Antonio or I will have to also come, just in case. It's our job to keep you safe and I don't want anything to happen," Ezra said. "Understand?"

He felt Sofia nod her head.

"Good," Ezra said. "I'll see you guys later."

Jaxson held onto Sofia as he watched Ezra leave the living room. He could still feel Sofia shaking in his arms, less than before, but she was still shaking.

He knew exactly what to do to help her calm down and it would also help him some.

"Let's go spend the evening in your room and you can be Little," Daddy said. "I'll take care of you, and you don't have to worry about a thing."

CHAPTER THIRTY-SIX

SOFIA

Sofia had been standing in front of the door to her Little room, staring inside. She didn't know what she wanted to do or if she even wanted to play. So many things were going on in her head.

"Come on, Little one," Daddy said as he placed his hand on the small of her back. "Let's go play."

She took another step into the room and looked around.

"Do you want to get changed first or do you want to play?" Daddy asked.

Sofia looked around before looking at her Daddy. She wanted to be comfortable, but she was worried that if she was comfortable that she would fall asleep. She didn't want to do that. She wanted to spend time with her Daddy.

"Sofia?" Daddy said her name.

She didn't want to make a choice because both sounded appealing.

"You picks?" she softly asked.

"Okay, sweetie," he said. "Let's get you changed into a

onesie, then we can play. Think about what you would like to do, but if you don't want to decide, I can choose for you."

Daddy picked her up, walked over to the closet to grab her cow onesie, before walking over to the changing table.

"Let's get you changed really quick and then we can go play," Daddy said as he started to take off her pants before he placed her on the changing table. "Do you want to wear a diaper or your undies?"

"Undies," she whispered.

She didn't feel that Little yet and she didn't know if she ever would. Daddy had bought a small pack of diapers in case she wanted to try them, but she hadn't had the courage, so far. She really didn't know if she would ever have the courage to try one on. She had never thought of herself as that young of a Little, but maybe she hadn't met the right person, until Daddy.

"Alright, Little one," Daddy said. "Let's get you into your onesie."

Daddy slowly put on the onesie before zipping it up and placing her back on the ground. She stood there, waiting for him to say something, tell her what they were going to do.

"Do you want to color or have a tea party with Trixie and Mattie?" Daddy asked.

She thought about it for a second.

"Tea party?" she asked.

"You go grab Trixie and Mattie. I'll get the cups."

Sofia walked over towards the crib and grabbed her stuffed animals out of it. Whenever she took a nap, Daddy would place her in the crib, and she felt safe. The bars made her think that no one could get to her unless they were her Daddy, and she would fall right asleep.

She turned around and saw her Daddy setting up the little table with the cups and tea kettle. Her heart warmed knowing that he wanted to do this, and he wasn't just doing it to get it over with.

"No, Trixie," she whispered as she stared at her stuffed animal. "I knows he's not wearings proper attires."

"What are you three whispering about?" Daddy asked. "Do I need to be worried?"

Sofia shook her head quickly and stared at him.

"So, what were you three whispering about?"

She didn't know if she should tell him, but when Mattie started to talk to her, she knew she had to.

"Somefings wrongs," she softly said, worried he wasn't going to like it.

"And what's that?"

"We've gots to change your clothes! Dress you up!" she started to get excited as she thought about it. "Cans I dress you ups?"

As seconds went by with Daddy just looking at her, she started to get worried. Would he say no?

"Okay," he said. "I'll sit here and let you dress me up."

A squeal left her lips, and she ran towards the chairs, gently placing down Trixie and Mattie in their seats. Then she dashed towards her closet where she had everything.

Sofia grabbed a tiara, tutu, and a frilly purple scarf before running back into the room. She was so excited he had agreed to letting her dress him up and she couldn't wait to do it.

"You going to looks so pretties!" Sofia exclaimed as she stood in front of him.

Even with him sitting down, he was still taller than her. It made her feel small but also protected.

Daddy grimaced as she looked at him, but she didn't pay any attention to it. She placed everything down on the table, covering up the cups, before she turned back to her Daddy.

Grabbing his cheeks in her hands, she leaned forward. "Daddy?"

"Yes, Little one," he replied, his lips smushed together so it sounded funny.

She giggled, stepped on her tippy toes, and leaned her forehead against his.

"So pwetty," she whispered.

"Not pretty," Daddy said. "I'm handsome, hot, sexy, but not pretty."

"Daddy pretties."

He sighed and closed his eyes. "I'm not getting you to change your mind, am I?"

Sofia stood up, but kept her hands on his face. "Nope." She gave him a smile before leaning her head forward, licking the tip of his nose, and leaning back.

She grabbed the tiara off the table before looking at Daddy.

"Did you lick my nose?" he asked.

She shook her head and couldn't help but giggle. His face was one of curiosity and disgust at the same time.

"No Daddy. Whys would I do that?"

"I don't know, because you're a naughty girl?"

Sofia gasped and shook her head. "I is *not* a naughty

girl."

Daddy snorted. "Whatever you say, but Daddy knows that you are, and you can't hide it."

She stayed silent as she looked at her Daddy. How did she respond to that?

"How about you start putting the tiara on me?" Daddy suggested as if he could tell she was struggling with what to do next. "But please do it gently. I don't want a bleeding scalp."

"I always gentles," She said as she moved to put the tiara on her Daddy.

"Of course you are," he replied and Sofia couldn't tell if he was making fun of her or not.

She would never intentionally hurt her Daddy. Sometimes she did things without thinking or realizing that it was hurting the other person. Even then, she always felt guilty and tried to make it up to the person.

"Ouch," Daddy said as he slightly pulled back.

"Oh no!" Sofia gasped and looked at Daddy's head. "Is you alrights?"

Worry filled her as she looked over her Daddy's head, but she couldn't find anything wrong.

"Little one," Daddy said, laughing but she didn't pay any attention to it.

Where was he hurt? Why couldn't she find anything? Did she need to get her eyes checked?

"Sofia," Daddy said. "I'm okay. I was just messing with you."

Her eyes filled with tears as she pulled away. Why would he do that to her? She didn't want to see him hurt and she didn't want to hurt him. Why would he poke fun at her like that?

"Oh Little one," Daddy said. "I didn't mean to make you cry."

She sniffled and looked away. She shouldn't be crying over something this little, but she couldn't help herself. Sofia hadn't cried in a while and was trying to be brave for her Daddy while everything went on. Maybe this was what pushed her over the edge.

"Little one," Daddy said. "Come here."

He opened his arms wide and spread his legs further apart. She rushed into his arms, tears dripping onto his shirt as he held her.

"I know, Little one," he spoke gently. "Everything is going to be alright. I've got you."

She continued to cry into his shoulder, releasing all of the pent-up emotions she had been holding in for several days. Everything had gotten to be too much, and she had just fallen apart when she got worried, and it was all because of a joke.

Why was she like this?

"I've got you," Daddy said as he gently rocked them. "Can you tell me what's wrong?"

She kept her head buried in his shoulder and tried to relax enough to stop crying. She didn't really want to talk about it right now, but she knew she was going to have to. It was probably the best thing to do.

"I justs am overwhelmed," she whispered, hoping he heard her.

"I've got you, Little one," Daddy said. "Let me worry

about everything. You just be my sweet, special girl who is naughty sometimes."

She giggled towards the end. "I is not naughty."

"You are and there's no arguing about that."

She completely relaxed into his embrace. He knew exactly what to do for her to calm down, to ground her.

"Now, are you ready to continue?" Daddy asked.

"Cans I put makeup on you?" she asked as she pulled away. "Pretty makeup to make you even prettier!"

Daddy shook his head. "No makeup."

"Buts Daddy!"

"No buts. No makeup on Daddy."

Sofia pouted and crossed her arms. "No fun."

"Do you want to cuddle in my arms?"

She thought about it a second, still pouting that she wasn't able to put makeup on him. Even though she was sad she couldn't, cuddles sounded amazing right now.

"Yes, Daddy," she whispered.

"Let's get into the rocking chair," Daddy said as he got up from his seat and walked over to the rocking chair. "Come here," Daddy said, patting his lap.

Sofia walked over towards him and crawled into his lap, resting her head on his shoulder. She loved falling asleep in his arms. She felt so protected and loved all at the same time.

"I love you," Daddy whispered as he started to rock the chair. "I'll always love you."

"Love you too," she yawned and snuggled into him.

"Sleep tight."

Sofia closed her eyes and felt herself being lulled to sleep.

CHAPTER THIRTY-SEVEN

JAXSON

Jaxson carefully placed Sofia down in the crib before he pulled her soft blanket on top of her. He quietly grabbed the pacifier she had been using for her naps and settled it in her mouth. She latched onto it and soothed herself back to sleep.

He could look at her for hours as she slept. She looked so peaceful and beautiful. She always did.

Jaxson walked out of the room and made his way down towards the living room. He could hear Ezra and Antonio talking and he wanted to talk to them about everything. To see if they had any leads on who this person possibly could be.

He didn't like seeing Sofia so overwhelmed and scared any time someone brought up the person who was terrorizing her. Everything in him wanted to help and make sure this never happened again.

Antonio looked up as he walked into the living room. "Is the Little Miss okay?"

It warmed Jaxson's heart that they were already concerned about Sofia, and not just because they were hired to protect her, but in a personal way. They were warming up to Sofia and treated her like they were friends.

"She's exhausted, scared, and worried. Sofia is down for a nap right now," Jaxson said. "Hopefully she'll sleep for a couple of hours so she can get some rest."

"Has she been sleeping okay? Eating alright?" Antonio asked.

"Sleeping not so well, but I wrap her up in my arms when she wakes up and she normally goes back to sleep. I'm making sure she eats enough. She's already tiny and I can't have her losing any more weight."

He had been watching her eating habits and making sure she was getting enough food. Sofia had gained a couple of pounds, but he wanted her to gain a couple more. Michael had said for her to gain at least ten pounds. So, that was Jaxson's goal, then they would reevaluate with a full checkup. She looked healthier as the days went on, well as healthy as she could be considering everything that was going on.

"Well, with you as her Daddy I don't think she'll be losing any weight. So don't worry about that, and the sleep will get better," Ezra said. "Just give it some time and maybe have her talk to someone."

He nodded his head. He had thought about having her talk to someone about this, so she could process it all, but he didn't want to push her. Not everyone liked talking to a professional and sometimes it didn't help them. He didn't want her to do something that would actually hinder her.

"Have you guys got anything?" Jaxson asked as he sat down on the chair.

He was hoping to hear good news; that they had found the person.

"I didn't find anything on my walk around the perimeter. They didn't leave anything," Ezra said. "And no one came back while you were up in the room with her."

Jaxson relaxed a little on the couch. That was good news, but it wasn't at the same time. They didn't have any clue who the person could be, and they didn't leave anything behind to indicate who it was.

"But we do have a lead. Or at least we have a suspect," Antonio said.

Jaxson raised his eyebrows in shock. He didn't think that they would have a suspect when they didn't leave anything behind. Maybe they caught something on the camera that he hadn't been able to.

"Who is it?" Jaxson asked.

"Monty," Antonio replied.

Jaxson stilled at the mention of Monty's name. That was not who he was suspecting and he didn't think she had a bad bone in her body. Could it really be her?

Monty and Sophia were close and the timelines wouldn't add up. Monty hadn't been at the club when Sophia started her shift. It was after Sofia got sick that Leo called Monty and she came in. Maybe she had someone else leave the note in Sofia's locker.

That was a possibility, but something just didn't sit right with Jaxson. Monty was sweet and he knew that she had a brother she was taking care of. He didn't think she would be up for it, and he didn't know what she would even gain.

It's not like Monty would get more shifts at the club if Sophia left the country. He had told the employees that if they needed more or less shifts to come to him and talk about it. They would discuss the employee's needs and figure things out.

Which means it wouldn't make sense for Monty to do it. Sophia didn't know anybody in the country, besides the people that worked at the club. Who would want Sophia to be gone?

Jaxson tried to make sense of it in his head, but every scenario he came up with, it just didn't add up. Monty couldn't be the person who wanted to get rid of Sophia.

It just wasn't possible.

"That doesn't seem like Monty," Jaxson said. "She's a sweet person. She and Sophia are super close."

"Do you know Monty well?" Ezra asked.

"I don't know her very well, but when I've interacted with her, she was really nice. She doesn't have a bad bone in her body. Everyone that interacts with her always sings high praises. She's one of my best employees," Jaxson said. He didn't know why she would do this. It doesn't make sense.

"Does Sophia have something that Monty would want?" Antonio asked.

"I don't think so," he shook his head. "Sophia came to the United States with nothing, and she knew nobody. She still doesn't have anything and only knows a couple people in the club. It just doesn't add up and make sense."

"Well, I'm going to dig a little deeper to see what I can find out. I'm not gonna rule her out though."

Jaxson nodded his head. "As long as you don't say anything or do anything to Monty before you have hard evidence. She has a brother, and I don't want him to get taken from her if she didn't do anything wrong."

He had too many siblings broken up because of a false accusation when he was in the police force. It was hard on him, but it was normally even harder on the siblings. Child services made it nearly impossible for siblings to come back to each other after an accusation was put against them, even if it was false. He didn't want that for Monty.

"I'll come to you before I do anything," Antonio said.

Jaxson relaxed and nodded his head. He figured that Antonio wasn't going to do anything until he had proof, but he needed to make sure. Just in case.

"What about any of the other employees?" Ezra asked. "Have you noticed anyone who could be suspicious or has treated Sofia badly?"

Jaxson thought about it for a second. If they would have asked him several months ago, he wouldn't have been able to say anything because he was never out on the main floor with the employees. Since Sofia came, he started being down there more whenever she worked.

But that didn't mean he was paying attention to the other employees. He was normally paying attention to Sofia and talking to her.

"I don't think so," Jaxson said. "Well, I haven't actually seen her be rude to Sofia directly."

"Who?" Ezra asked.

"What did this person do?" Antonio asked.

"Well, she didn't really do anything, but the way she spoke just didn't, and still doesn't, sit well with me," Jaxson said. He thought back to the day he was helping Sofia after he found out she had been mugged the night before. It was a nightmare of his that it would happen again, but he was going to do his best to make sure it never did.

"What did this person say?" Antonio asked.

"I didn't really think about it when it happened but looking back on it, something was up," Jaxson said. "Lucy is another bartender at the club. The day after Sofia got mugged, one of the bouncers stopped her as she arrived at work. That's when I saw the bruise on her face. When I was walking to my office, Lucy stopped me and told me to leave Sofia and help her."

"Did she know that Sofia was badly injured?" Ezra asked as he took a seat.

"No, I don't think she did. She seemed concerned that I was holding someone in my arms, but once I told her who it was, she changed."

"Hmmm," Antonio said. "I'll take a look into her. She was on my list, but I'll make sure I do her next."

"Has she done something like this before?" Ezra asked. "Around Sofia or in front of you and you just didn't register it?"

"I don't remember her doing anything in front of me or saying anything. Lucy has been sweet to customers but something about that interaction just doesn't sit well with me."

Antonio opened his mouth to say something, but before he could, a creaking noise was heard, and all their heads whipped to the stairs to see Sofia walking down.

What was she doing?

CHAPTER THIRTY-EIGHT

SOFIA

Sofia had woken up from her nap a couple of minutes ago. She had started to panic when she couldn't see her Daddy, but then she heard the faint voices, and knew that he was somewhere in the house. She didn't want to wait for him. Even though she knew that climbing out of the crib wasn't a good idea, she didn't care at this moment.

She just wanted her Daddy.

It had taken a lot out of her as she climbed over the railings and out of the crib. Scary even, when she realized that it was going to be harder to get down than she thought. But she had done it and now she was clutching Trixie and Mattie in her arms as she walked down the stairs, pacifier in her mouth. At first, Sofia didn't know if she was going to like the pacifier. Daddy had told her to try it at least once before she decided on anything, and she absolutely loved it.

She normally only used it when she was napping, but she

didn't want to part with it yet. It was giving her comfort when she needed it.

Sofia started to slowly walk down the stairs but stopped when she heard her Daddy start to speak.

"Lucy is another bartender at the club. The day after Sofia got mugged, one of the bouncers stopped her as she arrived at work. That's when I saw the bruise on her face. When I was walking to my office, Lucy stopped me and told me to leave Sofia and help her."

Why were they talking about Lucy and the incident in the club? What was going on?

"Did she know that Sofia was badly injured?" Ezra asked as he took a seat.

"No, I don't think she did. She seemed concerned that I was holding someone in my arms, but once I told her who it was, she changed."

"Hmmm," Antonio said. "I'll take a look into her. She was on my list, but I'll make sure I do her next."

"Has she done something like this before?" Ezra asked. "Around Sofia or in front of you and you just didn't register it?"

"I don't remember her doing anything in front of me or saying anything. Lucy has been sweet to customers but something about that interaction just doesn't sit well with me."

Sofia started to walk down the stairs again to hear better. But right as she took her next step, the stairs creaked, and she froze as all eyes were on her. Daddy immediately stood up from his chair and walked over towards her.

"What are you doing out of the crib?" Daddy asked. "How did you get out of the crib?"

Sofia continued to suck on the pacifier as she stared at her Daddy. She didn't really want to talk right now.

"That was naughty of you to climb out of your crib," Daddy said. "You should've called out to me, and I would've come and picked you up."

She looked at her feet as he continued to talk. She knew she should've waited for him, but she hadn't wanted to.

"It was also naughty of you to walk down the stairs by yourself. Little girls shouldn't walk down the stairs by themselves. They could get hurt," Daddy said. "Next time you call me, and I'll come get you."

Her cheeks started to go red from embarrassment. She hadn't thought it was a big deal but boy was she wrong.

"Do you understand?" Daddy asked.

She nodded her head and looked at him. He seemed satisfied with her nod, and she was glad.

"Good girl," he said.

Her cheeks went even redder as he said that. She absolutely loved it when he called her a good girl. She was embarrassed she was getting like this in front of Antonio and Ezra while also being scolded for getting out of her crib alone and walking down the stairs.

"Don't be embarrassed," Ezra said.

"We're both Daddies and completely agree with what your Daddy just said about getting out of the crib and walking down the stairs alone," Antonio said.

She looked over at them briefly before looking at her Daddy.

"They are right. You shouldn't be embarrassed," Daddy said. "Never."

She nodded her head and sucked harder on the pacifier. Her heart rate had sped up when he called her good girl but went even faster when Ezra and Antonio started talking.

"Come here," Daddy said as he held his arms open.

She took one step before wrapping her arms around his neck and her legs around his waist. If he didn't want her to walk down the stairs alone, then she wasn't going to walk at all. He could carry her.

"Any time you want to be carried, you let me know," Daddy said. "I'll gladly carry you around just to have you in my arms."

Her insides went all gooey as he said that. He was too sweet to her.

As they got closer to the couch, she remembered that they were talking about Lucy, and she wanted to know why. She struggled with the idea of taking her pacifier out and talking, but she knew that they wouldn't understand her if she didn't.

"Why are you talking about Lucy?" She asked, briefly taking the pacifier out before plopping it back in.

Hopefully, they wouldn't need her to talk anymore, and she could just listen to what they were saying. She didn't like being left out of things and right now she felt like she was on the outside.

"Just that she made a rude comment about you when I found out you had been mugged," Daddy said.

Sofia scrunched up her nose at that. She did remember

that, but it didn't shock her. Lucy wasn't a nice person, at least to her.

"Why the face?" Ezra asked.

She shrugged her shoulders. Should she tell them about Lucy and her ugly comments to her?

"What about Monty?" Antonio asked. "Would she want to do anything to hurt you?"

Her eyes went wide with the mention of Monty's name. Why would they think she would want to do something bad to her? They were great friends and had helped each other on multiple occasions.

She slipped the pacifier out of her mouth and held it as she sat on her Daddy's lap.

"No," Sofia said. "She wouldn't do anything to me."

Everyone was silent and Sofia couldn't help but speak again.

"Lucy on the other hand," she mumbled more to herself. She couldn't help it because Lucy was a problem.

Antonio raised his eyebrow at her, and she looked down at her lap. She shouldn't have said anything, but she couldn't stop herself. They were talking about who it could possibly be, and Lucy was a person in her mind that could be behind it.

"What did you just say?" Antonio asked.

"Look at him when you speak to him," Daddy said right after.

She looked up and stared at Antonio. Was she really about to talk to them about Lucy? Her Daddy had already mentioned Lucy to them, but they didn't know what all had happened. There was so much more than just the rude comment she made the other day, after she had been mugged.

"I said Lucy's name," she softly said. "I wouldn't be surprised if she was behind this. It honestly would make sense."

"Why do you say that?" Daddy asked.

She started to fidget in his lap, not knowing what to say. She didn't like saying mean things about people or really talking about people and how they were rude. Sofia just wanted to forget about it and pretend like it never happened.

Why dwell on what happened when she couldn't go back and change it. There wasn't any point and Sofia knew that she should've gone to her Daddy about this, Monty had even said that, but she didn't want to get him involved. He was their employer, but he was also her Daddy. What would people think when they saw him scolding an employee on her behalf?

Favoritism.

That was what she thought people would say. The whispers when they saw it, but it wouldn't be true. Lucy had been rude to her, several times.

"Sofia," Daddy said. "Why?"

"I don't want to say bad things about her," she whispered.

"I need to know so I can do my job well," Antonio said. "We won't judge you for telling us what she said or did to you, but we do need to know."

Sofia looked up at her Daddy, almost looking for permission to tell them what Lucy had said to her. He nodded his head and she relaxed a little.

"I'm here for you," he softly said. "Go ahead and tell them."

CHAPTER THIRTY-NINE

SOFIA

Sofia closed her eyes and she tried to relax in her Daddy's embrace. Right now, she had wished she listened to Monty several weeks ago, after Lucy told her that Jaxson was going to fire her. She had been rude to her, and Monty told her to tell Jaxson about it, but she hadn't. Nothing had happened yet, and she didn't want to do anything to make it worse.

Oh, how she wished she could go back in time. Maybe none of this would've happened if she went to her Daddy and told him that Lucy was looking at her meanly and being rude.

"Little one?" Daddy said. "Are you okay?"

She nodded her head. "Sorry, Daddy. Spaced out."

"No worries. Let us know when you're ready," Antonio said.

The sooner she told them, the sooner she would be able to get this over with. Everything. Part of Sofia hoped that it was Lucy so this could be over, but part of her felt bad for wishing that on someone.

"She had just said some rude things to me and given me mean looks," Sofia said.

"What has she said to you?" Daddy asked.

"She was hoping that you would fire me one time and said 'good riddance' after."

Daddy growled and she looked at him.

"She probably didn't mean it," She softly said, trying to make things better. "At first, I thought it could be because Lucy wasn't getting as many shifts as she wanted and that I was taking them from her. It could still be that way and I thought about talking to you about that. I don't want to take anyone's shifts just because you hired me."

"She hasn't gotten any shifts taken away. Her schedule is like it was before you came," Daddy said.

She furrowed her eyebrows. Then why would Lucy say those things?

"Well, then she probably doesn't like new people," she tried to justify it. "I'll grow on her at some point."

"I'll look into her next," Antonio said. "See what I can find out about her."

Sofia started to worry when he said that. What if it was her all along? But what if it wasn't? Sofia didn't want to get anyone in trouble.

"Leave the worrying to me," Antonio said. "I know that face all too well and I don't want you to worry about anything."

She chuckled and shook her head. "Easier said than done," she mumbled.

All three men laughed, and she snuggled into her Daddy's embrace. She hadn't meant to make them laugh, but she was glad she did. They needed a laugh in a time like this.

"Such big problems for a Little girl," Daddy said. "Let Daddy, Antonio, and Ezra worry about that."

It was a tall order for her to not worry about the person coming after her. How could she not worry about it? It was her life on the line and not theirs. That person had threatened her, not them.

How was she not supposed to worry about that? It was all she could think about right now. All she had thought about for the past day. No matter what she was doing, it was in the back of her mind.

Sofia looked over at Ezra and Antonio and she wanted to ask them questions. They were Daddies and she wanted to know if they had any Littles of their own or if they were all alone. Both of them were caring and protective which made her think they had someone in their life.

"Go ahead," Ezra said. "I can see that you're dying to ask us questions."

She blushed and nodded her head. She did have something to ask, and he had just given her permission.

"Go ahead. I'll answer them if I can or want to," Antonio said. "Not everything is okay for Little girls to hear."

She wondered what he could be talking about. What could she possibly not be able to hear?

"Do you have a Little of your own?" She softly asked.

She hoped that the question was okay to ask. She didn't want to make them feel uncomfortable or bring up something they didn't want to remember, but she was curious and wanted to know.

"It's okay if you don't want to answer," she whispered. "I'm just curious."

"Curiosity killed the cat," Antonio said. "But satisfaction brought him back. Your question wasn't bad and both of us will be happy to answer it."

Sofia looked back and forth between them, waiting for them to answer. Who would answer first?

"I'm talking to someone right now," Ezra started to speak. "But I'm taking it slow with her. She's a new Little and she doesn't know for certain if she is one."

"But he definitely thinks she is, and I would agree with him. She is just very unsure about a lot of things," Antonio said and Ezra glared at him. "What? You can't tell me that I'm wrong."

Ezra sighed and nodded his head. "She is very unsure about a lot of things, and this is one of them. She knows me and knows that I'm a Daddy. She wanted to see if she would like it or not, if it felt right. I'm hoping she realizes that she is Little and wants me to be her Daddy."

"Why don't you just tell her that?" Sofia asked.

It seemed simple and she didn't know why he wouldn't just bring that up to her.

"Because I don't want to pressure her into anything," Ezra said. "That wouldn't be right."

"There is a point that you should tell her, but I do agree that now might not be the right time," Antonio explained.

Ezra glared at him again and Sofia couldn't help but

giggle. They seemed like great friends, and she loved the little banter and glares they gave each other.

"For me, there isn't anyone right now," Antonio said.

"Bullshit," Ezra said. "And you know it. You told her about my girl, well more about her. If you don't say anything more, I'll tell her."

"Fine," Antonio let out a huge fake sigh. "I have my eye on someone right now-"

"For a while he has had his eye on this person."

Antonio glared at him. "But I haven't done anything yet."

"Why not?" she asked.

"Well, I'm not certain I'm the right person for her."

She could tell from his body language that he didn't want to talk about it anymore, and she didn't want to pressure him or make him feel uncomfortable. Sofia hoped that Antonio would find happiness soon, with that person or another person.

"Let's go feed you," Daddy said as he stood up. She snuggled into his embrace and let him take over.

CHAPTER FORTY

SOFIA

It had been hard to get her Daddy to agree to her working the rest of her shifts at the club. He hadn't wanted her to, but she had begged him to let her. She was going to go crazy if he kept her locked up in his office while he worked.

He had told her that it was unsafe until they knew who the person was. She understood his worries, but it wasn't like no one was watching over her. There were several Doms there and Ezra was there as well. She was totally safe.

Ezra had made good on his promise and had been walking around the club, watching her but also the other people in the room. No one knew about the situation, and no one batted an eyelash at Ezra. It was like they didn't even see him walking around.

It relieved her because she didn't want to make anyone uncomfortable while she was working. Since Ezra had to be down there, it would technically be her fault if someone was uncomfortable.

He had come up to her several times asking her if she was alright and each time her answer was the same. She was okay. No one had said anything, and she hadn't received any notes from anyone her whole shift.

Lucy wasn't scheduled for tonight and she was relieved. She hadn't heard anything from Antonio to know if it was her or not. Sofia was relieved that she wasn't here, if it was even her.

She hoped it wasn't, but her gut was telling her that it was Lucy all along. Her hateful looks and mean comments towards her and no one else. Sofia was the only foreigner working there and it made her think that Lucy didn't like foreigners.

"I'm going to go grab my stuff and clock out," Sofia said to Ezra.

"I'll come with you," he said.

"That's not necessary. It's just right around the corner. I'll be back before you know it."

As much as she was okay with Ezra being around her since he was her bodyguard, following her to grab her purse was unnecessary.

He looked uncertain but nodded his head. "Right there and back."

"Yes, Sir," she mock saluted him and giggled.

"Brat."

She skipped off to the employees room, feeling great. She was starting to feel herself again.

"Oh happy day. Happy day," she slowly started to sing to herself. "It's gonna be a good rest of the day. Spending it with my Daddy. Being bratty."

Sofia had been on thin ice around her Daddy. She had back talked one or two times to him before she went off to work and she left her water bottle in his office.

On purpose.

She was feeling naughty today and it felt great. She couldn't wait to go into his office to wreak more havoc and then again when they get home.

Oh she couldn't wait for that.

Sofia stopped in front of her locker, but before she could do anything, something was pulled over her head. A scream bubbled out of her mouth as she started to fight to get free, but arms wrapped around her.

"Shut the fuck up," a familiar voice said.

She tried to pinpoint who the voice belonged to as she started to panic, but she couldn't remember.

"Please," she begged. "Let me go."

She attempted to twist her body, but the arms tightened around her, making it even harder for her to breathe.

"I said shut the fuck up," the man growled.

Sofia stilled for a second when she realized this person was the man who mugged her several weeks ago. It wasn't a coincidence that this was the same man as before. Someone had hired him, but who?

She opened her mouth and screamed again. Someone had to hear her scream. The club had music on, but it wasn't that loud and the employees room wasn't far from the bar where Ezra was.

She just hoped that someone would hear her and investigate.

Hot searing pain erupted across her stomach as she felt a

fist connect with her. She yelled in pain and attempted to double over, but the guy's arms around her chest were holding her in place.

"I said to shut up you little bitch," the man growled in her ear.

"Let's go," another voice said. "Someone was bound to hear her scream."

Sofia wished that she didn't have the sack over her head, covering her vision. She couldn't see how many people were there with her, trying to kidnap her.

"Help!" She yelled. She needed to fight back, no matter how much pain she was going to be in. Sofia needed to alert someone that something bad was happening. "Help! Fire! Anyone!"

Her head flew to the right as a fist connected with her jaw. Pain ached all over her face and she knew she was going to have a bruise there later.

"Help," she weakly said.

"Shut the fuck up," another voice said.

Sofia felt herself starting to be dragged to who knows where.

"Good thing the lady said we could do anything to her," the same voice who she thought hit her said.

His voice was a tad bit deeper than the person who mugged her.

"Sofia!" she heard someone yell. It sounded like Ezra, but she couldn't be so sure.

"Shit," her mugger said. "Grab her legs and help me get her out and into the van."

She felt the other man grab her legs and she tried flighting, kicking, but his grip on her legs tightened and she whimpered in pain. Their grips were like steel and it hurt so much.

"Please," she begged. "You don't have to do this."

"Gettin paid," someone mumbled. "That's good enough for me."

Sofia tried to move her body to get out of their grip, but they only tightened their hold on her.

"Sofia!" Ezra yelled again.

Hope filled inside of her as his voice was closer. Maybe he would get to her before they could do anything to her.

"Ezra!" she yelled.

"In the van!" the mugger said.

She felt herself being thrown and hitting the floor of the van really hard. A groan escaped her mouth as her shoulder and side ached from hitting it so hard. She heard the van doors shut before it started to move.

Sofia moved her arms to try and get the sack off of her head, but someone gripped them super hard.

"Tie her hands," deep voice man said.

She felt something coarse being wrapped around her wrists really tight. She whimpered as she felt the rope dig into her skin.

"Stupid bitch was easy to get," the man next to her said.

"Boss lady said she was smart," the mugger said. "She wasn't very smart to leave her bodyguard behind to grab her things."

"Stupid cunt."

She flinched at the words they used. How was she supposed to know that someone was going to grab her in the employee room? Nothing had happened before like that in the club. Sure, the threatening notes, but they were just threatening notes. How did these men even get into the club without being seen?

"We're almost there," the mugger said.

Sofia had tried to pay attention to where they were heading, but she didn't have a clue where they started. Tears dripped down her face as the reality of everything was coming down on her.

She had just gotten kidnapped. She had no clue where they were headed or who this boss lady was. Were they going to kill her? Who was behind this?

"You grab her legs and I'll grab her arms," the mugger said as she felt the van come to a stop.

Sofia tried to wiggle around to see if she could get the sack off of her head, but a kick to the stomach made her stop and curl in on herself.

"Stop moving bitch," the man growled and she shied back as best she could.

"Just fucking grab her legs," the other man said. "The sooner we get her into the room and tied up, the sooner we get our money and can leave."

They were just going to leave her here? Where even was here? Panic rose in Sofia as she felt them grip onto her body and haul her out of the van.

"You get her arms and I'll get her legs," the mugger said. "Tie them tight to the chair so she can't get out."

The men tied her up to the chair and she tried to move around, but the ropes dug into her skin. She whimpered and tears ran down her face.

"Hello," the mugger said as he pulled the bag off of her head.

She saw the man's ugly face right in front of her.

"Aw look," he said. "She's crying. My favorite."

Sofia tried to stop crying, but her whole body ached, and she didn't do well with pain at all.

"Continue to cry," the man said. "It makes me fucking hard seeing the tears cascade down your face. Tears I made you have."

Sofia wanted to puke as he talked about her tears.

"Boss lady," the other man said.

She watched as the guy who mugged her stood up and stepped away. Standing right in front of her was the one and only Lucy.

Shit.

CHAPTER FORTY-ONE

SOFIA

Sofia stared at Lucy in surprise. She wasn't expecting Lucy to be behind all of this. Deep down, she had a feeling it was her, but she had hoped she was wrong.

She wanted to give Lucy the benefit of the doubt. She so badly wanted her to be innocent and have it be this horrible guy who is evil. But She was wrong.

So wrong.

Why would Lucy do something like this? What did Sofia ever do to her to deserve this much hate?

Sofia thought back to what the two guys were talking about earlier. Lucy hired a man to mug her and then kidnap her.

Had Sofia known Lucy before and done something? Had Lucy visited Chile while Sofia was trying to earn her money to come to the states? She was pretty sure she would remember, but it was hard to tell.

Sofia couldn't really remember a lot from the last year

she was in Chile. She had been working so much, and had gotten so little sleep, that everything had become a blur. Maybe she had met Lucy before but nothing about her seemed familiar.

Lucy continued to stare at her before she cracked a wicked smile. Sophia didn't have a good feeling about this. What could she have done to deserve this?

"Both of you can leave now," Lucy said. "Your money will be transferred to you in the next hour. I promise."

Sofia watched as the two men nodded their heads before they walked out of the room. She had lost hope that they would help her.

But she had to have faith that Ezra and her Daddy were going to come get her. Ezra had heard her scream for help, which put hope inside of Sofia. Maybe Ezra had gotten into his car fast enough to follow them. That's all she could hope and pray for.

"I'm finally going to get rid of you," Lucy said as she took a step forward. "You should've left months ago but now is better than ever."

"Why?" Sofia asked. "Why are you doing this?"

"Because you shouldn't be here!" Lucy yelled. "You shouldn't be allowed in this country! We don't need you here. We don't want you here!"

Sofia didn't know what to say. What did she mean? Just because she was not from the United States?

"We don't need you guys coming in here illegally and taking everything we've worked hard for!" Lucy screamed.

"I didn't," Sofia tried to reason with her. "I applied for a work visa and got it. Now, I'm applying for my Green Card."

Tears filled Sofia's eyes as she watched Lucy's face get angrier by the second. There was no reasoning with her, and she was worried. What was she going to do to her? Was she going to kill her or was she going to leave her here until someone found her? If they found her.

"You're finally going back to the country you belong in," Lucy said as she took another step forward. "And you can't do anything about it."

"Why?"

"I don't like immigrants. They should stay where they were born and not come to the United States."

The tears in her eyes streamed down her face. She didn't want to leave this country. She had just found a Daddy who wanted her for her and a job she loved so much. Sofia wasn't ready to give that up yet.

"I thought you were smart," Lucy said as she circled around her.

Chills ran up Sofia's spine as Lucy walked behind her. She couldn't see her and it worried her. Was she going to do something to her?

"Please," Sofia begged. "You can let me leave and I won't bother you."

Lucy chuckled and yanked on Sofia's hair and she whimpered. So much pain.

"You're not that lucky," she whispered in her ear. "You won't be getting off that easy."

She let go of her hair and Sofia let out a sigh of relief.

"I thought you would get scared after I sent the man to mug you," Lucy said. "I thought you would've left after you got the threatening messages from me."

It was starting to make more sense as Lucy spoke. Everything she hoped wasn't true was coming true. Lucy was the person behind all of this because she hated people, immigrants, who came to the United States.

"You don't need to do this," Sofia softly said. "I'll leave the city and you won't ever see me again."

Sofia didn't know if she would be able to do that since her Daddy was here. She didn't know if it would be better for her to leave the city or leave the United States in general. She loved her job at the club, and she had made friends. Would she be able to find that somewhere else in the United States?

It wouldn't be the same, that was for sure. And Sofia didn't want that. She wanted the people she had met here.

"Umm," Lucy said as she touched her chin like she was thinking. "I think not."

"I'll go to the police," Sofia threatened. "Show them the evidence of your threatening notes."

Lucy laughed. "You don't have any evidence. And are they really going to believe someone that is an immigrant? Someone who doesn't have her Green Card and who, according to a little bird, is about to lose her work visa?"

Sofia didn't know if they would believe her or not, but she had to try. But the first thing she needed to do was get away from Lucy and she didn't know how. She was tied to a chair, the ropes digging into her wrists and ankles. There was no way she was getting out of this.

"Security footage," Sofia said.

She had no clue if there was any security footage at the club or not, but she prayed that there was. Maybe then she could catch her in the act and have her arrested.

"I'm not dumb," Lucy said. "I hired someone to tamper with the security footage so they wouldn't see me come in or place the note. But someone would get framed if you did happen to show it to the authorities."

Her body went cold as she heard that. Who was going to get framed if she went to the police with the footage?

"You don't want your dear friend Monty to get taken away from her brother, do you?" Lucy said with fake worry. "That would be so bad for her brother and for her. An innocent person in jail and a young boy in foster care. Such a travesty."

Sofia didn't know what to say. What was there to say? She didn't want Monty to get framed for something that she didn't do. She didn't want her brother to go into foster care because who knows what would happen to him.

"They won't believe that," Sofia said, trying to sound so sure in that. "I'll tell the authorities that she didn't do it."

"Honey," Lucy said as she stepped closer to her. "The police won't believe you and it's kind of hard to go against evidence like that. Actual security footage of her leaving and walking next to your locker since hers is right next to yours."

She shook her head, not wanting to believe anything.

"I'll find a way," Sofia said. "Or I'll leave the city."

"Too late for that," Lucy said. "I've got people coming to pick you up."

"W-what?"

Sofia started to breathe harder as she thought about who these people were. What did Lucy mean she had people coming to pick her up?

"Oh yes," Lucy said. "People are coming to pick you up

and take you back to your country. It's great really. You'll be gone and then I can be the center of attention at the club again. And well, your dirty hands won't be anywhere near anything in the club. It's honestly too good for you and I don't even know how you got the job."

Sofia started to struggle in her chair, trying to get out of her restraints. She didn't care that they were digging into her wrists and ankles. All that mattered right now was her getting out and as far away from Lucy as she could.

"Tsk," Lucy took a step back. "I wouldn't try that. I told the men to tie them really tight so there was no way of you getting out of it. Sorry?"

She didn't sound sorry at all.

Lucy chuckled. "What am I saying? I'm not sorry one bit about anything. I couldn't care less that you could lose your hand from how tight those are. You deserve it by coming to this country when you weren't wanted. I mean, did you really think people were going to be happy you came?"

Sofia stayed silent and went limp in the chair. Her wrists were on fire, and she had no doubt she rubbed them raw.

She knew that what Lucy said was a lie. Daddy was glad she was in the country, and she knew that Monty was also glad. She had made several friends with the other Littles in the club. Lucy was wrong. So wrong in everything she had said.

If Lucy had said that when she first got here, she would've believed it because she didn't know anyone that well. But now, *now* she knew that Lucy was wrong. If none of the other Littles were happy she was here, she knew that her

Daddy was. He had made it clear several times and even told her he loved her.

"They should be here any second now," Lucy said. "I can't fucking wait to see you get dragged out of here and leave the country for good."

Worry went through Sofia as she thought about leaving. She didn't want to leave, but what could she do right now? She was tied to a chair and couldn't get out. Maybe when the men came in to get her, she could slip away or do something, anything to get away from them.

Both of them heard a door slam open and a huge grin spread across Lucy's face.

"Ah," she said. "That should be them."

"Please," Sofia begged as she started to cry again. "You don't need to do this. I promise."

But before Lucy could say anything, the door was pushed open, hitting the wall really hard and men filled the room. Men with guns and their faces covered.

Guns were fired, Sofia started to scream, her eyes going wide as she watched Lucy fall towards the ground.

Lucy was dead and Sofia was next.

CHAPTER FORTY-TWO

SOFIA

Sofia screamed as she stared at Lucy, lying on the floor. Her eyes roamed the floor, trying to see where she had gotten shot, but there was nothing. Was the bullet so tiny that it went in and killed instantly without leaving a trace? Was there such a thing like that?

A man stepped towards her and she screamed again. She pulled against the ropes hissing in pain as it dug into her wrists. She needed to get away from them. That was the only thing going on in her mind as he continued to walk towards her.

"Please," she begged. "D-don't do this."

Tears streamed down her face as the man took another step towards her. There were so many things she wanted to do in her life. She wanted to live with her Daddy and live happily. She wanted so badly to travel around the United States and see everything there was.

But most of all, Sofia wanted to tell her Daddy one more time that she loved him and he was the one for her.

She hadn't had the time to tell him before her shift started. She had been running late and couldn't visit him like normal. And now she was never going to get to tell him again. She was going to be dead soon and she couldn't do anything about it.

The man knelt in front of her. He wore a mask and every inch of his skin was covered in clothing. Was this the same man who mugged her? He hadn't said a word, but he looked about the same build as the mugger.

"Please," she begged again. "I want to l-live."

"Sofia," he softly said and she stilled.

That wasn't the mugger. That was her... Daddy?

He pulled off the mask and her Daddy's face appeared right in front of her. Tears filled her eyes as she took in his face. She didn't think she was ever going to see him again and yet here he was, right in front of her.

"I'm here," he gently said. "You're safe now."

Her eyes tracked over to the other man who had a gun pointing towards Lucy. Had he killed her? Even though Lucy was mean to her, Sofia didn't want her to die.

The man pulled off his mask and Ezra stood in front of her.

"Tranquilizer," he said as he kept pointing the gun towards Lucy.

She wasn't dead. Sofia let out a sigh of relief and looked back at her Daddy.

"Wait," she rushed out.

What about the two other guys? Had they left completely before they came? Were they still in the house somewhere?

"What is it, Little one?" Daddy asked.

"M-men," she stuttered. "Two men."

Both of them looked at her confused. Did they not see the men that had kidnapped her?

"What do you mean two men?" Daddy asked.

She shook her head and pulled against the ropes.

"Take a deep breath for me," Daddy said. "Such a good girl. That's it. Slowly in, hold it, now let it out."

Her eyes stayed on him the whole time.

"Now, can you tell us about these two men," Daddy asked. "I need to know if they are still in the house."

"They are the men who kidnapped me," she said.

Her eyes went around the room, trying to figure out if they were still in the house or not. She heard the door shut, both of them, but that didn't mean anything. They could've shut it but not actually left the house.

"Ah the two goons that were leaving when we arrived," Ezra said. "They have been taken care of. We have men who are giving them to the authorities right now."

She sagged into the chair to her best ability with her hands still tied.

"Let's get you out of those," Daddy said. "Sorry I didn't do it before. I wanted to make sure we got the men before I untied you."

Sofia nodded her head. She didn't really mind that her arms were still tied. Well, she couldn't really feel them that well, which was concerning her.

"I can't feel my fingers," she whispered.

"You're going to be okay," Daddy said. "We'll have Michael check over you when we get back."

Daddy picked her up after he got her untied and she relaxed into his arms. She was so glad he was here with her.

"I thought I wasn't going to ever see you again," Sofia whispered, her voice full of emotion.

She was going to start crying again but she didn't care. Sofia had just gone through a traumatic event and she needed to process her emotions.

"Never," Daddy said as he started to rub her back. "I would never let that happen to you."

Sofia pushed her head into his neck and silently cried in his arms.

"You're okay," Daddy whispered. "I've got you. Nothing is going to happen to you."

"Everything okay?" Ezra asked. "Do you need me to do anything?"

"No," Daddy said. "Everything is just hitting her all at once but she's going to be okay."

Sofia snuggled into his embrace even more and he held onto her.

"Let's get you home," Daddy said.

Daddy started to walk, and she clutched onto his shirt. She knew he wasn't going to leave her, but she needed to make sure, just in case. If she had her hand gripped onto his shirt, he couldn't go anywhere without her.

"How did you find me?" she finally asked.

She didn't know how long she was in the room with Lucy before they came in. Had it been an hour or was it just a couple of minutes?

"How long was I there for?" She asked.

"Twenty minutes or so," he replied. "The necklace."

She pulled her head away from his neck and looked at him in confusion.

"My necklace?" She whispered. "What do you mean?"

"Antonio knew that I was going to give you this necklace. He saw me looking at it and said he would like to place a tracking device in it," Daddy explained. "He wanted to make sure you were safe and, if anything happened, we could find you easily."

She looked down at her little cow pendant and smiled.

"Thank you, Daddy," she softly said.

"For what?" he asked.

"For saving me. For getting me this necklace. For showing me that you love me. It means a lot and I love you too. I love you so much and I don't want anyone else but you. I want you as my Daddy but I also want you as my husband."

A smile broke out on his face and she hugged him again.

"Let's get you home."

"I don't think Michael needs to look at my hands," Sofia whispered as they pulled into the driveway.

Ezra and Antonio were taking Lucy to the police station to turn her in. They had all the evidence from the cameras and eye witnesses to put her away. Sofia was relieved but she also felt bad for Lucy.

"I think you do," Daddy said. "Those ropes were tied really tight and bruises are already appearing on your skin."

Sofia looked down at her hands and ankles, bruises appearing where the ropes were. They ached any time she moved them, but some ice would most likely fix that problem. And medicine.

"I'm okay," she said.

"No," Daddy replied. "I'm not taking any chances. You wince when you move them, and I want Michael to check them out. It's the end of the discussion."

She nodded her head and waited for him to walk around and pick her up. He had told her on the drive that he didn't want her walking or moving much, until Michael took a look over her. He wanted to make sure nothing was broken.

She didn't believe anything was broken. She wasn't in a lot of pain, and she didn't feel anything snap while the men kidnapped her.

"I know you don't want this," Daddy said as he opened her door. "I know you don't like to be seen by doctors, but I need this. I need to know that everything is okay because, if not, I'm going to break into the jail, find those fuckers, and kill them."

Sofia's eyes went wide as she stared at her Daddy. She was not expecting that from him, especially since he was a retired police officer.

"You can't," she said.

"And why can't I?" he asked.

"Because, then you would leave me, and I can't deal with that. I need you."

Daddy sighed. "Okay, Little one. No going in and killing them."

She relaxed in his embrace as he picked her up and started to walk towards the house.

"Is she okay?" Michael said as he held the door open.

"I think her wrists and ankles are just bruised, but I want to make sure, just in case," Daddy said as he sat down on the couch and held her against him.

She didn't want to let him go yet and Daddy must have known.

"Does anything else hurt, Little one?" Daddy asked.

"Stomach," she whispered.

It ached a little from where they kicked and punched her, but nothing like her wrists and ankles. They hurt the worst.

"I'll check her ankles and wrists first, and then will look at her stomach," Michael said as he knelt in front of them.

He carefully picked up her ankles to examine them. He moved them in all different directions, while watching her facial expression.

"I think they're just really bruised. Put ice on them and keep off of them for a couple of days. If they get worse, come to me or take her to the clinic and they'll take some x-rays," Michael said as he started to look at her wrists and did the same thing. "And the same with her wrists. Ice and if they get worse, take her to the clinic."

"Thank you," Daddy said.

"Now, can I see your stomach?"

Daddy carefully lifted up her shirt and Michael took a look before gently pressing around. She winced several times when he pressed on the tender parts.

"Nothing seems to be seriously injured. I would give her

some pain medicine and let her rest a lot these next couple of days," Michael said as he stood up.

"Thank you so much for coming," Daddy said. "What do you say, Little one?"

"Thank you," she whispered.

She didn't like that he had to look her over, but she knew he took time away from Monroe to come examine her.

"You're welcome," Michael said. "Would you like to look at some of the stickers I have and pick out two for being such a good girl?"

Sofia sat up straighter and nodded her head. She wanted the stickers. Michael chuckled and grabbed two books, handing them to her. She briefly scanned the pages but stopped when she saw the cows.

"Ahhh," Daddy said. "I should've known she would go for those."

Michael chuckled and handed her two of the stickers she pointed at.

"Now," Michael said. "I hope I don't have to see you again for something like this. Next time it will be at the club when you're playing with Monroe and the other Littles or at the clinic when you come for your check up."

Sofia stilled at the mention of the check up. She didn't want one of those and she was going to do her hardest not to get one.

"Thank you again," Daddy said.

Michael left and she snuggled into her Daddy's body. She didn't want to do anything but relax in his embrace.

"I love you," he gently told her. "I love you so much."

"I love you too."

"When do you want to get married?"

Sofia thought about it for a second. When did she want to get married to him? She didn't want to wait a long time because screw that.

"A month?" she sounded so unsure but she didn't want to wait. "I don't want anything fancy. Just a small wedding and we can invite the other Littles, the Daddies and Mommies that we know from the club."

Sofia had never wanted a big wedding, if she was ever going to get married. The smaller the better. She wanted it to be intimate and meaningful with the people she knew best.

It was going to be sad that her best friend from Chile couldn't be here, but there was nothing she could do about it. Sofia knew though that her best friend didn't like weddings and probably wouldn't have come any way. She didn't go to her own sister's wedding, no matter how much her sister begged her to go.

Daddy kissed her forehead. "That sounds perfect."

"Maybe we could get married in your backyard?" Sofia suggested. "I think everyone could fit there."

"I think I have a better idea. You remember Gene, right?" Daddy said. "The farmer who delivers our produce."

Sofia nodded her head. Gene was a nice guy whenever she saw him.

"He owns the farm. They also have some houses there for people who need to get away or be somewhere safe," Daddy said. "But he also has an open field with the most beautiful trees and a barn. I'm pretty sure he would let us use it for the wedding."

"Yessss," Sofia said. "I love that idea."

"It's set," Daddy said.

She sighed in content and snuggled into his chest.

"I can't wait to spend the rest of my life with you," Daddy said as he held her closer.

"Me too."

EPILOGUE

SOFIA

"Are you ready?" Daddy asked as he held her hand.

They had just gotten married and were about to walk into the reception that was being held in the barn. Daddy had asked Gene about using the field and barn for their wedding and he had agreed to it. They had a lot of help setting everything up from the other Littles, Mommies, and Daddies from the club. She couldn't be happier with how it turned out.

She needed to remember to say thank you to everyone who helped make this day so special.

"Yes," she whispered. "I love you."

"I love you too," Daddy said, leaning down and kissing her briefly.

They stared at the entrance of the barn and waited for the doors to open.

"And last but not least, let's welcome the happy couple," Leo said into the microphone. "Introducing Mr. and Mrs. White!"

The door to the barn opened and they walked in, holding hands, and looking at all the happy faces in the room. People cheered and clapped as they walked towards their table. Twinkle lights were hanging on the ceiling, flowers on each table, and the soft glow of the fake candles.

Everything was perfect.

"I love you," Daddy said again. "I'm never going to get tired of saying that to you."

She blushed and kissed him on the lips. "I love you too."

Daddy held her chair out for her and she sat down. She was hungry and couldn't wait to dig into the waffles.

"Let me go get our food," Daddy said. "I'll be right back."

She nodded her head and watched him the whole time he made the waffles and put all her favorite toppings on.

"Thank you," she whispered when he sat the plate in front of her.

Sofia takes several bites and moans. Absolutely delicious.

Daddy leans so his mouth is next to her ear. "Those sounds are only for me."

She blushed once again and nodded her head.

"Where the fuck is she?" someone yells as they walk into the barn.

Her eyes went wide as she stared at this huge muscular man. He walked right towards Leo and Oliver. Who was he?

"Rogan," Monroe stood up. "Don't do this."

Sofia's eyes went wider at the mention of his name. Rogan. That was Monroe's brother's friend who lived in New York. She had heard that Monroe had someone staying at her house but didn't know who it was exactly and now it all made sense. His sister was staying with Monroe and Michael.

"Where the fuck is she?" he roared. "What did you fucking do to her?"

Daddy got up from their table and stood in front of her, almost like he was protecting her from Rogan in case he did anything. Sofia peeked around her Daddy's body to watch everything unfold.

Everything wasn't perfect.

This man had come in and was ruining things.

"Let's do this somewhere else," Leo said.

"Tell me where the fuck she is," Rogan yelled. "My sister was safe with Michael and Monroe before you two fucks took her."

Sofia flinched at all the language being used. She wasn't used to all of it and didn't enjoy it one bit.

"Rogan," Monroe said. "Stop it this instant. You're at a fucking wedding for heavens sake!"

"We're taking this outside," Oliver said.

Rogan turned around and looked directly at Sofia. She pushed herself into her chair as if she was trying to get away from him. There was so much distance between them, and Daddy was also in front of her.

He caught her eye. "Sofia."

She continued to stare at him. How did he know her name? Had she met him before? There wasn't any way she had met him before because she would've remembered him.

"I'm so glad you're married and in a better situation right now," Rogan gently said. "Especially not living in that dreadful apartment anymore."

Her whole body went still at the mention of her old apartment. How did he know she lived there? Had he been stalking her?

"I'm sorry for interrupting your wedding," he said. "Now, I'll be off."

Before she could stop herself, she found herself speaking. "All of you should go into time out for what you did. Especially you."

Gasps were heard all over the room, but she didn't look around. She didn't know what came over her, but she wasn't looking away from Rogan and losing all the confidence she had right now.

He cracked a smile. "I'm a Daddy, not a Little. I don't do timeouts."

Before she could say anything, he turned around and walked out of the room, Leo and Oliver following him.

What had just happened?

Daddy sat down and turned towards her. "Are you okay?"

She nodded her head but she didn't know if she was okay or not. Sofia leaned into her Daddy and took several deep breaths. So much for a perfect night.

"Let's get you home," Daddy said.

She whined and shook her head. "The guests."

They hadn't made their way around the room, talking to all of the guests and saying thank you for coming.

"They'll understand and besides, we'll see them soon. They all go to the club."

She nodded her head and he helped her stand up.

"We're going to be cutting this short," Daddy said. "Sorry

for the inconvenience, but you all can still enjoy the food and drinks here."

"Go and take care of the Little Miss," Pete said. "We'll make sure everything is cleaned up and put away."

"Thank you," Daddy said.

He gripped her hand and led her out and towards their decorated car. People cheered at them as they walked by, and she smiled at as many people as she could before they walked out of the barn.

"Ready to go home?" Daddy asked.

Sofia nodded her head and kissed him once again. She would never get tired of doing that.

"Wait for me to come around and get you," Daddy said. "I've got to carry my bride into the house."

Sofia giggled and watched as her Daddy got out of the car and around to get her. She loved him and how he wanted to do the small things with her and for her.

"Let's get you in the house so I can ravish you," Daddy's voice was husky as he spoke.

She shivered and he picked her up. Sofia started to kiss his neck, sucking on one part to leave a mark behind. He growled and picked up his pace.

"Such a naughty Little girl," Daddy said. "Are you my naughty Little girl?"

"Yes, Daddy," she said, kissing up and down his neck again.

Before she knew it, her body bounced on the bed, and she

looked at her Daddy. His eyes held hers and she could see the want and heat in his eyes. Oh, she loved that look.

"Let Daddy take off your dress," he said.

Sofia didn't have a traditional wedding dress. She didn't want one, so she had a simple white dress that went down to the floor. It hugged all of her curves and she absolutely loved it.

"Yes, Daddy," she said as she got off the bed.

The heat in his eyes grew as she stood up and he started to pull the dress off of her. The day before she had gone and gotten herself waxed. She decided before she walked down the aisle that she wasn't going to be wearing any underwear under her dress.

It was a bold move and Sofia was nervous the whole time. But it was worth it when Daddy sucked in a breath when the dress got pulled above her hips.

"No panties the whole time?" Daddy asked as he looked at her.

She nodded her head. Daddy groaned and kissed the top of her mound before pulling the rest of the dress off of her.

"Perfect," Daddy softly said. "Go lay on the bed. On your back with your legs spread."

Sofia climbed onto the bed, laying on her back and spreading her legs. She felt so exposed but she loved it. Daddy licked his lips as he stripped out of his clothes.

"Such a good girl for Daddy," he said. "Daddy's good girl."

Butterflies flew in her stomach and she felt herself getting wetter by the second. Daddy climbed onto the bed, slowly trailing his hand down her stomach, and to her perfectly waxed pussy.

"Such a pretty sight," he said.

His fingers slipped through her folds, teasing her as he went up and down several times, coating his fingers with her juices.

"Daddy can't wait to make love to you."

She couldn't wait either. Her hips moved down, trying to get his fingers to slide into her.

"Patience, Little one," Daddy said.

He gently slipped one finger into her and she moaned.

"Daddy," she moaned again as he moved his finger in and out.

"Daddy's going to add a second finger," he said right before he added it.

Sofia clenched around his fingers and raised her hips. She wanted more. She needed more.

"Daddy," she moaned. "I need you."

"Beg me," he said.

"Please! Daddy please put your cock inside of me."

His fingers left her pussy and she whined from the loss.

"I think you can do a better job than that," Daddy said.

She whined again and looked at him. "Please Daddy,' she begged. "Put your cock inside of me and make love! I'm begging. I need you. I need to feel your dick inside, filling me up. I belong to you and only you. My pussy belongs to you."

Daddy growled and aligned himself to her entrance.

"I love hearing that," Daddy said. "This pussy is mine. I own it."

He slowly started to push inside of her and Sofia did her best to relax the whole time.

"Such a good girl," Daddy said as he pushed the rest of himself inside of her.

She felt full, so full but it felt so good.

"Please," she said. "Please move."

He slowly pulled out of her before he rammed back in. Sofia moaned as the pleasure coursed through her body. She felt like little fireworks were going off throughout her body as he thrusted into her.

Daddy's hand slowly moved from her hip and found her clit. He moved his thumb in slow circular motions as he rammed back into her.

"Oooh," she moaned. "Please."

The pleasure inside of her started to build and she knew she wouldn't last long.

"Daddy," she moaned. "I'm close!"

"Come for me," he said as he picked up his speed.

He pressed down onto her clit and rubbed it harder as he continued to pump his cock inside of her. The combination of both sent her over the edge and she rode her release. Sofia clenched around him and felt him fill her up with his seed.

"Such a good girl," he said. "Take my cum."

She mewled and relaxed onto the bed as he pulled out of her.

"Daddy's going to clean you up now," he said. "He's going to take good care of you."

Sofia felt nervous as she saw several of their closest friends gather in the room. Daddy grabbed her hand, giving it a slight squeeze.

"Everything is going to be okay," Daddy whispered in her ear.

She knew everything was going to be okay. It was happy news they were telling everyone, but what if she messed up? What if words got the better of her and she screwed everything up.

"You're going to do amazing," Daddy kissed the side of her head.

Everyone looked at her and the room got quiet. Sofia took a shaky breath in and looked around the room. Their normal friends were here, but her eyes stopped on Oliver and Leo. Hedda was standing in between them and this was the first time Sofia had seen her.

Sofia had tried several times to invite Hedda to things. Their wedding, playdates, and sleepovers but each time she declined. She felt rejected, but her Daddy reminded her several times that Hedda had gone through a traumatic event.

"Thank you everyone for coming," Daddy said. "We really appreciate it. Sofia has some exciting news to tell you."

She looked up at her Daddy and he gave her a nod of encouragement. Five seconds of courage.

"After months of applying and waiting, I'm excited to tell you that I got my Green Card!" A big smile spread across her face.

Everyone erupted into cheers and people started to congratulate them.

KEEP UP WITH EVERLY!

Sign up for my newsletter to get teasers, cover reveals, updates, and extra content!

Everly Raine Newsletter

SCAN ME TO SIGN UP NOW!

Get a free short story when you do!

ACKNOWLEDGMENTS

There are so many people I want to thank.

Thank you to all the beta readers for taking your time to read my rough draft and point out things that needed to change, things that needed to be clarified more, and overall everything.

Thank you to my ARC readers!

Thank you to Lori for helping me edit this book. I absolutely appreciate it and I couldn't have done it without you.

I really appreciate everyone I mentioned and didn't mention. Thank you to everyone who has taken the time to read this book.

ABOUT EVERLY RAINE

Everly Raine is an emerging author of age play books. Want to follow along in her journey as an author?

FB Group: https://www.facebook.com/groups/878978066732860/

IG: https://www.instagram.com/authoreverlyraine/

Goodreads: https://www.goodreads.com/author/show/30503603.Everly_Raine

ALSO BY EVERLY RAINE

Missouri Daddies

1. Daddy's Little Cupcake

2. Daddy's Little Survivor

3. Daddy's Little Foreigner

4. Daddies' Little Spitfire (March 1, 2024)

5. Daddy's Little Mama Bear (April 19, 2024)

Ricci Crime family

1. His Perfect Little Storm

Made in the USA
Columbia, SC
12 August 2024